# THE WAGON DRIVER

# David Berardelli

# THE WAGON DRIVER

GRAVESTONE PRESS

# PART 1 - THE YELLOW MONSTER

# Chapter 1

"You the new driver?"

The petite young girl scowled behind the desk. Her scowl said she didn't believe he was the new applicant—that maybe someone was playing a joke on her.

"That's what they tell me." Kyle wasn't getting a warm fuzzy about this place. Too many negatives. The chick's attitude, for one thing. The olive drab wall behind her reminded him of Army film clips. The paint job looked old—peeling in places, bubbling in others. And the room's musty smell took him back to the bathroom at the State Home.

"You have a sheet?" Her large brown eyes zeroed in on the thick tan folder he held in the crook of his arm.

"Got a bunch of stuff." At the Employment Center they'd loaded him down with a ton of papers, forms and leaflets. The fat man in the rumpled blue suit—"call me Ralph"—crammed even more crap in his folder after the interview. A necessary evil, Ralph explained with a sly wink. "They live for paperwork. They'll want your work history, blood type, I.Q.—everything. It's the Government we're talking about, Sonnet. They can't function without it."

The girl forced a hand through her short black hair. He caught a whiff of lavender perfume. At least there was *some*thing positive about this place.

The tiny reading glasses hanging by a black elastic band above her small breasts shifted. She wore a watch with a plain black leather band on one wrist, a tiny gold bracelet on the other.

"The sheet you filled out at the Employment Center." She sounded bored. "I need form thirty-three seventeen. It's got all the information we'll need for your profile plus the results of your last physical."

He laid the folder on the counter, opened it, glanced at the top sheet and handed it over. She snatched it and squirmed onto a metal stool, which squeaked like a baby mouse. The glasses were now balanced on the tip of her small upturned nose. More lavender drifted in his direction. He wondered if she ever smiled. He tried not to appear obvious studying her breasts beneath her sleeveless tan shirt, but sometimes a man just had to give in to his urges.

She skimmed the report. Without looking up she said, "Sonnet. Kyle. Age eighteen. Your last known address was the Children's Foster Home of Pleasant Valley."

"I know all that," he said, grinning.

Her blank expression didn't waver. "Where are you living now?"

"Home is where the heart is."

When her dark eyes met his, they told him she was not amused.

She obviously liked her men reserved and businesslike. He could be that way—at least until she understood just how complex he was for his tender years. "They told me I'd be staying here at the Station."

She blinked. "They already *gave* you the job?"

"They called here during my interview. Someone here said I could start any time. The sooner, the better. They said a Mr. Stoner okayed it."

"The Stone hired you without an interview?"

"The stone*?*" Another not-so-warm fuzzy.

"Our Chief."

"They said you were desperate for drivers."

"We're desperate, all right. But that's a real hoot, giving you the job without references or a formal meeting. They mention salary?"

"They said Mister Stoner would give me the details."

"By the way, he's a captain. You call him mister, you might as well get yourself primed for one long, lousy day. The Stone's a former Marine. He headed up the National Guard a few years back. His unit was recalled during all that trouble with those medical school closings. You heard about those, didn't you?"

He recalled something like fifty closings that were covered on CNN. The National Guard was called in to handle the rioting at the affected locations. The Guard threw heavy nets at the crowd and used rubber bullets on the rioters. One elderly woman whose apartment was teargassed fell from a third story window and landed on a parked car. Two dozen people struck in the face with rubber bullets were suing the police. Many deaths resulted from others being trampled or run down by police vehicles.

"The Home has TVs all over the place," he said. "Even in the bathrooms. Yeah, we heard about the riots."

"The people who sent you here. They tell you anything else?"

"They told me Mist—Captain—Stoner would give me the details. But they said it was a County job, and the County pays top wages."

"That's it?" She sounded disappointed.

"A job's a job. Money's money, right?"

"When you're talking about this job, some think it's better to sponge off the State."

She wasn't exactly your basic high-pressure salesman. His feeling that he hadn't made the right choice for a career move jumped up another notch.

"You know what this place is, don't you?"

"The Department of Refuse Removal."

"Know what that means?"

"Refuse removal. Bodies. Burial. It's not exactly rocket science."

The girl sighed. "You just said you had news access at the State Home. Didn't you pay attention to the stories about this place?"

She was probably referring to clips of the attendants slipping bodies into the wagon at fires and traffic accidents. But since he didn't know what she was getting at, he just shrugged.

"Ambulances are equipped to handle only two bodies at a time," she said patiently. "Wagons follow them, collecting and transporting corpses for burial. It's necessary—especially when you find yourself in a situation where a dozen bodies need to be picked up."

"Actually, the process sounds fairly simple."

"Sonnet, you'll be driving a meat wagon. Did anyone tell you that?"

None of this mattered much. He had virtually no work experience to his credit. He was just starting out and he knew he had to accept whatever came his way. Up till now he'd relied on the state for his meals, lodging, and what little spending money the Government entitled him to. The system was all right when he was a kid, but the last couple of years had been rough. Accounting for your whereabouts and actions is much more aggravating at eighteen than when you're younger.

"I need a job," he said. "How bad can it be?"

"Take it from me, you're not gonna be popular. But I'll let the Stone fill you in."

"Why do you call him that?"

She barked out a short laugh, causing jagged cracks to fan out from the corners of her eyes. He had the impression she didn't enjoy laughing at all. That it probably hurt. The cracks surprised him because he didn't think she was much older than he was.

"You'll see." She produced a yellow card almost magically. "Fill this out, bring it back and leave it on the counter when you're finished. You can sit at that table over there. The Stone'll buzz when he wants to talk." She snatched up a pamphlet from underneath the desk top and handed it to him. "Read this. It tells you all about the Point System."

"What's *that*?"

"The Department offers medical coverage, but you need to accumulate a certain number of points to qualify. It gives you an idea what's covered and what's not."

"I thought the County took care of everything. Doesn't this entitle me to—"

"It doesn't entitle you to squat." She flashed yet another scowl. She probably had a batch of them ready for all occasions. "You'll see once you read this."

"What's your name?"

"Parsons."

"First name?"

"Allie. Why?"

"I like to know a person's name while I'm talking to her."

The trace of a smile flickered across her lips, softening her eyes and almost making the sharp vertical line between her brows disappear. He figured he'd just hit pay dirt.

"I'll fill this out now."

"That would be nice."

"I'm almost always nice."

She made no comment.

"Thanks for your help."

She'd already slipped through the open doorway.

Beyond it, a big room done in the same plain olive drab flickered beneath the overhead fluorescent. Covering the far wall, a huge computer screen displayed a map, where glittering colored dots jumped around like fireflies. In front of the screen, a long slanted table extended the length of the wall. A row of stools was lined up in front of the table. On each stool sat a female wearing a headset.

Kyle counted twelve. Most had long hair tied in back, probably to stay clear of the headsets.

Allie Parsons was nowhere to be seen.

She was probably standing in front of a mirror off to the side, perfecting her vast assortment of scowls.

He sat down at the table in front of the grimy window and opened the pamphlet.

*The Point System*
*"Man's Newest Form of Survival"*

He skipped the introduction, flipped a page and tried making sense of the Table of Contents:

Reading matter to sleep by…
He stifled a yawn and flipped to Chapter 7.
The "brief" list covered eight pages.

| Complaint | Points | for |
| --- | --- | --- |
| | Treatment | |
| Abdomen pain | *1* | |
| Abrasions | *1* | |
| Addison's disease | *4* | |
| Adenocarcinoma | *28* | |

11

| | |
|---|---|
| Adenoidectomy | *3* |
| Adrenal tumor | 10 |
| Aerophagia | *2* |
| AIDS | *100* |
| Allergies | *2* |
| Alopecia | *7* |
| Amenorrhea | *5* |

And so on...

Outside, gray clouds covered the tops of the super structures like tufts of smoke. Across the street, six lanes of creeping vehicles sent tendrils of exhaust vapors spiraling upward.

A sloppy-dressed black man rushing through the crowd yanked the purse from a middle-aged woman burdened with packages. He was tripped at the corner by a black-haired leather-clad female and sent rolling to the curb. The purse flew out of his hand and was picked up by one of the tough's two female partners. The thief scrambled to get up. The trio surrounded him and kicked him repeatedly with their leather boots. Then, growing bored, they turned and walked away.

Kyle sighed. *I'm part of the grown-up world now. Here people were loud and abrasive, pushed you around and stomped on you if you resisted. They took what they wanted and didn't care who liked it.*

Not much difference between this place and the school playground.

The State Home suddenly seemed a million miles away, its crammed classrooms a part of someone else's past, the daily pandemonium in the lunchroom a dark, distant memory, the rowdiness in its dormitories some- thing he constantly forced from his mind.

So why didn't he feel good about it?

Could it be because the grown-up world didn't look much better?

He slid the pamphlet into his folder and reached for the form Allie Parsons had given him.

This one didn't call for much concentration at all. His cup of tea. He could do it with his eyes closed. It required detailed contact information about relatives and designated beneficiaries.

No problem. As an orphan you didn't waste much time filling out information about relatives or beneficiaries.

# Chapter 2

The man behind the desk had a face that could have been carved by a sculptor who really went apeshit for cracks and slashes. His small square head sat snugly on a corded, columnar neck. His cheekbones and jawline were razor-sharp, the skin covering them pulled Spandex-tight.

He wasn't big, but his compactness suggested strength and calculated power. The short sleeves of his starched khaki shirt stretched over a pair of well-developed biceps and triceps.

Stoner's seated rigidity was similar to that of a Rottweiler protecting its property—the spine perfectly straight, the head held high. It looked like someone had shoved a three-foot length of rebar up the man's ass.

A large white mug sat beside a corded forearm. An intercom and pencil sharpener took over the opposite corner. The sparsely decorated room, partially lit by slivers of early afternoon sun poking through the parted blinds, gave the atmosphere a solid bleakness.

The brass nameplate on the desk said *Captain William Francis Stoner*. "The Stone," as Allie Parsons referred to him. Kyle could tell how the dude had earned the nickname. Nothing soft or yielding about him at all. Probably shaved with a blowtorch and did his nails with a rasp file he'd bought at the local hardware store.

"Kyle no middle name Sonnet." Stoner's voice, a series of abrupt barks, substantiated the Rottweiler persona.

"That's me."

The close-cropped salt-and-pepper dome shifted as Stoner raised his face. His steamy gaze sliced into Kyle. "That's me...*sir.*"

*Something tells me this dude ain't kidding.*

Allie Parsons should have said Stoner was one tight asshole. The Marine thing, no doubt. He'd always heard Marines were a very select breed of sociopathic killers.

Or maybe there actually *was* a length of rebar shoved up that ass...

"That's me, *sir,*" Kyle echoed.

"You're eighteen," Stoner announced, making Kyle wonder if the statement was supposed to be a question.

"Yes, sir."

"And this will be your first job."

"Second."

The coal-black eyes dropped back to the sheet on the desk blotter. "You delivered laundry for six weeks."

"Just before I left the Home."

"You've done nothing since."

"No, sir."

"Why not?"

Kyle wanted to say he was waiting for the right management position to present itself but suspected this man wouldn't appreciate such humor. Stoner's DNA undoubtedly lacked a humor gene.

"Well, sir, when I quit the laundry job—"

"You were fired."

"Yes, sir."

"This says you have trouble with authority."

15

*Good ol' Harris…* Kyle figured the sorry dude would put out the word. The man was barely five-four and had a problem with taller people. It was no doubt a serious pain, looking up at nostril hairs all day long. Harris, well over forty, also had an age phobia as demonstrated by his abrupt treatment of the younger workers. But Kyle knew better than to voice these opinions. Stoner seemed about the same age. "That's not exactly so," he said.

"What *is* exactly so?"

"The man I worked for—"

"I'll bet he was a tyrant."

"Well, he—"

"He picked on you, didn't he?" Stoner's face had tightened.

Kyle could sense the bitterness in the air. Grownups stuck together but seldom shared their hang-ups. Harris wouldn't likely confide in Stoner about his nostril-hair complex and probably fabricated things about Kyle so it wouldn't reflect on him.

"Well, sir—"

"He didn't recognize your true potential, did he?"

The heavy dark vibes oozing from the other man were like waves of black smoke. The "stone" definitely said it all. Kyle wondered if an X-ray would reveal a knotty rock wedged inside the man's skull where his brain should be.

"Let's get this out in the open right now. Any objections?"

Before Kyle could respond, Stoner said, "You're young. A punk. Worse, you're a stupid punk."

Stoner stood sharply—with a definite *snap!*—and circled the desk. Much smaller than Kyle guessed. Around five-eight and probably one-fifty, every bit of it muscle, gristle, and sinew. He moved like a caged tiger in a zoo, giving the impression he could easily maneuver his way through a herd of stampeding elephants.

At six-one, Kyle felt small and insignificant in this man's presence.

"You think the world owes you. You're young, so you're smarter than everyone else. You—"

"But sir—"

"Don't interrupt."

Kyle sank into his chair. Oh, to be back in those woods... No stones out there, just some antsy squirrels, a few feisty chipmunks, snakes, ants, spiders, and poison ivy.

Stoner put his hands behind his back, interlaced his fingers and slowly circled Kyle's chair. "You figure you're better than anyone else. That's why you couldn't make it at Laundry World. Isn't that why you were fired?"

"It's a long story—"

"I don't want to hear it." Stoner resumed pacing. Kyle decided a riding crop would complete the picture. That and a pair of those funny trousers the Nazis wore.

"That wasn't a job. You drove a truck, picked up laundry and listened to people bitch about how long it

17

took you to get there. Then you took the stuff back when it was clean and you were done for the day."

The job also included driving to bad neighborhoods and getting hit with rocks, bottles, toilet lids, bullets, and other equally messy debris. Other times kids would dash across the street to see how close they could come without being hit. But this dude probably didn't want to hear about that.

"This is a *job*." Stoner put his face within six inches of Kyle's face, sending over a warm, sour bubble of onions and a hint of whiskey. "You like working, Sonnet?"

"It's not a question of *liking* it, sir."

"Good answer. Any objections to taking orders?"

He knew better than reply. He suspected Stoner was probably the biggest order-giver in the civilized world. "If you do, you might as well pick your pitiful ass right up and haul it out of Dodge. I give the orders. In fact, I give lots of orders. And when I give an order, it's obeyed. If it isn't obeyed, I get upset. When I'm upset, I'm nasty." He aimed his smoldering eyes at Kyle. "You know what I do when I'm nasty?"

He couldn't see Stoner slipping into the confessional booth for some quick penance, or listening to a tape of ocean sounds. But he could visualize him munching on a handful of carpet tacks fresh from the box.

"No, sir." Sweat gathered on his brow. He knew better than wipe it off. Stoner would disapprove.

"You don't want to." Stoner returned to his desk. "This job pays well, but you'll put in a lot of hours. Any objection to good money?"

"No, sir."

"Any objection to long hours?"

"No, sir. Not if I like the job."

Stoner crossed his arms. Veins swelled across columns of muscle running from his elbows to his wrists. "I see a definite problem cropping up. We've got to make this job *likeable* for you. We've got to give orders in such a way that you consider them *requests*. What else have we got to do to make things easy for you, Sonnet?"

A bevy of large-breasted slave girls would have been the icing on the cake, but Kyle figured that wasn't an option.

"You can either work here or try living on that so-called shared allotment program the Government hands out to the shiftless users taking over this country. If you don't have a certified profession they'll make you sign up for the program—which will last for six months maximum. If you don't find a suitable job in that time they'll stick you in a relief barracks. There you'll shack up with sixty other losers. You'll share a shower stall with four shower heads, six urinals, and six toilets. You'll have breakfast, lunch, and dinner with three hundred others from the compound and you'll be trucked all over God's creation to mow grass, clean up trash, wash out dumpsters or empty holding tanks for the airlines. You'll work side-by-side with convicts and other useless dregs for twelve hours a day, and most of your pay will go for your board. Would you prefer that?"

"No, sir."

"Wouldn't have much money for incidentals, would you?"

"No, sir."

"You know what incidentals are, don't you? They're things you don't need."

"Yes, sir."

"Like entertainment."

"Yes, sir."

"Or women."

Kyle considered women essential but didn't want to cause more trouble.

"You won't even have enough money for cigarettes. You smoke?"

"No, sir."

"Good. Filthy, disgusting habit." Stoner's face wrinkled up. "But there *is* something else about this job you should know." He blinked. "There's no quitting."

"Sir?"

"Since you were referred here by the State, you're required to fulfill your contract with them and work here for six months. In a nutshell, if you quit before that time, the State people will think we're not doing something right. Inspectors will come down from the State Capital and look for reasons to close us down. They'd enjoy that because they don't think too highly of us. We remind them of their own mortality. We're a department of the State, and subject to the State's regulations and standards. And when something happens to draw attention to us, those assholes hightail it down here with their cameras and technological equipment to dissect us all like a bunch of stupid laboratory frogs." Stoner's face flushed. "Do I appear the laboratory frog type?"

It was difficult holding back a laugh. Fear of being sent to a relief barracks helped greatly. From what he'd heard, they were no better than the World War II prison camps he'd learned about in history class. "No, sir."

"Then I suggest you keep your mouth shut. Understand?"

"Yes, sir."

Stoner sat back in his chair. "What do you know about this job?"

"I'll be a driver."

"Driving what?"

"An ambulance or a wagon."

"We have more than enough ambulance drivers. We need wagon drivers. Know what they do?"

"They follow the ambulances around."

"We're a cleanup crew. The ambulances can't handle the volume. They need us for disposal work."

Disposal work. Cleanup crew. Coming from Stoner, it sounded like they'd be hauling trash.

"Ever seen a body before?"

"Yes, sir."

"Been close to one? Touch it? Sniff it?"

"Yes, sir."

"Where?"

"At the Home."

"Tell me about it."

A couple of years ago, some of the older guys had been drinking and smoking pot. When they fell asleep, a smoldering joint dropped out of the ashtray and rolled onto a pile of test papers, torching the floor.

"There was a fire, and some kids were trapped on the second floor." Kyle didn't think Stoner would want to hear about the drinking and the pot-smoking.

"How many of them?"

"Seven."

"Bother you?"

"Not much, sir."

Stoner squinted. "They were your classmates, your friends. You studied with them, shared rooms with them. Didn't it bother you to see them sizzling like T-bones on a grill?"

They were big, dumb jocks with attitudes. A year before the fire, they'd stuffed Kyle in a trash can behind the cafeteria and tossed in the uneaten contents of their lunches before stacking sacks of potatoes onto the lid.

Kyle had never cared for the preferential treatment the athletes were given or how the teachers turned the other way whenever one of their "star players" cheated on exams. He'd experienced a strange sense of relief the night the firefighters carted out the bodies. A sense of relief coupled with the elation of justice being served. "I wasn't close to any of them," he said   diplomatically. "None were good friends."

"Did you know any of them, Sonnet?"

"A couple, but not very well."

"And it didn't trouble you to see them crispy-fried."

"Not really, sir."

Stoner's features relaxed. "Good. You might do well here. As I said, we're cleanup. When we're full we make a trip to the rendering plant. We dump our load, come back, and follow the ambulance till the shift's over."

The rendering plant. The news had mentioned it briefly but did very few in-depth stories. He'd seen a shot of it one time from the lens of a CNN helicopter. A huge concrete building out in the middle of nowhere, the land surrounding it stripped bare.

"Where's the rendering plant, sir?"

"Why?" Stoner's thick brows slid upward. "Got a hot date there tonight?"

"Just curious."

"No need. I give you orders and you follow them. You follow them and I'm happy. I'm happy and you're paid. You're paid and you're happy. Understand how the process works?"

"Yes, sir."

"Good. Now...how much experience do you have driving something the size of a bus? Your records say you've got a commercial license but it doesn't go into detail."

"You mean like a school bus?"

"That's what I mean."

"None, sir."

Stoner shrugged. "It's not difficult. They're all automatic. Power steering, brakes—the works." His eyes lowered. "You're kind of skinny. You've got shoulders, but not much meat there to speak of."

*I'm what you'd call wiry.*

"No, sir."

"How much weight can you lift?"

"I'm pretty strong. The football coach said I have good tendons."

"You played football?" Stoner looked surprised.

"No, sir. We were all tested the year of the fire because five key members of the team died in the blaze."

"Why didn't you play?"

"Never cared much for the game, sir," he said flatly. Or spending his time with jerks who liked stuffing skinny kids into garbage cans for entertainment.

"No matter. We're talking dead weight here. You might be strong enough. We'll see. Think you'll have trouble moving something that might weigh two hundred and fifty pounds?"

"Won't know till I try."

"Another good answer." Stoner raised his left arm and, holding his forearm horizontally in front of his face, read his watch. "Next run's in about thirty minutes." He lowered his arm. "Ready to start?"

"Yes, sir."

"You're already on the clock, so you'll need a locker. Take one without a label on it. You can have any suit hanging in the locker room. Find a marker, print your name legibly on one of the self-stick labels in the box, and slap a label on an empty locker. Suit up and I'll pick you up."

"Suit up?"

"We dress in airtight yellow vinyl suits. Haven't you seen us on CNN?"

The news reports focused on the bodies being wheeled by gurneys. The uniforms—Fire Department, police, wagon drivers, ambulance attendants, county workers—meshed into a single entity. A flurry of colors. Yellow, blue, orange, and black. They all seemed to stand for something seriously bad.

"Problem?" Stoner asked.

"I never paid much attention to the uniforms."

Stoner sighed impatiently. "We wear the same type of outfits the astronauts wore before the space program went belly-up. Suits are comfortable and really work." He scanned Kyle's sheet. "You're not inoculated. Go see Irene. She's down the hall in the room marked Infirmary."

Kyle shifted uneasily. Shots. Bummer. "Irene?" he asked softly.

"She's got the inoculation gun. One jolt gives you more than a hundred immunizations. Fixes you right up. You never know what we're going to find out there. This way we don't have to worry about you suddenly foaming at the mouth, or shitting your drawers."

At the Home, several older kids were selected to administer the shots. Their "training" amounted to a single demonstration. They were usually clumsy and had trouble finding veins. Kyle's were almost impossible to locate. Being stuck over and over was not his fondest memory.

"Sir, I was immunized a year ago and—"

"You were immunized *two* years ago, this report says. There's everything under the sun out there. I'll be damned if I let one of my men make himself susceptible because he was too chickenshit to let Irene juice him up. Besides, the State requires it. Get it?"

"Yes, sir."

"Irene's gun takes two seconds. Then get suited up. I'll meet you in the garage out back."

Kyle stood rather shakily.

"You okay, boy?"

"Yes, sir," he said, a little light-headed.

"You're not gonna faint on me, are you?"

"No, sir." The urge to dump chowder on the man's spit-shined shoes was overwhelming.

"Good. Go do it now. That's an order. Chop! Chop!"

His legs stiff and heavy, Kyle shuffled out of the room.

# Chapter 3

In the dimly-lit stall, the metal monster snoozed.

The beast was an old school bus that had been gutted, then fitted with enclosed compartments much like a morgue storage locker. Two rows of six compartments started behind the driver's seat, extending to the rear of the vehicle.

It smelled nasty. Instead of the normal gas/oil reek gripping most vehicles, something else clung to it. A sweet/sour hint.

Kyle had seen distant shots of the wagon on CNN. He'd even seen bodies being loaded into it. But up close it seemed much bigger. And on CNN you weren't aware of its stench.

"A lot of compartments, sir," he said uneasily. "Do you use them all?"

Stoner sprayed his visor liberally with Windex. Using circular strokes, he rubbed it carefully with a soft cloth. He screwed the helmet onto his peppered skull and gently pushed down the visor using only the fingertips of one gloved hand. "One never knows. A riot like that anti-euthanasia rally that broke out in town two years ago might erupt out of the blue. By the time we show, there could be twenty, maybe thirty bodies to cart away. There's trouble, and we're the only available unit, we'll have to cart as many to the plant as we can. We're on a time table, you know."

"Time table?"

"Rushed, Sonnet. Always rushed. Even if there are only a couple of bodies to pick up." Stoner jerked his head at the wagon. "C'mon. The ambulance starts out in five minutes."

His arm still stinging from Irene's hypo gun, Kyle climbed the metal steps.

Stoner pulled the folding door shut and situated his compact butt on the padded bench slightly behind the driver's seat.

Kyle examined the gearshift, dials and dash. The truck he'd tested in had twice as many controls and gauges. He didn't think he'd have a problem.

"At least this isn't a high-volume day like Saturdays or any of those damn holidays." Stoner pulled the clipboard dangling from the hook on the dash. "Starting out slow is best. You'll learn more. You need to concentrate on keeping close to the ambulance and learning the route. Understood?"

"High-volume days?" This sounded more and more like your basic classic downer.

"Weekends can be killers. People get drunk, stoned, and stupid. They start fights and someone ends up hurt or dead. Or maybe they just do some serious thinking about things in general. Also dangerous. Any time an idiot tries using brain cells he doesn't have or normally use, all hell breaks loose. Think you can handle this rig?"

"Yes, sir."

"Let's get going. Clinic's down the street at the end of the block."

\*\*\*

Humanity—an immense bloated carcass oozing over the sidewalks—swelled and shuddered like a dying mammal. Occasionally parts of it broke off, becoming a well-dressed man talking to his earpiece, a woman pushing a stroller, or a couple of street kids yanking purses.

Kyle kept close behind the ambulance, brushing past jaywalkers and parked cars. A passerby spat something at the wagon, forming a shiny brown teardrop on the windshield. Others glared or mouthed strings of angry cusswords.

*You're not gonna be popular.* Allie Parsons hadn't lied. It didn't matter. Kyle had always been a loner. When you loved music and art and went for long walks in the woods while everyone else screamed from the stands during a football or baseball game, you didn't enjoy much of a fan base.

A high-pitched voice erupted from the console. "Get us a new recruit, Captain Bill?"

"Fresh meat, Logan. Can't be picky. Times are hard."

"Tell me about it. Lost one of our drivers."

"Which one?"

"Miller. The tall blonde? Gargantuan knockers? You knew her. Wore too much perfume."

"When did this happen? Parsons didn't mention it."

"Didn't show for roll. Problem with her mother last week."

"What's the story?"

"Woman's over sixty, has a serious drinking problem. Been to AA, Detox, SAA—all the funded programs. Anyway, Mumsy pours herself into her car one night and takes out the neighbors' patio wall. Confused reverse with drive, she said. Last night she went on a large bender and ended up out

29

in the street in her nightgown, screaming bloody murder about goblins."

"I remember the patio incident. Heard it on the scanner on my day off."

"We had to go out there last night to pick her up and take her back to Detox. We're in the locker room suiting up and there's Miller, pulling a giant tantrum. Scary situation. Miller's a big girl. She gets a wild hair and your life flashes before your eyes."

"She go out on the call?"

"Only after I reminded her of the Federal Desertion Decree."

"What happened this morning?"

"Didn't show. No one's heard a word."

"Told 'em not to hire her," Stoner said. "You don't hire anyone with family—especially when they live in your Sector."

"Just got a call, Chief."

Stoner flicked on the dash-mounted twelve-inch screen. A network of flickers danced brightly. "Where?"

"Area Seven."

"*That's* a section we don't get to very often."

"Mostly lawyers out there. Lawyers and bankers. Homes are too pricey for regular folks."

Stoner fished for his fountain pen. "How far?"

"About six blocks. Talk more when we get there. Out."

Stoner scribbled busily.

Kyle's pulse quickened. This was it. The beginning. He would soon know what all the fuss was about. And what he was made of.

"How large an area do we cover, sir?"

"About a quarter of the city. It's not bad—maybe twenty square blocks. At least we don't have to cover the state capital. Those boys have a hundred and fifty square blocks divided by four units. And their man- power isn't much bigger than ours."

"But this job pays pretty well."

Stoner's face wrinkled. "It's not the money. It's just like what happened with Miller. In the city you've got families and friends living close, so naturally no one wants to work for us. Relatives and friends complicate matters, make things messy. Especially relatives. Friends are bad enough. You got friends, Sonnet?"

"No, sir."

"Good." Stoner's features relaxed. "You'll do just fine, then."

*I have no friends, so I'll do fine.*

He had the sinking feeling he was off to a really bad start.

\*\*\*

A paved drive swept up a grassy knoll to a large colonial house. Manicured hedges lined the front of the two-story brick building, a flower garden running along the side. Well-tended bushes surrounded a white gazebo in the backyard. The neatly-trimmed lawn added to the image of order and serenity.

Only the two bodies lying in the grass out front spoiled the effect.

The man and woman were both around sixty years old. The man, about six feet tall, probably weighed two hundred pounds. He wore a dress shirt, knit slacks and expensive Oxfords. The light-boned woman lying beside him couldn't have weighed more than a hundred pounds. Serenity shrouded her pretty face. Her makeup had been applied carefully. Her manner of dress—long-sleeved cream-colored blouse, form-fitting gray slacks and shiny open-toed black heels—indicated the same high level of meticulousness.

Blood pooled darkly on the trimmed grass beneath the woman's carefully-styled silver hair. Her companion's head wound was identical except for the red drops pitting his cheeks and lips.

Two police cars sat unattended in front of the carport, their lights flashing.

A large-framed man squeezed out of the ambulance. The creases slashing his square forehead and close-cropped red hair were visible inside the visor. His light-weight blue uniform—tight in some areas, loose in others—couldn't accommodate his awkward size.

His partner, tall and knife-blade slender, sported a black brush cut. He had the rough, grizzled face of a badger. His deep-set iron gray eyes rested comfortably beneath a wide, slab-like forehead. Dressed like his partner, he carried a shiny black leather bag. He dropped to his knees between the bodies and placed the bag on the grass in front of him.

Across the street, a tall slender woman with frizzy blond hair stood on her front stoop, hands on hips. When Kyle glanced her way she straightened an arm. Even at that distance he recognized the gesture. *Not very cool, lady*, he wanted to say.

"Over here, Sonnet."

Dwarfed by the ambulance driver, Stoner waited patiently, the late morning sun reflecting off his visor. Two black bags were spread out on the grass at their feet. Two gurneys had been removed from the ambulance and were positioned nearby.

"Where's the gun?" Stoner asked the big man.

"Police must've taken it."

"Already?"

The ambulance driver pointed to the observers across the street. "Probably didn't want it to walk. Handguns are now going for two large."

"Point taken, Buster. Can't have any cowboys running around."

"At least, not while we're out in the field." Buster laughed. "I'm too old and too lazy to dodge bullets."

"Another point taken."

"Apparently these two did the deed out here, for whatever reason."

"Maybe they didn't want to get blood and brain matter on their good furniture."

Buster nodded. "So they decided to christen the lawn?"

Stoner shrugged. "Maybe they're doing a spread in House Magazine and thought blood spatter on the carpet might offend some subscribers."

The other ambulance guy removed the stethoscope from his ears. "This one's simple."

"Here's where we find out what you're made of, Sonnet," Stoner said. "At least your first two aren't that big."

33

Kyle grabbed the man by the ankles while Stoner slid his hands beneath the shoulders. They lifted the body onto the bag, zipped up, picked up the bag and swung it onto the gurney.

The procedure was repeated for the woman.

Stoner jerked a gloved thumb. "Open 'er up."

Kyle unlatched the heavy metal door on the side of the wagon and pulled it open. A mixture of mildew and disinfectant whooshed out, collecting beneath his visor.

Stoner and Buster wheeled over a gurney and positioned it in front of the opened door. Stoner stood directly across from Kyle. "Just grab one of the handles and push. It'll slide on in."

Kyle gripped a rubber handle. The bag slid easily into its slippery square metal sheath, thumping the opposite wall. The corpse's head stopped several inches shy of the opening.

Stoner slammed the door shut and latched it.

"How long are those compartments, sir?"

"Seven feet and some change."

It seemed more than adequate. But his curiosity flared, and he couldn't help wondering about the inevitable.

"Something on your mind, Sonnet?"

"What if...what if the body's...longer than the compartment?"

Logan boomed laughter. "A new recruit with questions! *That's* always good for a chuckle or two, eh, Chief?"

Stoner didn't reply. He was staring at Kyle. Even beneath his visor Kyle could feel the annoyance emanating from the man's eyes. "Now just who in hell would be taller than seven feet, Sonnet?"

Kyle could tell he'd just entered forbidden territory, but it was too late to back out now. "Cops. Basketball players."

The ambulance guys snickered and turned away.

"No policemen of that height work in this Sector, Sonnet. No professional basketball players live in this entire county, either."

"Yes, sir."

"According to our Internet data, only two men of that height reside in the central part of this state. That is, those fitted with a chip. I think we're reasonably safe."

"Yes, sir. I was just curious."

"No need to worry. But there's something else you should know, now that we're on the subject. Would you like to know what it is, Sonnet?"

Kyle hesitated. He knew Stoner was going to say it anyway, so it would be wise to agree. "Yes, sir…"

"If a body's too long for the box, we make certain adjustments. Understand?"

Certain adjustments. Kyle's mind reeled.

"In other words, Sonnet, we make it fit. Understand *now?*"

"I…think so." He glanced at Buster and Logan. The humor had drained from their faces.

The smoldering coals in the center of Stoner's face grew. "I take it you haven't noticed the chainsaw under the bench seat in the wagon."

Chainsaw. Make it fit. *All right, Sonnet, take out that chainsaw and let's make those adjustments. C'mon now. Hurry. Chop! Chop! We're on a time table, you know.*

"I...think I get it now, sir."

"Good. Good. Now help Logan with the woman. I've got to get the paperwork signed. Once that's finished, we'll be merrily on our way."

\*\*\*

Twenty minutes later, Logan's voice crackled through the radio. "Another call, Chief. Hostage situation. Domestic."

"Damn family shit. Nasty." Stoner reached for his clipboard. "What's our ETA?"

"About two minutes. Take a right on Virginia, then halfway down the block. Residential area. Section's mostly state-assisted."

"Police been notified?"

"Their ETA's between five and seven minutes. You're the only one available with a grade triple-A rating, Chief."

Stoner unzipped the side pocket of his suit and reached inside. A large stainless automatic pistol emerged, gripped tightly in his palm.

*A gun. Terrific.* Kyle froze, losing his grip on the wheel.

The tires of the wagon bumped the curb.

"Careful, Sonnet." Stoner grabbed the metal pole for balance. "Mind your driving."

"A *gun*, sir?"

"Yep, that's what this is. Good observation."

"But...no one told me—"

"Told you what? That we use guns?"

36

Kyle nodded.

"Guess what, Sonnet."

"Someone didn't...tell me everything...about this job?"

"Another good observation. But don't go having a heart attack on me. Not yet, anyway. I probably won't have to use this if the police show."

Kyle steadied the wheel but couldn't steady himself. No one during his interview had mentioned guns. Ralph hadn't even hinted that anyone would be carrying a gun, nor was it suggested that there would be a need for firearms.

Stoner removed the mag, gave it a thorough examination, slammed it loudly into the butt and jacked a round in the chamber.

The man's efficiency was frightening. Allie Parsons had said Stoner was a Marine. Marines were competent with firearms and other forms of weaponry. Shouldn't that make the situation less tense?

A domestic hostage call. And the cops were only a couple of minutes behind them.

Why not wait?

Kyle was led to believe this job would be fairly easy. A commercial driver's license, good health, and a desire to learn was all that was required. Keeping your eyes straight ahead, oblivious of everything else going on around you.

The perfect job for someone like Kyle, who'd been specializing in being oblivious since he was little.

"What's a...grade triple-A rating, sir?"

"I'm allowed to act in accordance with Martial Law if the situation requires it. I was a Marine Captain in the National Guard more than ten years ago, when the National Police Force was first assembled. This came about when the Gun Confiscation Law was voted in. Marine officers—as well as Army, Navy, and Air Force—are viewed by the Government in the same category as civil law enforcement officers, and are given the same authority. I'm allowed to own and carry this firearm. I'm also allowed to use it if I believe the situation warrants extreme force. In other words, I've been given the same authority as a sworn-in police officer. Answer your question?"

# Chapter 4

The streets ran mazelike for miles.

Soot-smeared one-story brick houses formed endless rows, separated from one another by slim walkways. Each back yard extended approximately twenty feet to a wooden privacy fence backing up to the houses lining the next street. The roofs were all severely weathered, the front lawns neglected. Trash littered the curb. Hispanic, black, and Asian men and women in their twenties and thirties watched the activity from their front stoops while chattering away on their earpieces. A few had assembled in small groups on front lawns. When the wagon came into view, many disappeared indoors. Others ducked behind parked cars or bushes.

A beefy black man stood on a front stoop, his left arm applying a chokehold to a short, pudgy young black girl. The girl's face was frozen in terror; tears glistened in her eyes. A shiny black revolver grew from the man's free hand. Its short barrel pressed against the girl's right temple.

Kyle inched the wagon to a stop at the curb and applied the brake. Stoner flung open the door, scrambled down the steps and rushed over to where Buster and Logan hunkered behind the open rear door of the ambulance. Kyle followed.

"Any word from the police?"

Logan peeked at his watch. "They just told us they'd be another ten minutes. Road rage dispute near the Turnpike."

"Road rage?" Stoner shook his head. "Not even their damned job. National Force handles that.

That's why they've got certified snipers on their payroll."

Buster shrugged a beefy shoulder. "Sounds like a management problem, Chief. That staffing thing they're always harping about."

Stoner's face wrinkled behind his visor. "Three-quarters of a billion in this country and everyone wants to sponge off the State or peddle trinkets from their stupid home computers. No one wants to work anymore."

"What's the plan, Chief?"

"Got to get that damned gun away from that moron. Logan, you circle around to the other side and stay behind the ambulance. Buster, switch on the radio. Let me know everything the cops tell you. Sonnet, don't move till I tell you. I don't want us too close together in case that idiot decides to open fire. Logan, fetch me a loudspeaker."

Logan reached into the rear of the ambulance and pulled out a black and white unit.

Stoner positioned it tightly in his gloved fist. "You three do as I told you."

Staying close to the door, Stoner pushed up his visor, flicked on the speaker and brought it up to his face. "You!" His voice echoed loudly. "In front of the house! Drop that gun and let the girl go! *Now!*"

The big man did not move.

"I repeat, drop that gun and let the girl go*!*"

The man shook his head. "You ain't the po-lice! I ain't got to do anything you say!"

"Sir, I am Captain William Stoner of the Department of Population Control. I am a Grade triple-A Officer and as such, am licensed to carry this firearm." He raised it, the slab barrel pointing skyward, then lowered it to his side. "I am fully authorized to use this if necessary. In other words, I can and will shoot you if you do not comply with my orders."

The girl whimpered.

"You, sir, are committing several felony crimes. You are unlawfully detaining another person, a minor, with a firearm. The firearm you are holding is illegal and falls under the category of—"

"Fuck you." The man jerked, pulling the girl. A high-pitched squeal escaped her throat. "I'm dead anyway, so I don't give a damn. You and your Grade triple-A asshole can get outa my face!"

Stoner switched off the speaker. "Sonnet, have Buster get busy with the computer. The satellite dish should already have the filter positioned for a visual scan. The computer'll take care of the rest. Just in case that moron hasn't been chipped. I want his sheet and I want it *now*."

Kyle climbed into the ambulance. Buster sat at the dash, eyeing the house through the side window. "The Captain wants—"

"Heard him." After logging on, Buster worked the digital. The dish mounted to the ambulance roof already pointed to the house. It took only a millisecond to get a sharp image on the display screen. A close-up of the man's face appeared. Buster punched more keys. The hard drive hummed quietly. A printout whirred from the printer underneath and slipped softly into the plastic tray. Buster handed it to Kyle.

Outside, Stoner grabbed the sheet and held it close. The speaker was instantly switched back on.

"Sir, you are Nathaniel Odell Johnson, thirty-four years of age, born in Chicago. The minor you're holding hostage is your own daughter. Her name is Ophelia LaShonda Johnson. She is eleven and is one of your two children. You, sir, are a convicted breeder. Both you and your wife were chemically sterilized in accordance with the Family Planning Act passed by Congress. You have been living in this house for eight years. Your wife's name is Latrina Femalia Lewis-Johnson. Her blood type is O Positive. Your blood type is A Negative. You have been arrested three times for shoplifting, once for petty larceny, twice for smoking marijuana, and six times for drunk and disorderly. Your wife has been arrested twice for prostitution and has been brought up on multiple minor drug offenses. Both you and your wife have been living on extended State Welfare, and you, sir, haven't—"

"I *know* who the hell I am, goddammit. I also know what my wife done for a livin' 'fore she met me." Johnson lowered his gaze to the ground at his feet.

"Listen, Johnson—"

"*You* listen. If you know so damn much, you must also know I don't care no more. Got nothin' to lose, know what I'm sayin'? So you can stick that loudspeaker where the sun don't shine."

"Johnson, this is serious. I suggest you—"

"Don't I *look* serious?" The man trembled. "Think I'm havin' a Jim Dandy time out here? Think there's a *party* goin' on in this house?" He

42

raised the barrel of his revolver. "This here ain't no gun—know what I'm sayin'? It's a party favor." He shook his head. "You County folks are the stupidest bunch of honky morons I ever seen."

"Johnson." Stoner studied the printout. "This says you were at the Clinic the other day."

"That's right, moron. Go to the head of your class."

"It also says—"

"I'll tell you what it says. Says they did tests on me. Found masses in my lungs and bladder. Been coughin' blood for three weeks. What's *that* tell you?"

"It tells me you're a sick man."

Johnson barked laughter. "Somebody coughs up blood and you say he's sick. That should make everyone feel better. We can *all* sleep better now—know what I'm sayin'?"

"Johnson, this chart says the cancer can be controlled. It says you should be able to—"

"That's crap. Don'tcha know what it means to be on Welfare with a terminal disease? They stick you in a room with a hundred others and strap your ass down. When they got the time, they come in and say they're gonna give you somethin' for the pain. Then they give you the juice and your ass is on its way to the Plant. I ain't got no money—understand? We chumps on Welfare ain't got nothin'. And if I'm sent to the Clinic, I'm gonna be dead in two weeks, tops."

"Listen, Johnson—"

"I'd rather die right here, right now, than go to that Clinic. Damn state won't give no expensive drugs to no one on Welfare."

"Johnson, let the girl go."

"Fifi goes with me."

"Johnson, listen to me."

"Fuck you."

Stoner lowered the loudspeaker. "Sonnet, tell Logan to do something to distract this moron. Anything he can. Pull down his pants, crawl around on the pavement, scream like a chicken. But tell him to keep close to the ambulance for cover."

Kyle's stomach made a loud protest. He didn't like the way Stoner's thumb was resting on the hammer of the pistol. "Sir, the police should be here in—"

"No time for that."

"But—"

"Do as I say, dammit. Now! Chop! Chop!"

Logan was squatting near the front tire when Kyle snuck up behind him. "What's up?"

"The Chief wants you to distract Mr. Johnson any way you can. Get his attention. But you know what? I really don't think—"

"That's right, kid," Logan said flatly. "You *don't* think. Do yourself a large favor. Do what you're told. Understand?"

There was no way Kyle understood. He was barely a grown man, had never been on his own before. He hadn't heard anything about these people using guns and acting like police officers. Or about distracting a man with a gun or doing what you were told without thinking about the consequences.

Using the front bumper for leverage, Logan climbed up and began waving wildly, his hands high above him.

The roar of a pistol shot shattered the afternoon silence.

Something slammed into Logan's shoulder. Blood spattered the ambulance's hood and windshield. Tiny drops sprayed Kyle's visor and a portion of his yellow cap.

Gasping, Logan thumped to the pavement.

Johnson's daughter wrenched free, landing on her stomach in the grass. Wailing, she crawled frantically toward the ambulance.

Johnson aimed the gun. His arm shook violently.

A deafening gunshot reverberated behind the wagon. Johnson swayed, a cold emptiness welling in his remaining eye. His arm dropped to his side; the gun fell silently onto the grass. His mouth gaped open. He looked like he was about to say something. His face lifted toward the heavens.

Then he collapsed.

\*\*\*

"Lose your breakfast, Sonnet?"

Kyle knelt on the ground, his gut burning like a bucket of hot coals. His nose was running and his eyes were wet.

"No, sir," he managed. "Not yet."

"Good. Don't let's make this a habit, now. Time table, remember? Things to do."

Stoner sounded like was having a good time. Kyle half-expected him to suddenly execute a

45

cartwheel on the pavement. *Nothing like blowing someone away to get the juices flowing, eh, Sonnet?*

Maybe all that stuff Kyle had heard about Marines being psychos was true after all…

"Didn't that…bother you, sir?" Kyle straightened to his full height. "You just…blew a man away."

"I know what I did, Sonnet. I was there, remember? Had the best seat in the house. Look…you have to see things objectively. Johnson was a dead man. He wanted to take his daughter with him when he cashed in his chips. He might even have killed someone else with a stray bullet. When you've got a lunatic waving a loaded gun, it usually goes off. And it did, didn't it? Enough of this nonsense. We need to look after Logan. So clean your chin and wipe off your visor and helmet. There's blood all over it."

Three police cars blocked the street. Two cops examined Johnson's body while a third stood on the front stoop, talking with the family. Johnson's widow—a tall, heavyset woman—sobbed into a handkerchief. A skinny boy about nine or ten and the girl Johnson called Fifi pressed against her ample bosom. Neighbors watched from front porches and behind bushes. Others remained indoors, peeking behind half-closed blinds.

A tall, broad-shouldered cop approached Stoner. The name 'Roarke' was stamped in white letters on the shiny black plastic nametag pinned to his shirt pocket flap. Stoner handed the cop several forms he'd taken from his satchel. The cop laid them on the hood of the cruiser, scribbled something, and returned them to Stoner. Stoner signed his name, carefully ripped off both the pink and yellow copies and surrendered the originals to the cop.

"Documentation for everything, Sonnet." Stoner followed Kyle up the wagon steps and pulled the door shut. "Death certificate, accident report, incident registration, witness report, justification examination, euthanasia certification—although that last item doesn't apply here, so we won't have to sweat that one out. Cops take the originals. We keep a copy for our files and send copies to the state capital. Our lawyers study everything very closely before anything is filed or sent out."

"For everything, sir?"

"Wherever and whenever a death occurs. Especially if I have to discharge my firearm."

"Do you...discharge your firearm...a lot?"

"How's that?" The glint in Stoner's eyes told Kyle he'd wandered into forbidden territory again.

"I mean, like, every day? Once or twice a week?"

"If I have to use it every day, that's what I'll do. Sonnet, when someone forces me to use my firearm I'm going to oblige them, because it happens to be my job."

47

# Chapter 5

Dwarfed by the jagged mountainous shapes of glittering skyscrapers, the Clinic sat silently, its mirrored windows reflecting the ambulance and wagon as Kyle followed Buster up the paved drive.

Beneath the *Emergency Admittance* sign, the glass doors slid open. Two burly men in green scrub shirts and baggy white trousers rushed outside. In a flurry of well-coordinated movements, they removed the gurney containing Logan's covered shape from the ambulance, locked it into position and rushed it up the walk. Kyle could feel Stoner's eyes on him as he applied the emergency brake and switched off the ignition. "You need to come in and observe, see how the process works," he said.

"Yes, sir."

"Know what observe means?"

"Yes, sir..."

"What's it mean?"

"To watch and learn?"

"Exactly. It *doesn't* mean that you can ask stupid questions. Get it?"

"Yes, sir."

***

A middle-aged woman with gray hair tied in a severe bun waddled into the waiting room, her overstuffed orthopedic shoes making tiny squeaks on the tile floor. Her square face sat above folds of loose flesh covering her neck. The lipstick didn't do much to soften the severity of her mouth, which was nothing more than a slash mark pulled down at each

48

corner. Her small hazel eyes seemed lost behind the puffy lids. The material of her white smock stretched Saran Wrap-thin over the expanse of her hips and waist.

"Captain Stoner?" she said in a loud, low-pitched voice.

Stoner straightened. "Yes ma'am."

"We need to know Paramedic Logan's medical situation before we proceed."

"Of course."

"This way, please."

Stoner and the nurse disappeared around the corner.

Buster, his normally ruddy complexion a sickly white, slumped in a chair in front of a window.

Kyle sat down beside him. "This might not be so bad. It was only a shoulder wound."

"Kid, you don't know what you're talking about."

Kyle knew he was naïve, but he'd been right there when Logan was shot. The wound was serious but not life-threatening. "It just didn't look very—"

"Logan's only got five years with the Department. That doesn't buy you too damned many credits."

Kyle didn't like Buster's grim tone. "But...a *shoulder* wound?"

"Kid...when you see how the system operates, you'll understand."

*The system.* That pamphlet Allie Parsons had given him to read. He'd chosen to daydream instead, to watch the activity out in the street.

At the desk, the gray-haired nurse filled out a form on her clipboard while Stoner looked on.

"You say Paramedic Logan's got five years with your department?" she asked.

"Yes."

"His rating?"

"Logan was due for an appraisal in three weeks. I was about to recommend a promotion. Would've bumped him up to a twelve. I was gonna recommend the promotion be retroactive."

"But he's only a ten as we speak?"

"I'm afraid so."

"How long has he been a ten?"

"Three years."

The woman consulted her chart. "Three years as a grade ten. That gives him two points per month, for a grand total of seventy-two points. His first six months earned the minimal monthly quarter-point. That brings it to seventy-three-point-five. What was Paramedic Logan's rating between that time and the time he was made a grade ten?"

"He was a four for six months, then a six the following year."

"I didn't see a history when I pulled up his files earlier. Has he been treated for anything recently?"

"No."

"Nothing to subtract from this, then. Good." The nurse removed a small calculator from her hip pocket. "Six points for the rest of the year as a four, twelve for the second year. At fifty medical units per point, this earns Paramedic Logan an allowance of forty-five hundred and seventy-five dollars."

"I'm aware of that."

"I'm sorry, Captain Stoner…"

"Shame Logan couldn't have been a twelve before he was shot. This would have given him more than enough allowance points."

The nurse double-checked her chart. "A rating of twelve earns the individual a full five points per month. Grade twelve would have put Paramedic Logan in the Elite category, automatically giving him a year's bonus, or another sixty points. Added to his forty-five seventy-five, he would have had more than enough points to have his shoulder repaired. But as it stands, the care he's facing—the operation, medications, and at least three days' stay in the hospital, which is over two thousand dollars per day even in a shared room—will easily surpass his present allotment."

Stoner made no comment.

"We've got no choice, Captain Stoner."

"I understand."

"With our current work load, not to mention the strict policy handed down directly from Washington—"

"We're all aware of the policy. Logan was given the handout like the rest of us. Just make sure he's comfortable."

"No need to worry. Paramedic Logan will be given every consideration. The paperwork will be ready in just a few hours along with the death certificate. We'll fax everything to Washington as quickly as possible. Your department should have copies this afternoon. Will that be satisfactory?"

"Yes. Thank you for your consideration."

"And Captain Stoner?"

"Yes?"

"Will your unit transport Paramedic Logan to the rendering plant?"

"We'll be delivering bodies we picked up earlier. I don't think we'll have time to make another trip within the hour." He gave her a curt nod. "You can call for another unit. We've got four. There's always a backup at the station."

"Thank you, Captain."

Stoner turned and nearly bumped into Kyle.

"Do I understand what's happening, sir?" Kyle couldn't believe what he'd just heard. "Is Logan going to be all right?"

"Not here."

***

"You're heading in the wrong direction, boy." Stoner's tense form filled the wagon doorway. His eyes sizzled. "Your first day on the job and you've already managed to get on my bad side."

Kyle sat behind the wheel, trying desperately to understand.

A shoulder wound. According to what he'd learned in school, nothing vital there but bone, cartilage, muscle, and skin. But it didn't matter because they were going to kill Logan anyway.

Allowance points.

Make sure he's comfortable.

"Why should this put your panties in a knot?" Stoner's voice expressed no remorse, no regret. Just some dude trying to understand what the fuss was all about.

"I don't know. It just does."

"We all die, Sonnet—every last one of us. Even young troublemakers like yourself will bite the dust one day."

"But Logan was hit…in the shoulder…"

"Logan knows the rules, what to expect." Stoner's tone was simple, direct. No fuss, no muss. No need for complications.

"Shoulder wounds aren't fatal. Are they?"

"Not having sufficient medical coverage makes a shoulder wound fatal, Sonnet. In plain English, Logan can't afford to stay alive any longer. Clear enough?"

No. It wasn't clear. Nor was it fair.

"Didn't Parsons give you a copy of the Point System? The State requires all State, County, and Federal employees—"

"Yes, sir…"

"You're not going to tell me you didn't read it, are you? You're not going to sit there and tell me you didn't deem it necessary to open the pamphlet, stick your nose in it and read the damn thing."

"Well, I *started* to—"

"Dandy. Just dandy." Stoner's rough features tightened. "The Point System is the single most important document published nowadays. It tells you everything about health benefits in plain, simple language. It's a slim volume, Sonnet. Twenty-four pages. It was written so anyone with average intelligence can understand it. I read the damn thing in twenty minutes. And since your files state—for whatever reason—that your intelligence is *far above* average, it should have taken you even *less* time."

"I know I should have read it, and I feel really badly for not doing it. I just don't see why Logan should have to—"

"Don't be stupid, boy. You've been around long enough to have observed certain things. Damned world's been going down the shitter for years. People kill one another, squirt out babies, piss away our natural resources, pollute the air and dump toxic chemicals into our drinking water. They kill off wildlife and fill in all the nice spots of the world with shopping malls, condominiums, and toxic dumps. Because of their stupidity, we all have to suffer."

Kyle wondered if Logan was conscious. If he knew what was going to happen. If they had already euthanized him.

"Sonnet, the population of this country has been in drastic need of thinning down for decades. Fifty million are cluttering up this state alone. The Government's been forced to step in and take care of people too stupid to take care of themselves. They've cracked down on healthcare, and for the last forty years they've been sticking it to these worthless assholes that insist on running around, making babies every fifteen minutes. You know all this. You were in a State Home, not a damned cave."

Kyle was only half-listening.

"Sonnet, can you honestly tell me that you came from a place that wasn't overcrowded?"

Overcrowded was an understatement. Hundreds of unruly kids turned the cafeteria into total pandemonium three times a day. Fights, flying food, yelling and screaming were the norm. The bathrooms sounded like a zoo at feeding time. The classrooms were even worse. The dormitories were so chaotic—even after lights were out—that a good night's sleep was a rarity.

Kyle frequently gulped down his meals and hurried outside so he could sit on one of the playground swings to escape the noise and the heat of chaos. Many times he'd avoided supper altogether, choosing instead to take a walk in the woods to enjoy the serenity of nature.

He'd managed to go on one field trip before Government aid dwindled down to nothing. The bus took them to the biggest theme park in the state. There were crowds of people everywhere. One exhibit, shot years ago from satellites, featured a panoramic film of different parts of the world. The exhibit required you to walk down a ramp and stand in a dimly-lit tunnel until the doors opened. Kyle got there twenty minutes early and waited with a couple of other people. In five minutes, twenty people stood in front of the doors. Five minutes later, there were fifty. Then a hundred. The entire tunnel was soon jam-packed. You couldn't raise your arm to scratch your ear.

The confined area quickly grew hot. People began to sweat. A few minutes later, the reek made his eyes water. The crowd fidgeted, coughed on one another and complained about the wait. Deodorants stopped working. Mouthwashes died. Bored kids jumped up and down and wailed. The adults with them raised their voices to hear themselves over their kids. Shouting ricocheted off the walls. The screaming worsened.

When the doors finally opened up, the gush of the crowd penetrated the doorway like a broken dam. Kids and small women were dragged along like debris in a strong wind. Clutches, keys and earpieces lay discarded on the hall floor, grim reminders that humanity had recently left its mark.

Despite his reluctance, Kyle had to agree that Stoner definitely had a valid point.

But he just couldn't help thinking about Logan being pushed into a dark room where a masked figure waited, a hypodermic in one gloved hand.

"Sir, Logan doesn't deserve—"

"Sonnet, stop your damned whining. This is how things are. Get used to it. And do it fast. That's an order."

# Chapter 6

Gum wrappers, cigarette butts and crushed beer cans lined the road outside the city. A beat-up couch rested in the brush. A gutted garbage bag sat near the curb, its contents strewn across the two-lane highway.

As Kyle drove, he couldn't stop thinking about his first day at his new job. Or about the bodies he was hauling to the rendering plant.

Two people living the good life who suddenly didn't want any part of it anymore.

A troubled man who didn't want to die a long agonizing death in a hospital ward.

Logan lying in the street, blood gushing from the bullet hole in his left shoulder.

Do what you're told.

The nuns had told him that same thing many times. Sister Maria Francesca, Sister Mary Benedict, Sister Agnes, and the others.

*You're a child, Kyle Sonnet. You don't know what is good for you. You can't see the overall picture, can't judge for yourself the right thing to do.*

Now he was in the real world, and the overall picture still wasn't clear.

As a child, doing what he was told meant obeying his elders. But now that he was a grown man, it meant becoming deaf, dumb, and blind.

*You wanted a job where you could be oblivious, didn't you? Well, now you've found one.*

Ten miles from the city limits, a large sign

*D. P. C. Rendering Plant*

painted in bold black letters on white metal reflected the penetrating glare of the afternoon sun.

"Turn here." Stoner pointed with his pen. "Then go straight for about five miles. There're signs everywhere. You can't miss it."

Kyle eased the wagon onto the dirt road. On their right, an overgrown pasture showed no signs of life. Deadfalls rotted in the tall grass. Withered, crippled trees formed an endless line of defeat in the background.

"No one owns this land, sir?"

"Confiscated."

"Why?"

"Farmers were squeezed out, so the places were condemned."

"Squeezed out?"

"Because of the oil shortage years ago, most farmers started growing corn for ethanol and let everything else go. Not many people want to live near a farm. The smell bothers them."

"But now there's no one to take care of the land."

"The Government'll do something with it eventually. A landfill, if nothing else. Or another plant. Where do you think all the trashed computers end up? Anyway, the Government can always use more land. Look what they've done on your left."

Rows of condominiums appeared lost in the middle of the sloping countryside, backing up to a large retention pond. Beyond the condos, barren land stretched as far as the eye could see. Felled trees lay in scattered piles, remnants of what was once lush woodland.

A small guard's station appeared. A large man in a seamless khaki uniform stood smartly behind a *STOP! WAIT FOR GUARD!* sign. A white mask covered the bottom half of his face; thick goggles covered the top half. A compact assault weapon hung from a black leather strap across his chest.

"Why the gun, sir?" Kyle asked uneasily.

"Heavy equipment out here. Expensive stuff. Black market thrives on it. This is Government land. Squatters, you know."

Recognizing Stoner, the guard saluted. Stoner returned the salute. The guard scrambled to unhook the big silver chain blocking the entrance.

"Go ahead, Sonnet."

The bumpy dirt path eased into a steep downgrade lined with pine trees. Barbed wire spanned its length in front of the tree line. A sign said, *"Proceed With Caution!"*

"Watch out for stray dogs. People drop them off out here all the time."

"Out *here*?"

"People buy animals because they're cute, but when the critter grows up, the cute turns to ugly. Their owners don't want anything ugly living with them so they dump them."

"Isn't there a Humane Society in town?"

"Costs five dollars to drop off an unwanted pet. That's a lot of money when you can just drive out here and do the deed for nothing."

"Isn't there a penalty for dumping animals?"

"Two years in prison for the first offense, compliments of the Animal Rights folks. When the State decreed euthanasia for the second offense, most of the dumping stopped. The morons too stupid to be scared still come out here at night. There are only a dozen guards, and everyone knows they can't watch everything. This place covers more than ten thousand acres, for Christ's sake. Over fifteen square miles of raw land. They've got cameras, but the dumpers are smart enough to wear caps and ski masks. Since they do the drop-offs at night, you can't work up a good ID. They haven't installed infrared yet." Stoner pointed. "Down this road. We're almost there."

A huge concrete building grew visible through the trees. Workmen in gray suits operating backhoes and shovels roamed the area. All wore the same white mask and goggles. A sign posted *Deliveries* on one side of the building near a guard's station.

"Drive on over to the station and stop on that inclined ramp. Make sure your side of the wagon faces the building. Workers will open up the release doors on your side. With the angle of the ramp, the bodies will slide on out and fall down a chute, which empties into a large tub. When a certain poundage is reached, the bottom is released. The load drops into a bucket, then onto a conveyor belt. The bodies are then removed from the bags and carried to a vat, which emulsifies them into a paste that is later dried and pounded into chips. Everything's recycled and turned into fertilizer, or electrical power."

Kyle was silent. *Poor Logan.*

"You'll get used to it. Twenty, maybe thirty bodies from now?" Stoner grinned. "You won't even bat an eyelash."

Kyle remained silent. *Remember—stay oblivious.*

"Lower your window, Sonnet."

Kyle did so. The thick stench made his eyes water.

"Kind of rich, eh?"

Kyle wiped his eyes. The smell made him think of the bodies that had been removed from the fire at the Home. "Is it always this bad, sir?"

"Didn't you ever get a good healthy whiff of human fertilizer?"

"They used it at the Home, but I guess I got used to it. Why is it so bad out here?"

"You're catching it before the chemicals bombarding it can tone down the aroma. Too damned fresh."

"It doesn't seem to be bothering you."

Stoner shrugged. "I've been doing this for so long, it no longer wrinkles a hair on the old schnoz. You'll be a regular trooper after a few of these trips."

Kyle nodded dutifully. *A trooper.* More *good news.*

A tall, skinny guard approached the window. His white mask was pulled down and shoved to the side, exposing the protruding walnut of an Adam's apple.

The guard's voice boomed over the steady hum of the machinery. "How many, Chief?"

"Just three, Aaron!" Stoner yelled. "But the day's young!"

"Heard about Logan! Sorry!"

"Those are the breaks! How long's the wait?"

"Just a few minutes! We're pretty busy, but we'll fit you in!"

Someone yelled at Aaron. He turned, nodded and waved at Stoner. "Gotta go! Later, Chief!"

Kyle closed the window. "The smell doesn't seem to bother him," he said.

"Boy's had bad sinuses ever since I've known him. Couldn't smell shit if you smeared it all over his face."

*Now* there's *an image I can live without...*

Stoner sat back. "Settle in, Sonnet. Sometimes 'just a few minutes' turns out to be half an hour."

***

Half an hour later, as they were just a few miles from the city limits, Stoner shifted in his seat. "Tell me your problem, Sonnet."

Kyle flinched. "Problem, sir?"

"Those stupid questions you've been asking all day."

"Stupid questions?"

"What part of that don't you understand? You ask questions all the time. Don't you realize they're stupid?"

"I always thought asking questions was the best way to learn, sir."

"It's not the asking, it's the questions themselves. They're irritating things a little kid asks his father. Why is the sky blue? Why do birds sing? What happens if the body's too long for the

62

compartment? Sonnet, it makes me wonder if those nuns taught you anything."

The nuns taught him how happy they were in their world of total abstinence and misery. They also taught him how much they hated males. But he knew Stoner wasn't referring to stuff like that.

"This is my first real job, sir. And I *am* only eighteen. I haven't been on my own very long…"

"It's more than that. You act like you haven't actually *seen* anything."

"I haven't. Not really."

"Sonnet, the pamphlet explains everything. All you need to know is in there, but you didn't read it. If you *had* read it, everything would be as clear as glass, and we wouldn't be having this conversation."

Nothing in the pamphlet could have possibly warned him about Logan's fate.

"I'm not so sure, sir."

"It would have given you the complete picture. What happened to Logan happens a *lot*."

"But Logan was one of us."

"The decree has been passed. We all have to abide by it. Each month you accumulate a certain number of points. Logan simply didn't have enough to pay for his operation. Since he didn't have enough coverage, we couldn't expect the Clinic to donate its valuable time and money to repair his shoulder, could we? Especially when people who *can* afford treatment would be pushed back in line. Understand *now*, Sonnet?"

"I hear what you're saying, sir."

"Good. We're halfway home, then."

63

Lunch hour traffic cluttered the roads. Lines flocking the fast-food takeout windows reached the main drag. The front lots of stores and shopping malls had become an endless sea of screaming kids, roving teens and angry drivers fighting over parking spaces.

At a filling station, a bald-headed man around fifty pumped gas into his van. As Kyle passed, the man yelled something inaudible above the sound of the engine. A fat woman emerged from the rest room behind the store. She turned around, bent over, and hiked up her checkered skirt.

"What do you like, Sonnet?"

"Sure don't like *that*," he said, frowning.

"Who the hell does?" Apparently Stoner had seen her, too. "Anyway, what interests you? Any hobbies?" The question was innocent enough, but Stoner wasn't exactly the *what's going on, dude?* type. As a Marine, his testosterone level would be more suited for smashing a beer can with his forehead or wrist-wrestling for drinks at the local bar.

"I enjoy music and writing. I also love movies. I've always wanted to see the really old ones. At the Home I read about the flicks they made in Hollywood in the early part of the Twentieth Century."

"They're corny and stupid. No one lived that way. The ones they made fifty or sixty years ago are a lot better. That kick-ass stuff with computers, wires, and special effects. Like them?"

"Some of them, but I'm really interested in the old films."

"What the hell for?"

"I've read that the classic movies made you feel good inside."

Stoner straightened in his seat. "You need a *movie* to make you feel good inside, Sonnet?"

"I've never seen any of the old ones. In those days folks would flock to the movie theaters and wait in line to see a film."

He'd read about *Casablanca, The Wizard of Oz, Gone With the Wind, It Happened One Night,* and many other classics. The short video clips he'd downloaded fascinated him. They never showed those films at the Home. Most were on the condemned list for the Catholic students. Some were considered satanic, some anti-Semitic. Others were thought to be anti-American, or anti-religious.

"Not enough blood and guts in 'em to suit me," Stoner said. "But I guess some would have a taste for them. I only saw a couple and never wanted to see any more. Much too unrealistic. They appeal to fat old ladies with sex problems." Stoner chuckled. "Hollywood's come a long way since, eh?"

"In what way, sir?"

"The way they priced themselves right into oblivion. Those narcissistic jerks getting close to a hundred million bucks for six weeks work, and it didn't matter one damned bit that people had stopped going to see them. When the theaters finally went under, that was the kiss of death. The movie producers knew what they were doing when they started working with the computer geeks to make movies without using flesh-and-blood actors.

Computer-enhanced images are where it's at. I like all twenty *Spiderman* flicks, the third *Superman* series, the *Matrix* remakes, and the James Bond films they've made with that new model prototype— what's its name? BondImage. Best thing Hollywood ever did. Now you've got the option to select who you want to play your Bond. Like those, Sonnet?"

"I enjoyed the books."

"They were *books*?"

"At first."

"Well, I really get a hoot out of the flicks. The star's image and individual voice are filtered in and you're all set. Once I programmed one of the Three Stooges to play Bond—just for the hell of it. Bald, fat guy? Curly?" Stoner's laugh bounced sharply off the walls of the wagon. "Hilarious. Curly and Goldfinger made a good team. You couldn't tell who was who."

Kyle hoped Stoner would soon tire of talking. Kyle wanted to get back to the station, take off his suit and have a long shower.

"What kind of music do you listen to?" Stoner asked.

"Big band stuff. Rock'n Roll. Jazz. I tried playing a trumpet at the Home, but the State stopped the music program because of budget cuts."

"Trumpet?"

"Yes, sir."

Stoner scratched his cheek. "Brass instrument?"

"Yes, sir."

"They used to use 'em for bugle calls before the Military got smart and used recorded piped-in stuff, right?"

"Yes, sir."

"Why in hell would you want to learn to play an instrument when you can just buy a CD?"

"I've always wanted to learn to play. It's...a challenge. Something to learn."

"Waste of time. Why do you think so many musicians have gone hungry? It's just like what happened with the movies. No one cares any more. You go to a bar, drink, and listen to piped-in stuff. It adds atmosphere. Take a mural on the wall. If it's there, good. If not, you don't even notice. Buy a CD. It doesn't appeal to you, take it back and exchange it or get a refund." Stoner shrugged. "Economical."

Kyle said nothing.

"Same thing with writing. Why bother? All the books have been written. What can you say that hasn't already been said? Nobody even reads any more. Why do you think all the big publishers went out of business? Reading is no longer necessary. They take books and make them into movies so you don't have to waste your time reading them. Instead of spending days poring over a stupid book, buy the damned movie and crack open a beer. You drink beer, Sonnet?"

"Yes, sir."

"Good. For a second you had me worried."

# Chapter 7

A few minutes later, Buster's voice crackled through the radio.

"Pickup, Chief. Three miles south of the Clinic, two blocks from Taylor County High School. Heart of the Doomsday district."

"Dandy. Just dandy."

"*Doomsday* district, sir?" The name didn't give Kyle a warm fuzzy.

"Not exactly our favorite section of town," Stoner replied.

A bleak quagmire of gutted buildings, scattered trash and rotting skeletons of automobiles awaited them. Bullet-riddled signs leaned against crumbling brick walls and shattered doorways of vacated businesses. Deserted liquor stores and filling stations sat in misery, the blank stare of their broken windows revealing the bleak emptiness within them. Graffiti embellished the walls. The deteriorating pavement gave the area an even more emaciated appearance.

Stoner removed the automatic from his hip pocket as they crept into the area. "All sorts of gang and drug activity out here. Five murders a week is considered slow. No need to take chances."

Twenty yards ahead, the bodies of four teenage males sprawled in the street. Gunshot wounds riddled all four. Blood pooled the pavement.

Kyle stopped behind the ambulance. Buster and Falworth, Logan's successor, got out cautiously.

Kyle locked the emergency brake with a shaky hand.

Stoner had already hustled down the steps.

68

As Buster and Falworth examined the bodies, one of the young hoodlums tried crawling away.

"Bastards can't even kill one another without fucking it up," Stoner said sourly. "Go help Buster, Sonnet."

Screaming, the boy lashed out, but was too weak to administer an accurate blow. Blood gushed from a gaping shotgun wound in his lower gut.

Buster knelt beside the boy, pulled a plastic-wrapped syringe from his leather bag and held it up. "Thebusol," he told Kyle. He ripped the plastic away and dropped it in his bag, then removed one of the packets. "It's more potent than the old stuff, which didn't work when we were in a hurry, or if the victim was on drugs."

The kid began choking. Blood dribbled down his chin. "*Fuck* you assholes" came out hotly, but without sufficient lung power.

Buster carefully filled the needle. "The old concoction consisted of five grams of sodium pentothal, fifty cc's of pancuronium bromide, and fifty of potassium chloride. Each was a lethal dose by itself but just didn't work well enough." Buster grabbed the teen's exposed arm. "This is what we've been using for lethals the last ten years. It's got a synthetic drug in it that gives them one last but very brief high."

The teen hacked up blood.

Kyle's stomach contents rumbled.

A shot rang out, slamming into the side of the ambulance just above the rear tire. Stoner spun on his heel and let loose with three quick deafening blasts. A distant scream reverberated down the street. The sound of garbage cans slamming against one another echoed likethunder.

Buster put his equipment away while the teen slipped away peacefully. "Let's bag 'em and get the hell out."

Within minutes Kyle, Buster, and Falworth shoved the bodies into the wagon while Stoner kept watch.

There were no more shots. Shadows lurked behind the stripped cars a block away.

While Stoner stood in the open doorway of the wagon, his gun pointed outward, Kyle followed the ambulance out of the area.

When they were a safe distance away, Stoner closed the door, pocketed the pistol and sat down heavily. "A good day's work, Sonnet."

Kyle barely heard him; he was trying to rid his mind of the blood.

# Chapter 8

Stoner's loud voice crackling from the p.a. system wrenched Kyle from a restless sleep.

"Up and at 'em! Early runs this morning, men! Sonnet, chow down your eggs and sausage and meet me in the garage in half an hour! That's six o'clock *sharp!*"

Three bleary-eyed men wearing bath towels and rubber flip-flops shuffled around beneath the humming florescent in the L-shaped bathroom. Kyle hadn't seen them when he chose his bed the previous evening. Brief introductions were mumbled as he approached one of six urinals fastened to the tile wall.

Tracy—short and square, reddish hair, and tiny blue eyes—swatted Kyle on the shoulder on his way to the sink. "You must be the kid with all the dumb questions the Stone's been grumbling about."

Heavy laughter bounced off the block walls.

Kyle smiled sheepishly. *Terrific. Just one day and I'm already the resident clown.*

He'd been similarly marked in grade school, when the nuns observed him wandering off by himself. But nuns seldom laughed, and swatted someone only as punishment.

"Keep 'em coming, kid." Wilcox, tall and dark, his face covered with black stubble, had the tiny blinking eyes of a mouse. He meticulously arranged his shaving gear on the sink. "Just get something kicking around up there, then jump the Stone about it. As long as you keep him busy, he'll leave the rest of us alone."

71

"I'll do my best," Kyle said flatly.

Wilcox turned on the hot water tap. "We got confidence in ya, kid." He smeared his cheeks and neck liberally with creamy white lather. "The Stone'll probably want to keep you here a long time just so he can say he straightened you out."

*Cool. Something else to look forward to...*

"How long have you guys been here?" he asked.

"I was about your age when I started," Wilcox said. "That's twenty years."

Tracy flushed the urinal and belched loudly. "Twelve for me. And believe me, we all asked stupid questions at first. You've got to. This job's weird."

Wilcox rinsed off his razor. "That bum there?" He jerked a sharp elbow at Tracy. "Had the brass *cojones* to ask the Stone if we could keep the jewelry we found on the victims."

Tracy glared through the giggling. "I figured after twelve years, even a mental midget like you would forget that."

Kyle picked up his shaving bag. "Was Captain Stoner here when you started?"

Younger—medium height, with a muscular body, short gray hair and chestnut eyes—hawked out a white burst of toothpaste into the sink. "Stone's been here since the dinosaurs ruled the Earth, kiddo. That steel-assed bastard built this place."

"I sorta thought he was maybe forty-five or so," Kyle said.

"Stone's sixty if he's a day." Tracy opened his shaving kit. "Keeps himself in top shape. Once a Marine..."

Younger nodded. "A two-mile run and two hundred push-ups each morning before breakfast. Then an hour in the weight room before bed. I've tried keeping up with him but it's impossible, and I'm only thirty-seven. Stoner's a monster. Been with the County thirty years. He'll *never* retire."

"I were you, kid," Wilcox said, "I'd learn the job. Stone ain't the guy you want on your ass."

"I already figured that out," Kyle said.

Younger rinsed off his toothbrush. "Stay on his good side. Job pays well and it'll take care of you—especially if something happens."

"Like what?" he asked nervously.

Younger chuckled. "There he goes again, asking those dumb questions."

\*\*\*

Glass slivers twinkled like jewels on the asphalt.

A red pickup truck lay on its side twenty feet from the curb. An airport limousine, flipped upside-down, obstructed three lanes of highway. Two compacts formed a jagged entity of twisted metal on the macadam.

The accident had occurred at a crucial twelve-lane intersection. Double lines of cars at takeout windows and impatient gas station traffic turned the area into a labyrinth of hot metal, flared tempers and exhaust fumes.

Police filtered the swollen flow down to a one-lane trickle in each direction. Cars, trucks, motorcycles and buses inched nervously past the orange cones.

"This one will be easy." Stoner assayed the scene from the bench seat of the wagon. "The two in the compacts are probably toast. And judging by how the roof of the limo is squished flat, the limo driver is probably also worm-food. The trucker's no doubt in bad shape. I see kids in the back of the limo, but I don't think they'll be major problems."

Stoner's relaxed tone suggested he approved of the situation. Bodies were easy: just bag 'em, load 'em and haul 'em. No fuss, no muss. Only the living presented problems. The living got drunk, turned stupid and tried using brain cells that just weren't there.

As long as everyone was dead or dying, Stoner was happy.

The compact drivers, both around forty, were pronounced dead from massive head wounds. No problem there. The driver of the pickup was slammed senseless against the passenger's side when his truck was knocked over. Another easy one. The limo driver lay unconscious. No biggie—especially when the needle poked its ugly nose out of Buster's leather bag.

Two females around ten or eleven lay shivering on the pavement. One whimpered, "I want my father," in a heavy British accent. A male about thirty-five had been sitting with the two girls in the limo. Judging from the strong resemblance, he was undoubtedly their father. His chest was crushed after being slammed into the front seat. The roof caving in on him had pulverized his spine.

"How bad?" Stoner asked.

Falworth knelt between the girls. "Two broken legs, a broken arm and a severed artery. One's got shattered ribs and a sliced femoral. Probably when they pulled her out through the window."

Kyle couldn't turn away. The little girl's eyes were glossy and unfocused. She seemed so helpless lying beside her sister, whose eyes were closed. "Are both…going to die?" he asked no one in particular.

"Would *you* want to live through this?" Stoner asked curtly.

"But they're—"

"Tourists." Stoner's brows mashed together beneath the visor. "And tourists fall under our jurisdiction as soon as they touch American soil."

"I wasn't going to say 'tourists,' sir."

"What *were* you going to say?"

Blood spurted from the little girl's upper thighs. Her pink flesh, visible beneath her brown and white plaid skirt, seemed so fragile. She moved her mangled hand awkwardly in Kyle's direction.

A lump gathered in Kyle's throat. He wanted to take her in his arms and tell her everything would be fine. They'd get her to a hospital and make her well.

But she was going to die; Buster would see to it. No problem. There were just too many damned people in the world.

"Nothing to say, Sonnet?"

Kyle forced down the anger. "They're…little girls, sir." He was surprised the words came out so coherently.

"Well, now they're road-kill, and it's our job to take them to the plant. Isn't that what we do? What we're being paid to do? Whatever happened to that 'dead bodies don't bother me' bullshit you handed me yesterday morning? Did you lie to me, Sonnet?"

"I didn't think I did, sir…"

"Then what's the problem?"

Stoner was the problem because he wanted everyone dead. He enjoyed it. It was the job, yes, but the fact that he'd taken it to another level was frightening. There was something seriously creepy about a man who obviously liked being around death.

"I…don't know, sir."

"Then it must not be important. So get your mind clear. That's an order."

"What about their relatives?"

"State Department's responsibility. They're the ones who communicate with our international visitors. Don't worry. All the necessary paperwork will be filled out, everything properly notarized and delivered. All the t's will be crossed, the i's dotted. Nothing to worry about."

Kyle forced himself to turn away.

"Anything else?"

Despite the hot wave of disgust sweeping through him, Kyle shook his head.

"Good. Just shut up and do your job. That's another order." Stoner gave Kyle a scowl. "People are staring. Don't want them doing that, do we?"

"No, sir. We sure don't want people staring."

"Go help Buster. I'll help Falworth with your little girls. Now hustle right on over there. Chop! Chop!"

*** 

A gray-haired man lay half-hidden in the high grass in front of a one-story brick house. Behind him, an aluminum ladder leaned against a rusty gutter.

As Kyle stopped along the curb behind the ambulance, the fallen man regained consciousness, jumped to his feet and scurried back up the ladder.

Stoner shook his head.

"What now, Chief?" Buster said from the dash unit. "Who called this in?"

"Concerned neighbor. False alarm?"

"Looks like it. You and Falworth head on back and take off for lunch. We'll be there shortly."

Kyle waited for Stoner to tell him to start up the engine, but Stoner just sat there, staring at the house.

This didn't feel right.

"Back to the Station, sir?"

"False alarms are serious, Sonnet. We're on a tight schedule and don't have time for nonsense. Do you realize what would happen if we were called every time some idiot tripped or fell?"

"Not really, sir. What would happen?"

"What the hell do you think would happen?"

"We'd be out on a lot more calls?"

"We'd also need ten times the manpower. We'd have to requisition a damned shuttle for the rendering plant. I've been trying for three years to get those Government morons to grant us a shuttle, but they don't seem to have the time for an in-depth

77

study. How's *that* one for a healthy sweep under the rug?"

Kyle didn't reply.

"Jerks have all kinds of time for parties and international trips, but are squeezed much too thin for a shuttle service study. Doesn't that sound stupid to you?"

"Yes, sir." Kyle hoped he looked serious enough. "So…are we going back to the Station?"

"I have to remind these folks what's what. First, the asshole on the ladder. Then, of course, the nitwit that called this in."

Stoner sprang to a standing position and pulled open the side door. "I'm going to give them a short version of the law because they've obviously forgotten it. One false alarm is tolerated, but logged in our books. A second time entitles us to prosecute the offenders to the fullest extent of the law."

"*Offenders*, sir?"

"You have a better term for it?"

"Victim sounds more like it to me…"

"Victim. Good one. Sometimes you're a real hoot, Sonnet." Stoner looked like he wanted to laugh.

# Chapter 9

Kyle coaxed the wagon into its dark stall. He put it in park and killed the engine, and felt honest relief for the first time since breakfast.

Stoner sat finishing his log entries under the interior light. A minute later he snapped the book shut and jumped up. "Chow time, Sonnet." He pulled open the side door. The strong reek of machine oil, grease and exhaust fumes spiraled up the steps. "Chow hall's open twenty-four hours. All County workers are entitled to free meals. They also serve all patients and workers shuttled over from the Clinic." Stoner nodded solemnly. "A good deal, Sonnet. Any idea how scarce good food is in this town?"

"How scarce is it, sir?" Kyle found that he wasn't hungry. He also found that he really wasn't in the mood to talk to Stoner but knew that keeping quiet would cause even more trouble.

"Pretty damn scarce."

Kyle nodded but made no comment.

"The food-service workers were appropriated when the County Hospital went out of business and turned the buildings into Government storage. We lucked out because we knew important people who knew how to move the right papers around. Otherwise, everything would have been shipped to the state capital to fatten up those fat politicians even more. Eat well, Sonnet. We may have a busy afternoon ahead of us." Stoner hopped down the steps and disappeared in the darkness.

Kyle stepped down from the wagon, tried not to take in the exhaust-laden air and headed sullenly for the hall door. He wanted to take a walk but figured he should eat something.

Ten minutes later he sat alone, picking at his food while the afternoon sun glinted off the windows of the buildings across the street.

Kyle saw only darkness and death.

Wasn't that what everything was about? We offer death—quick and painless. What could be easier? When you're in pain, do not fear, Stoner and his band of death-dealers are near. Just hold out your arm. No fuss, no muss. We take care of everything—the shot, the ride to the plant. Everything above board and proper. All the t's will be crossed, the i's dotted. Can't have problems or complications.

"Mind if I join you?"

Allie Parsons slid her tray toward his. She wore a sleeveless tan tee shirt and faded jeans. A slender gold necklace decorated her neck. Her faint smile nearly erased the vertical line between her slim dark brows.

Kyle's previous thoughts of death evaporated like a book snapping shut.

"How are you, Miss Parsons?"

"Call me Allie." She lowered herself onto the bench seat.

"You can call me Kyle."

"I know. I remember you from yesterday." She picked up her fork.

"You remember everyone who comes in for an interview?"

"Just the ones asking too many questions."

*Here we go. The Clown strikes again…*

"News sure does spread fast."

Allie fitted a small forkful of steaming mashed potato between her lips. "Want some advice from someone who's seen just about everything in the last five years?"

"Let me guess. Stop asking stupid questions. Shut up and do your job. Don't worry about things that don't concern you. How's that?"

Allie forked up a slice of smoked salmon. Her sober expression did not change. "That basically covers it."

"Thanks, but it's already out. Stoner doesn't exactly keep things buttoned up inside."

"Not much stays hidden in this place. The least you could do is let me try to help you." She sounded sincere, but the hardness covering her pretty face didn't match the soft, caring voice. She could be one of those softies who didn't appear that way on the outside. He'd known a couple of people like her at the Home. Abe, the janitor, a hard-faced old guy with a gruff voice, would give you the shirt off his back. Albert Doane, a music teacher Kyle once knew briefly, always looked like he'd just swallowed something sour, but was available any time of day or night if you displayed the slightest interest in music.

But women seemed different. If a woman appeared hard, chances were very good that she *was* hard.

Allie Parsons, for example.

Yesterday she didn't seem the least bit interested—maybe because she didn't want to be caught fraternizing. The cafeteria could be neutral ground. Here you could fraternize to your heart's content.

"What's the problem?" she asked. "Yesterday you didn't seem too concerned about what the job was."

"I've learned a lot since yesterday."

"By the way, keep your voice down." She jabbed an index finger at the ceiling behind him. Above the wide entrance, a black box sat mounted just above the camera. "Those speakers work both ways, you know."

Speakers as well as a camera. Cool. They had cameras in banks, service stations, supermarkets, the laundromat and public rest rooms. Why should this place be any different?

In the Home, cameras monitored activity in every classroom and hall, each bathroom, the dormitory halls and the cafeteria. Kyle had longed for the day when he no longer had to worry about being watched.

"What's bumming you out?" Allie sipped some iced tea through a straw.

"The wagon."

"Whaddya mean?"

"The part where I get in the wagon and drive."

"You don't like driving?"

"Driving's cool. In fact, I really get off on it. I get to see places I've never seen before. It's almost a rush."

"Then what's the problem?"

"Stopping, getting out and shoving bodies inside the wagon."

She blinked. "But Sonnet, that's—"

"I know. It's the job."

"A job you applied for. A job you knew about."

"I thought I did."

"What's changed?"

"Capping the people still moving around. I guess they didn't consider that minor tidbit worth mentioning at the Employment Center."

Allie made no comment, but he could tell by the way she lowered her eyes that she understood. He hoped this meant she didn't care for any of it, either. An ally would be nice to have in this. Her name even fit.

"We find people who are hurt or dying and give them a shot to make them croak faster. Does that seem cool to you?"

"Didn't the Stone give you his speech?"

"He sure did."

"Didn't you read between the lines?"

"What lines are between 'there are just too many damned people'?"

"There aren't enough jobs or enough housing. Welfare and other state aid are nearly all tapped out. The Family Planning Act has helped quite a bit. At least it prevents people from making too many babies—which has been our biggest problem—and forces those who don't know or care about birth control to be chemically sterilized. But the underdeveloped countries are still at fault, and there's little we can do about that. And since this country and all other major countries have been

83

taken over by giant international conglomerates, declaring war would be like slitting our own throats. There just aren't enough people dying to keep the population balanced. Sonnet, where have you been? I'm only four years older than you but it seems like I've seen way more than you have."

"I grew up in a State Home. We were kind of isolated out there."

"If you had CNN, then you must have *some* idea what's been going on."

"I got in the habit of tuning out. People used to laugh at me for zoning out all the time."

"Why'd you zone out?"

"I wanted to be by myself."

"Hard to do, isn't it? Especially when you're up to your ears in kids."

"I could zone out anywhere."

"Must have taken a lot of concentration."

"After a while it became second nature."

"How about the cafeteria there?"

"What about it?"

"Could you zone out there?"

"Sometimes."

"How many were usually in there at a time?"

"Three hundred."

"Ouch."

"We waited in line for trays and silverware, then waited in line for the food. We were given twenty minutes to eat. We got up from the table when the buzzer went off and waited in line to drop the dirty dishes and silverware into the bins. We stacked the trays and waited in line to leave so we could go back to class."

"See what I mean? Too many people."

"Right about that…"

"Sonnet, a few years ago, most hospitals went under because they were so swamped they could no longer function. Because of hospital downsizing, they were forced to turn down nearly everyone who came to them for treatment. There were no nurses. No technicians. No doctors. State aid flushed itself right down the tubes. The remaining hospitals had to close entire wings and hire early-release felons, vagrants and veterinarians just to keep up with the workload. This was all so crazy because the hospital moguls were getting filthy rich in other avenues. They systematically eliminated most of their staff and used investment money to buy non-medical commodities such as oil, real estate, foreign money, solar power—anything that could make them richer. But people were still lining up outside. When nobody could tend to them they died on the sidewalk and in the grass. Something had to be done."

Kyle stared at his uneaten cheeseburger. He saw only Nathaniel Johnson lying in the grass, staring up at the sky with his remaining eye, Logan sprawled on the pavement, his shoulder soaked in blood, and the broken bodies of two little girls being pulled out of a smashed limo. But what really disturbed him was Allie trying to convince him everything was okay.

"You knew you'd be driving a meat wagon," Allie said. "Tell me what's really bothering you about all this."

"I figured they'd already be dead."

85

"Well, now you know the whole story. Didn't the Stone ask during your interview if you'd ever seen a dead body?"

He nodded.

"What did you tell him?"

"There was a fire at the Home, and some kids I didn't like died in it."

"All right, then."

"It's *not* all right. They were dead when I saw them. They weren't squirming around on the ground like smashed roaches."

Allie glanced at the doorway.

"I just think there's a world of difference between a dead body and someone lying at your feet, reaching out for you."

"These people you saw euthanized," Allie said a few moments later. "Were they healthy and strong?"

"No…"

"Were they dying? Suffering? Almost dead?"

"Logan was perfectly healthy."

She took a breath. "He was shot, Sonnet."

"In the shoulder…"

"He didn't have enough points, did he?"

He didn't reply. Once again, she'd made her point.

Allie put her fork down. "Trust me, Sonnet. It's the only solution we have right now. And if I were you, I'd get with the program. Otherwise…"

"What'll happen?"

Allie hesitated.

"Will I get fired?"

"The Stone doesn't fire people," she said very softly.

"I know. He doesn't like quitters. Makes him look bad. Maybe he forgot to dot an 'i.'"

Allie dabbed at her mouth and dropped the napkin on her plate. She got up. "It was nice talking to you, Sonnet." She picked up her tray. "Let's do it again some other time."

The sound of a tray cracked smartly onto a table. Stoner sat down at the table directly behind him.

# Chapter 10

The afternoon passed quietly.

Kyle lay on his bed in the dark room. When he closed his eyes, he imagined he was back at the Home. It was the weekend, everyone attending a Saturday afternoon baseball game. Normally he'd be in the library, but he wanted to lie here for a while. Only when everyone else was gone could a guy get some serious thinking accomplished. You had to take advantage of times like these because there weren't too many of them. In an hour or so the game would end and everyone would be stampeding back to their rooms—half the guys celebrating, the others moping around. Chains of insults would bounce off the tiled walls of the bathroom down the hall. Chaos would ensue as the winners showered triumphantly with the losers. The steady hum of cascading water could not drown out the stinging sounds of slapping butts and cries of pain.

*Click! Smack! Thump!*

"Shit!"

"Dammit, Tracer man. You made me scratch!"

"Cue ball's *mine* now."

"Ya lucked out, dammit."

Guys shooting pool in the rec room down the hall.

The Station.

The grownup world…

Kyle turned on his side. The speaker was fastened to the wall above the doorway. When it squawked there would be more work. And more bodies to be picked up.

But it had to be this way. Stoner said it. So did Allie. There were too many people. Kyle knew it as well as anyone. Anyone who had spent any time in the Home knew it. Anyone who had driven on the roads—or gone into the city or anywhere else— knew it.

You waited in line. For everything.

The only thing you didn't wait in line for was death.

At five-thirty Stoner, still in his khakis, appeared in the doorway. The man's face was impassive as usual. It was impossible to determine if he was angry or happy. "Not much going on, Sonnet. Take off. I'll let you know if something comes up." Then he was gone.

Cool. A good night's rest to drain the unpleasantness from his bones. After a long shower and some sleep, he'd be as good as new.

But what about tomorrow?

Would he be able to face another day? To turn a blind eye and do what he was told?

It's necessary. Remember that.

*It's not like you'll be as guilty as Stoner, is it? You won't have a gun to coax the process along. You won't have a hypodermic to expedite the works. All you'll be doing is driving the wagon. Your conscience will be clear.*

He was doing too much thinking. A shower. A good night's sleep. He could do more thinking at breakfast tomorrow morning, when he was refreshed. And as the saying went, tomorrow would take care of itself.

He stripped down to his shorts and opened his locker.

Sharp clicking noises on the tile floor echoed down the hall, growing louder. Dressed in a light blue tank top, black skirt and spiked heels, Allie Parsons slipped through the open doorway.

On impulse, he held his trousers in front of him to hide his near-nakedness. "What's up?" he asked timidly.

"I was wondering if you'd like to go somewhere tonight."

"Where?" He tried not to notice her eyes summing him up. The blinds were closed; the room was pretty dark. But he could tell he was being evaluated.

"The Tech Novel." She accented the last syllable of the third word. "A new place that opened a couple of weeks ago. Everyone says it really rocks. Wanna go?"

"You...want me to go with you?"

The prominent vertical line, never completely gone, appeared boldly between her brows. "Am I talking to you, Sonnet? I don't see anyone else here."

"I *guess* so..."

"Is there a problem?"

"I...didn't know you liked me."

The vertical line remained. "I'm not proposing marriage. I'm only asking if you'd like to go. Personally I think you could use a night out."

"I don't have a car."

"I do."

"Cool."

"Does that mean you want to go?"

He nodded.

"Sonnet, no one can ever accuse you of talking too much."

\*\*\*

Six blocks from the Station, fireballs of blinding neon splashed off the cars parked at the curb and across the street. Four lanes of heavy traffic growled and moaned impatiently at the intersection. Spike-haired partiers wrapped tightly in leather, chains and rawhide congregated at street corners, sharing blunts and lines of cocaine while mumbling into their earpieces. Long lines at the fast food mall down the block mixed with the crowds at the gas pumps, forming a swollen boil of anxious humanity.

Inside the block building, rotating strobe lights transformed the huge room into a disorienting fireworks display. A monolith of jerking limbs and flashing jewelry covered the polished floor.

Allie shouted something, but it was impossible to hear anything above the throbbing sound system.

She grabbed his elbow and pulled him close. "Wanna dance?"

The minty smell of her breath and the vanilla scent of her hair perked him right up. It took him several seconds to examine the heart-shaped mole on her lobe above the diamond stud. "Don't know how!"

"How about we just sit for a while and have a drink?"

"Sounds good…"

Small round tables sitting on metal posts bolted to the floor and flanked by padded bar stools were lined up along the psychedelically-painted walls. Flickering candles floating in glasses highlighted their centers. Kyle and Allie squirmed onto stools. A waitress emerged from the crowd and stuck her sweat-glazed face between them. "What's your order?"

Kyle wanted a beer but didn't know if he could afford one. Everyone leaving the Home was given one month's living expenses which were deducted from their first month's salary when employment or state aid was obtained. Kyle's six weeks at the laundry hadn't enabled him to accumulate much financial independence. And since the state wasn't noted for promptness regarding monthly allotments, he was almost certain his account was empty.

"I don't know how much money I've got in my account," he said.

The waitress frowned.

"Is this your first time in one of these places?" Allie said.

"I guess you could say that."

She moved closer. "Here's how it works. Your card was read at the door. Since there's a two-drink minimum, you're automatically billed. Any more and you've got to give them your card so they can swipe it again. If there isn't enough to pay for the drinks, an electronic charge is sent to your employer and the amount is deducted from your paycheck. This way everyone gets his money. Understand?"

"I think so."

Allie turned to the waitress. "Two drafts."

She whispered into her mouthpiece then disappeared.

"Well?" Allie asked. "Whaddya think?"

Blocking out the chaotic thumping of the electronic music was impossible. He could understand Allie by reading her lips—which was cool. However, surviving the booming p.a. system was going to be difficult. "I think I'm going to have a headache in the morning—but not from drinking."

"You'll get used to it. This is truly your first visit to a bar?"

"Nuns aren't exactly party animals. Their habits keep them from doing the latest jigs."

"I've heard that they don't like anyone having fun."

"Pretty much."

"I guess they don't think much of society."

"Actually they don't think much about it at all."

"What *do* they think about, Sonnet? Aside from God and abstinence, I mean."

"Mostly they just think about God. And when they're all together, they either have lengthy rap sessions about abstinence or just say the rosary."

The waitress put their drafts on the table between them. She wiped off some spill with a wet cloth and disappeared again.

Allie pushed her stool closer. "I've been meaning to ask you something."

"Shoot."

"You got a girlfriend?"

"I don't *think* so…"

She frowned. "You're not sure?"

"Not really."

93

"You really don't know if you have a girlfriend?"

"Last I checked I didn't."

"How about friends? Someone from the Home, maybe?"

"I wasn't what you'd call a mixer."

"You're quiet and all, but you seem to be a really nice guy. That is, unless you're hiding your dark side from me."

"I like hiding my dark side from women."

"What's your dark side?"

"I'm not sure. I guess I haven't given it much thought."

"Very funny."

He shrugged. "It's a gift."

"You've always stuck pretty close to yourself, then?" she asked.

"Me, myself, and I have been buddies for years. We're usually too busy hanging out to bother with other stuff."

Allie drank some beer. "You act like you've never *done* anything. All those questions you ask. It's as if you're from another world. Like you just landed a few days ago and haven't been able to find out anything because you don't know where to look."

"At the Home you got into trouble if you were caught looking at stuff they didn't want you to look at."

"What did you do for entertainment?"

"Went to the library, listened to music and audio books and took long walks. The Home was surrounded by woods. When you share a bedroom and bath with twenty guys, sit in a classroom with sixty or seventy and eat in a cafeteria with hundreds of others, you go out of your way to be by yourself. At least I did. Everything was quiet and peaceful in the woods. It became my fantasy world. When everyone else was busy with games or sports, I went off by myself. I never paid much attention to what was going on. The news never interested me because it was so depressing. Someone was always dying or getting blown up. And most TV shows are plain stupid."

"I feel that way, too. I've been living alone since I left home. I really like it. You can come and go as you please. If you can't sleep and want to take a walk, you don't have to tell anyone what you're doing, where you're going or when you'll be back. There's a really neat pond behind my apartment. If I wanna take a walk at three in the morning, I'll do it. At the station they call me 'Iceberg.' You've heard that, no doubt."

"Actually I hadn't heard anyone talk about you."

"Truly?"

"I only actually saw the other guys once. In the bathroom this morning. They were busy razzing me."

"Those guys are basically okay, but some are real jerks. Especially the night shift. Your group is about the best, and I'm just not saying that to be nice."

"I guess they're all right. They'll probably be even better when they quit razzing me."

On the dance floor, people jumped up and down to the music.

"You're the first guy from work I've ever gone out with," she said.

"I guess that makes me special."

"You *are* special, Sonnet."

This chick was full of surprises. Her cold, businesslike persona showed clearly, even in dress clothes. In her eyes, her features and the way she held herself. Her attitude said she knew she was attractive but wasn't about to let her looks soften her.

"You really think so?"

"You're quiet, funny, don't bother anyone, and don't like to see people dying or suffering. Not too many people are like that nowadays."

"Neither are you or you wouldn't have even noticed it."

"You could be right."

"I think I am, but you're putting a hex on it."

"How?"

"We're obviously two of a kind, with the same opinions and outlook. But this job and what it means doesn't seem to bum you out at all."

"It did when I first started."

"And now you don't care anymore?"

"It's not that…"

"Tell me how it is, then."

"I understand things better. But you're right. I was sensitive about it at first."

Kyle drank some beer and wondered what he was going to be like a few years from now. He hoped he wouldn't be as insensitive as Allie seemed to be.

"What do you think of me, Sonnet?"

"As a person?"

"As a woman. How do you feel about me?" Something in those big dark eyes told him Miss Iceberg could turn into a serious fireball if nudged the right way.

"I like you."

"Really?"

This was beginning to get a little hairy. Even with his limited experience he'd learned how easy it was to upset a chick. They wanted to know the truth but went crazy if you told them something they didn't want to hear.

"Tell me, Sonnet..."

"You're pretty, smart, and look really hot in jeans. And that skirt's doing a serious number on me."

She looked down at the water-stain near her beer.

"That was slightly un-cool, huh?" He figured he'd embarrassed her.

"I asked, didn't I?"

He had more beer and wondered what was next on her agenda. He couldn't tell by her body language. She was leaning forward, her cleavage easily visible. It would be so much easier if women turned a different color when something bothered them.

Finally she said, "Would you like to fool around?"

*Whoa. Iceberg* wasn't exactly the right word for this chick.

"Did I embarrass you?"

"Just around the edges."

"Does that mean you don't want to?"

"Not exactly…"

"Then you want to."

He nodded.

"Good. How about if we—"

A large yellow-gloved hand shot out from the crowd, resting heavily on Kyle's left shoulder.

Stoner, dressed in his yellow suit, pointed to Kyle, then jerked his thumb toward the front entrance.

# Chapter 11

The wagon blocked three lanes of heavy traffic.

His gloved hands clearing the way, Stoner led Kyle out of the bar.

Small disjointed crowds, their backs to the wagon, remained a safe distance away. Occasionally someone shot them a glare or mumbled something.

Stoner's smoldering eyes stayed on Kyle. "Emergency," he said. "We need everyone we can spare."

"What about Allie?" Kyle glanced behind him. There was no sign of her among the glossy-eyed leather-and-steel crowd hunkered beneath the flashing neon.

"What about her? She's not qualified for any of this…"

"She's inside."

"So?"

"I can't just leave her here…"

Stoner stabbed a gloved thumb at the wagon. "Parsons is a big girl. Let's move. Your suit's on the seat."

\*\*\*

Angry tongues of fire lit up the black sky. Thick pillars of smoke billowed toward the heavens. The overpowering stench of scorched flesh soured the night air.

Lights flashing, police cars blocked both ends of the street. Some were parked on the knob of the hill, others at the curb.

Fire trucks surrounded the apartment building. Firefighters wrestled giant hoses, forcing fat columns of water into the inferno. White-haired folks in bathrobes and pajamas lined up on the sidewalk, shivering.

Kyle parked beside the ambulance. Stoner had already scrambled out of the wagon. He was arguing with the fire chief by the time Kyle joined him.

A row of at least twenty bodies had been spread out on the lawn. Half a dozen squirmed in the grass, coughing and hacking.

Buster prepared an injection for an elderly man covered with horrible third-degree burns. Falworth, kneeling beside someone farther down, went through similar preparations.

"Pin him down for me, kid," Buster said. "Can't give him the shot when he's moving around like this."

Kyle swallowed. "Pin him *down*?"

"Haven't you ever wrestled before?"

Wrestling. Gym class. Sure. Pin him down, Sonnet. Get those shoulders down. Flush to the mat. You want to win the match, don't you?

But this wasn't gym class. This was—

"Sonnet!" Stoner's voice broke sharply through the chaos. "Do what you're told!"

Ignoring the smoke and the gagging reek of cooked flesh, Kyle dropped to his knees and straddled the victim's shoulders. Blood and saliva from the man's pursed lips spotted Kyle's protective visor.

"Get *off* me, goddammit!"

Kyle kept his body weight on the man's shoulders. *Close your eyes. Make believe this is gym class. Don't forget, this is necessary. The way things are.*

He opened his eyes. Another hot jolt of bloody froth had smeared his visor.

Buster prepared the hypodermic.

"Fuckers! Murderers!"

Buster administered the injection.

With one last burst of strength, the man tried squirming free, nearly knocking Kyle off-balance. "You're *all* murderers! Every last *one* of you! If I—"

The old man went slack.

A woman lay shivering in the grass. Well over seventy, she was nothing but flesh and bone. Most of her gray hair was singed to dark stubble, her pink housecoat blackened and scorched by flame. A large ugly bruise discolored the side of her head. She watched Kyle closely as he gently took her wrist and held it steady.

"Got a mother, boy?"

"I'm an orphan, ma'am."

The woman squeezed out a painful smile. "Had a boy…like you…long time ago. Tall and skinny, too. Sure was a caution. Had to watch him…all the time."

"Where is he now?"

The bloodshot eyes blistered. "Dead. You County people, you're killers. *All* of you…" Her face tightened. "Killed my boy! My sweet, adorable—"

Then she was gone.

101

Kyle's skin turned ice-cold beneath his sweltering suit.

"C'mon, kid." Buster got to his feet. "There's more. At least six are still moving. And they're bringing out two more from the building."

His head hot, Kyle followed Buster down the walk, where elderly people squirmed around in the grass like dying fish.

*** 

Kyle drove mechanically, unaware of the bumpy country road sliding beneath his headlights.

He couldn't stop agonizing over the old woman—the heat oozing from her body, the wrinkled mask of hatred on her face. She was a nice old lady—much like others her age he'd seen. Living out her days quietly with a few friends, the TV and her family album. Just a handful of years ago she was young, vital and attractive. She had a husband, a son, friends, relatives, hobbies. Church functions to go to. PTA meetings to attend. Business luncheons. Vacations. Mornings spent at the kitchen window, enjoying a cup of fresh coffee while the sun peeked at her from behind the rose bushes. Afternoons shared with friends over bridge, gossiping. Evenings relaxing on the couch, enjoying her favorite TV shows with her family.

But only an hour ago she lay dying in the grass, the yellow-hooded figures hovering over her providing her last glimpse of life.

Kyle's thoughts shifted back to the beginning of the evening.

The Tech Novel.

How did Stoner know where they were?

Allie?

How else? She wasn't wearing an earpiece. If she'd brought along a monitoring device, he hadn't seen it. Any hint of a bulge beneath her tight-fitting clothes would have been conspicuous.

As far as Kyle could remember, he had never been chipped. The Catholic Church stubbornly maintained its opposition to modern ways, including birth control, the Internet and the internal chip program. Due to pressures from the education system, the Church lost its petition against the Internet. Mass overpopulation had made it necessary to forfeit its exemption from birth control. But it won its exempt status from the chip program based on its ancient belief that marking someone brought society one step closer to demonic possession. In the eyes of the Catholic Church, the "Mark of the Beast" translated easily into the Government's chip program.

But how about Allie?

He didn't think she was Catholic. And since she'd been with the Department the last few years, she was probably carrying an implant. If so, Kyle had his answer. She showed on the screen. They recognized her code, took down the coordinates, and presto! There they were. No problem. Right on schedule.

*Rushed, Sonnet. Always rushed.*

"Rough night, eh?" Stoner's voice sounded less menacing. He sat on the padded bench, less rigid than usual.

"I've had better, sir."

"It happens."

What was this? Understanding? It didn't seem natural that such an emotion should belong in the man's psychological wardrobe.

"We're all on call, Sonnet. Every last one of us. There were twenty-eight bodies in that fire and we had to tend to them quickly. The firefighters battled the fire *and* handled the rescue efforts while the cops manned crowd control and searched for looters. It wasn't like we were out there alone."

Kyle didn't reply. He had no words left.

"We need to find 'em, shoot 'em, bag 'em and dump 'em. Health Department's always on our ass. They're forever snooping around, looking for violations."

"Violations?" he asked, suddenly curious.

"Anything they don't like. Anything they consider wrong."

"What would happen...if they found one?" he asked.

"They'd slap us with a healthy fine and send out an inspector to ride shotgun with us until he's satisfied we've done everything right. Washington hears about it. Then we've got every last political rat bastard in the country using us as leverage for more healthcare reform." He scowled. "We've already got more than enough healthcare reform to keep us neck-deep in bodies."

His thoughts racing, Kyle drove in silence.

"This job's difficult enough without us having to put up with bullshit from the Health Department, Human Rights, and Washington."

"Have you ever been hit with a violation, sir?"

"We run a tight ship, Sonnet. You ought to know that by now."

"Yes, sir."

"Answer your question?"

"I guess so, sir…"

"Something else on your mind?"

"No, sir."

"Good. Good. Let's get back, then. I'm tired. You tired, Sonnet?"

"Yes, sir."

"We need our rest. Tomorrow's another day."

# Chapter 12

Kyle spent the night staring at the dark ceiling, the loud snoring in the room gradually turning into the steady moaning of the wagon engine. When he did manage to doze off, his world became a hazy collage of dark shapes writhing on the ground, crying and whimpering.

His breakfast remained untouched on his tray. The cafeteria had become a bright blur. The mixed smells of sausage, bacon, coffee, and toast ceased to exist.

This room had somehow become the woods, the laughter and chatter, the banging of trays, the pounding of pots and the clatter of silverware all ebbing into a peaceful silence.

Kyle could almost hear the wind whispering through the trees. The cheerful songs of birds. The distant gurgling of a stream.

A man's loud, irritating guffaw resonated behind him.

Kyle's fantasy world disintegrated like smoke in a sudden burst of wind.

Buster and Wilcox sat six tables down, exchanging jokes. Falworth flipped pages of a magazine at the table behind them. Four girls from Dispatch huddled close to one another at a table near the rear entrance.

There was no sign of Stoner. He was probably doing his pushups or his two-mile early morning jog.

"Heard you had a rough night." Allie placed her tray next to his and sat. She gave him a brief smile before adding cream and sugar to her coffee. "Sorry we had to cut our date short. How about we try it again the next time you've got the evening off?"

Kyle didn't reply.

"Something wrong?"

He was trying to decide just who this chick really was—if she was as she appeared, or if it was just an act. She was so nice to be with—why did he suddenly distrust her?

"Tell me what's on your mind."

"Did you tell Stoner where we were going last night?"

"Of course not." The vertical line between her brows thickened. "Is *that* what's bothering you?"

"You must be chipped, then."

"Of course I'm chipped, silly. We *all* are."

She was wrong—she had to be. That fallacy had been flickering around ever since he could remember. In history class they were told that it was against every principle in a democratic society to inject a microchip into private citizens because it was a violation of everyone's Constitutional rights.

"That's illegal," he told her. "Besides, the Catholic Church is exempt."

"You honestly believe that?"

He swallowed. "That's what we were told."

"Sonnet, I hate to tell you this, but you've been lied to."

He didn't reply. Her attitude was not only irritating, it was frightening—especially if she was right. But she *wasn't* right. She *couldn't* be.

"While we're on the subject, you never did tell me how you got stuck with nuns."

"When you're sent there they put you into one of five groups—Catholic, Presbyterian, Episcopalian, Methodist, and Lutheran. They try to keep the groups the same size. When I went there, the Catholic wing needed bodies."

"I heard about those places. Strictly Nineteenth Century."

"We were taught the old ways. Lots of kneeling, penance, confessions every week, church every morning. They don't approve of modern technology, computers, birth control, or—"

"Welcome to the real world."

He frowned. That was something Stoner would say. "Would the Government really ignore Catholic doctrine?"

"They're the Government, Sonnet. They do what they like. You know that."

Maybe, but it was one of those things he'd shoved into the back of his mind. It sickened him to think the United States Government would chip its citizens to monitor their every move, confine them to a relief barracks when they couldn't find work, and euthanize them when they were sick or injured.

"I'm surprised the nuns even let you watch CNN."

"CNN broadcasts current affairs, which were supplemental to our schoolwork and essential in our preparation for the outside world. The Home was Government-subsidized, so they couldn't very well tell it where to go—even though they wanted to."

"Tell me what you know about internal chips, Sonnet."

He'd learned about the program in grade school. Because of mass starvation in underdeveloped countries, livestock theft grew rampant in North and South America, Europe, and Australia. The black market be- came disgustingly rich when it developed an international pipeline providing fresh meat to specified countries. To fight this, the American Government developed a program to chip all farm animals. In a very short time, livestock theft came to a standstill.

"It started with horses," he said. "People stole them and shipped them overseas for dog meat and gourmet steaks. After that, the prison system used it to monitor felons."

"The prison experiment actually came much later." Allie had some coffee. "The livestock program worked so well that the Government decided to use chips to track stolen vehicles. They altered the chip so it could be used to immobilize a vehicle during a high-speed pursuit. The police were given direct access to every chip-implanted vehicle, and that worked well. The number of pursuits and stolen vehicles dropped dramatically.

"That forty-year war against terrorism also preceded the felon chip program. There were an estimated fifty thousand terrorists living over here in sleeper cells, so they started a kind of electronic witch hunt under the guise of an inoculation program against chemical agents. This enabled them to inoculate nearly everyone. They added a light sedative to the mixture and injected the chip when the patient grew woozy. During interrogations they managed to chip all sorts of suspicious characters.

In five years, nearly all the terrorists in this country were caught and euthanized."

Allie nibbled on a strip of bacon. "The prison program was inevitable. Drug lords were among the first. It didn't take long to chip lesser criminals—muggers and petty thieves. Then it went right down the line— traffic offenders, deadbeat fathers, tax evaders. For the last ten years, everyone's been getting it. It's easier to control everyone when you know exactly where they are."

"But when did they do *me*? I'd remember, wouldn't I?"

"When was the last time you were inoculated?"

"Just the other day, with Irene."

"Before that."

"Two years ago."

"What for?"

"Boosters, mostly. We'd get them annually, but there was a budget crunch and they changed the program."

"Were you unconscious for any length of time?"

"No."

"Did you ever get hurt playing? Break or sprain anything? Didn't you ever get into a scrap with anyone?"

"I was in a couple of fights."

"Were you hurt?"

"Not bad—wait a minute." The memory made the back of his head warm. "It happened when I was around eleven. One of the few times I played baseball. I hit a long one that made it to the fence. I was running toward third. When the third baseman saw me coming, he tripped me. I went down hard and my leg doubled up underneath me. The fall sprained my ankle."

"Did they treat you there?"

The nurse—a big square woman with heavy jowls, smelling of talcum powder and antiseptic—made him lie on a padded table. She plodded over to the sink and did something in front of the mirror. When she turned to face him, a hypodermic appeared in her large pink fist.

"Sonnet?"

"Shit. She *did* jab me. She said there could be infection."

"Did you watch?"

"I grew woozy, then lay down and crashed. But it was only for a minute or so."

"That's how they do it. You doze for a few minutes, only it's more like half an hour, because they've got to jam the implant inside the muscle. And when you wake up it's all over."

Kyle couldn't believe it. They'd lied to him. The doctors, nurses, the United States Government—even the nuns. He didn't know who he should be angriest at.

Allie had more coffee. "For the last twenty years, anyone who's gone in for any kind of shot or operation has been given a chip. Anyone who's ever had a checkup…or a tooth pulled. Face it, you've got one. We all have."

# Chapter 13

At one-thirty, Kyle coaxed the wagon to a stop behind the ambulance.

Endless rows of one-story brick homes huddled so close together, only a narrow walkway separated them. Cigarette wrappers, French fries and mashed beer cans littered the curb. Hopscotch squares spray-painted a light-blue embellished the cracked sidewalk.

Stoner waited at the curb while Buster and Falworth got their equipment ready.

The house in question, like many of its neighbors, cried out for a new roof and serious landscaping. Inside, a family of three—a husband, wife, and the man's invalid mother—awaited them. According to what Buster had said earlier on the radio, the wife wanted the State to take the mother-in-law away.

"Can't remember her own name." The heavyset, round-faced middle-aged woman wore a loose-fitting flowered dress and smelled strongly of cigarettes. "She'll sit in the living room chair, stare at the TV, and dirty herself. We've had to throw out *two easy chairs*, for God sake. *Two* of 'em. Trashed. Garbage. Know how much those suckers go for nowadays?"

The victim—about seventy-five, fat, and sloppy— slumped in an armchair, her glazed smile unable to hide the vacant look in her small green eyes. The smell of urine hovered around her like a thick cloud. Buster took out his stethoscope and applied the diaphragm to her misshapen chest. She giggled.

"Why isn't she in a rest home?" Stoner asked.

"No money," the wife said curtly.

"You the son?"

A tall slender man wearing thick glasses slumped near the kitchen archway, his hands buried in the pockets of his dark dress slacks. The clinking of change was the only sound he made. He nodded slightly.

"You don't have enough insurance?"

"The premiums were putting us in the poorhouse, so we had to drop her."

"What about State housing?"

"They put us on their damn list," the wife chirped in. "Said three years, for God sake. *Three years!* Think we're gonna put up with *this* for three more years? Damn place needs fumigating. You oughta smell her room." She raised a flabby arm and pointed toward the hall. A cloud of b. o. drifted in their direction. "Last room on your left. Got to keep the door closed or we'll all puke. Go 'head, have a whiff."

"We'll take a rain check on that," Stoner said. "You willing to sign a Surrender of Support waiver?"

The man hesitated. His wife nodded eagerly.

"You understand that in surrendering support, you're giving the State permission to authorize this Department to euthanize all individuals over the age of seventy, provided the individual in question can no longer support him- or herself, has no health insurance, and suffers poor health?"

113

The man lowered his head. His wife shrugged indifferently.

"And do you realize this entitles the State to confiscate this woman's possessions?"

"She's got nothing." The wife shoved a hand through her dirty brown hair. "Drawer full of old clothes. She gave every damn thing to his idiot sister before we took her in." She shot a quick glare at her husband. "That's what we get for takin' in a nasty old woman nobody else wanted…"

***

A maroon Camaro, now a twisted mass of metal and broken glass, glimmered in the afternoon sun. Firefighters struggled to extricate the driver from his squashed metal prison.

Kyle parked a safe distance from the fire trucks. His thoughts reeled with images of the heavy, urine-soaked body of the old woman he and Buster had loaded into the wagon compartment ten minutes earlier.

All his life Kyle had longed to be a member of a family. Having a brother or sister to play with, a mother to wake you in the morning and welcome you with a plate of freshly-baked cookies when you came home from school. A father to share projects with. Engaging in happy conversation during family meals. Visiting relatives. Going on weekend excursions. It sounded so wonderful. But what happened earlier made him realize that his notion of a family had come from books and old TV sitcoms. Harsh reality was a different animal.

The old woman was the man's mother. She'd given birth to him, raised him. It wasn't her fault she'd grown old.

But that didn't matter now. She'd become a problem. And no one dealt with problems anymore.

Across the street, the firefighters removed the man from the wreckage. His chest was crushed, his back was broken and his legs strips of flesh peeled from the bone. He screamed for a strong drink while Buster administered the injection.

Kyle wandered over to the curb and tried to zone out.

This was necessary. How things were done. The way things were.

"Problem, Sonnet?"

"Sir?"

"You're standing here like you're waiting for a bus."

"Is this a bus stop, sir?"

Stoner looked around. "You see a sign anywhere around here?"

"No, sir…"

"Then I'd say this isn't a bus stop."

"I guess I need to stop waiting, then."

"Are you serious, Sonnet? Or just being a smartass?"

"I guess I'm just being a smartass, sir."

"Any particular reason why?"

"Just a little bummed-out over our last call."

"Why?"

"She was the man's mom."

"And?"

He realized right then that, like their other conversations, this wouldn't go well. But he was determined to let Stoner know what was on his mind. "She was his mother."

Stoner pushed up his visor. "You're upset because we've got someone's mother in the wagon?"

"Yes, sir."

The visor was flipped back down. "Sonnet, I honestly don't understand you."

"You know something, sir? Sometimes I don't understand myself."

"Do us all a huge favor, Sonnet."

"What's that, sir?"

"Forget the self-analytical bullshit for now and concentrate on the job. We need to bag that worthless pile of drunken dogshit and load him."

# Chapter 14

Kyle peeled off the suffocating yellow suit and stood in the shower for twenty minutes, letting the intense warm spray shed away the heavy layer of sweat, fumes, and the clammy film of death clinging like flypaper to his flesh. Refreshed, he dried himself off, put on street clothes and left the station.

He needed different air.

By seven o'clock, the streets swelled with swarms of traffic. Filthy, shabby-dressed men and women pushed shopping carts piled with junk. Animal carcasses and tossed garbage—grim reminders that the Department of Health and Sanitation had downsized severely—rotted near the curb.

Four blocks from the station, the world turned even bleaker. The streets were lined with two-and-a-half-story houses. Skinny boys around nine or ten years old played stickball in the street while others crawled underneath parked cars, scrounging for whatever they could find. Another group of boys circled two teen girls rolling around on the pavement, kicking and scratching one another. Dogs sniffed the garbage scattered along the curb.

An old man sat rocking on the front porch of a small two-story block home behind an old picket fence with several of its rails missing. Smoke billowed brightly from his curved briar pipe. He waved. "Evenin'!'"

The old man's long bony face was all lit up. Kyle experienced an odd sense of well-being. It was the first time a stranger had ever greeted him.

What should he do? Wave and politely walk away? He wanted to stay, but common sense told him he shouldn't linger among such chaos.

"C'mon over!" The old man pointed to the glider beside him. "Set a spell."

Had he heard the old man right? Whatever he said might have been distorted by the screaming kids. Perhaps he'd said *Go away,* or something worse.

"Got a heavy date?"

"Not that I'm aware of…"

"Then c'mon over, set yourself down."

Kyle pushed open the creaky gate and climbed the four rickety wooden steps. The second step was loose. He stepped over it to keep from losing his balance.

"New to the neighborhood?" The old man's face, gray and filmy behind the tendrils of pipe smoke, remained animated. Kyle figured the old guy was lonely and needed someone to talk to.

"I guess you could say that. I work for the County."

"Got your own place? Or live with 'em?"

"I live with them." Kyle sat down in the glider.

"Figures. Look a tad young for your own spread. Especially these days, houses bein' so dang pricey. Whaddya do for the County?"

Kyle hesitated. Saying something like *I pick up bodies,* or *I haul people to the dump,* would definitely put out the sparks in this little chat. "A little of this, a little of that."

A high-pitched giggle escaped the old man's throat. "Don't sound too dang sure about things…"

"I…drive for them," he said softly, and hoped the old man didn't hear him.

The fight among the two teen girls had ended down the street. One of them ran screaming into a three-story gray brick house. At the end of the block, two skinny boys fought over something they'd found in the garbage.

The old man watched the activity for a few moments before blinking out of his trance. "Been here fifty years now. While ago, these homes were only big enough for one family. Now they got three, four, even five families apiece living in 'em. Had to turn over my own place, rent out the upstairs to two families. Didn't want to, but when the big boys from Washington serve you with one of their famous official notices, you gotta oblige. Shame, ain't it? Folks all bunched up like that?"

Kyle nodded. "A real bummer."

The old man nudged a smoke ring out of his mouth. It stayed intact until a whiff of warm breeze broke it into tiny gray snippets. "What kinda drivin' you do? Ambulance? Or the meat wagon?"

"I…drive the wagon."

The old man fell silent.

That was it. The punch line to end all punch lines.

End of smile. End of conversation.

Kyle stood. "I…guess I ought to split."

"Like what you do, boy?"

"Not at all."

"Why do it, then?"

"The County job was the only one available at the time. They told me they'd send me to a relief barracks if I don't make the grade here."

"They'll do that, all right. Government boys sure like pushin' us around. They always done it, but lately they been gettin' a genuine knee-slappin' hoot from the whole business. Makes 'em feel important. Powerful. They pay good?"

"I haven't been paid yet, so I really don't know."

"How long you gonna do it, son?"

Kyle hadn't thought too much about it. He was still trying to convince himself that the job was necessary.

After a few weeks, he'd be able to ignore things better. He might even be able to ignore putting someone's mother into the wagon. Or little girls. Or convince himself that doing all this actually did make sense. He might even eventually believe that if they *didn't* do it, this world would be even worse than it was.

But he didn't want this nice old man to think he was enjoying himself. "Until I find something else," he finally said.

"Name's Elden." The old man's hand was dry and very warm—probably from the pipe.

"I'm Kyle."

"How old are ya?"

"I'll be nineteen in six months."

"And what would you prefer doin'? If ya had the choice."

"Stuff no one does or even thinks about any more."

"Such as?"

"Music. Writing. Art. Sculpture. Things people create—*used* to create. I've never done any of it. I don't even know if I can. But I've always envied anyone who could."

Elden grinned. "Played the sax once. Used to paint, too."

"Really? When?"

"Long, *long* time ago."

"Before I was born?"

The old man's face relaxed. "Before your *folks* were born, most likely."

"How long was it before you could produce a good sound?"

"Few months, I guess. Takes longer to sound good than play songs. You can learn to play a song in just a couple days once you learn the fingerings. Buzzin' the mouthpiece ain't so hard. Soundin' good? Now that's *somethin'* else. Tone quality takes a while. And lots of patience. That's why there ain't many players no more. Or painters. Not many folks wanna take the time to get really good at anything." He shrugged. "And not too many have the time or the patience. They're all too busy makin' ends meet."

"You still play?"

The old man sighed. "Naw."

"How come?"

Elden tapped his bottom teeth with the stem of his pipe. "Fake choppers won't let me. 'Sides, the ol' ticker just ain't what it used to be."

121

A shame the old man had given up the things he loved so much.

"I'll bet you could still play if you wanted to."

"No sense in it."

Stoner's words. Everyone seemed to be spouting them.

"What makes you say that?"

"Boy, I'm ninety-four years old. I've seen things most everyone else these days can't even imagine. Seen this country go through some rough times, seen it prosper. I grew up in another world. Back then, people talked about peace and love. Folks seemed to care more about one another. But when those fellas started buildin' their computers, it got the country all steamed up and excited about what else they could do. Wasn't long before everyone decided they just couldn't live without 'em. That's when folks started pullin' away. Always thought that was dang ironic. Computers bring the modern world into your home, but what they take away is somethin' nobody even wants to think about."

"The only thing I like about computers is that I can learn how things used to be."

Elden nodded. "They're good for a few things, I guess. Heck, if folks didn't abuse 'em, everything would turn out just fine. But people don't know how to use *anything* without ruinin' it. Look at how everybody's runnin' around, chatterin' away like monkeys on those tiny pieces of plastic jammed inside their ears. Who they talkin' to? And why? Ever hear some of those conversations? They're a real hoot. Hey, I'm goin' to the store, should be there ten, maybe fifteen minutes, then I'll be in the car, then I'm goin' to the office, then I'll probably be in the rest room…" Elden sat back and shook his head. "Stupid. Even stupider when ya figure whoever they're talkin' to is probably sayin' the same dang thing right back."

"When you put it like that, it's *real* stupid."

"But as far as computers go? No one seems to understand what we've all lost. The young ones don't know 'cause they weren't around before this new world started up. The older ones mighta just forgot. I don't think they even care anymore. To care about somethin', you gotta think about it first. People don't do much thinkin' anymore. They let their computers do it all."

"I never thought of it like that."

"Nobody does. That's the problem. Everyone's too busy with themselves these days, but what they're busy doin' really don't matter much. When I was a kid, one of those creative fellas ya don't see or hear about no more wrote a song called "Dust in the Wind." I was only a little sprout when it came out, but I'll never forget it. Made sense, those words. Summed everything up pretty well."

"What did the song say?"

"Nothin' really matters. Everything's just dust in the wind."

"That's depressing."

"Yep, seen lots of changes over the years, but what I seen in the last twenty makes me wish I was never born. When you kill off creative thought and expression, you know the end's not too dang far off."

"You make it sound like there's nothing left." Kyle couldn't help feeling even more depressed than before he'd left the station.

"Nothin' worthwhile, in my opinion. But I'm an old man, and I guess I seen too much. When you've seen too much, you tend to read into things more."

"What exactly…do you see?"

The old man fell silent. Kyle didn't like the fear emanating from the glossy blue eyes.

Suddenly Kyle needed to know what the old man was thinking. "You can tell me. I'll believe anything you say."

"Quit doin' what you're doin'. Society's comin' apart at the seams. You don't wanna be anywhere near when it rips wide open. When they make it okay to kill folks just 'cause it's too expensive to keep 'em healthy, it's time to make tracks. Get out and hide. Hell's just around the corner."

"But…where can I go?"

Elden's smile was tired—nothing at all like it was when Kyle had first seen him. "You're a good kid. Don't want anything bad happenin' to ya. Go wherever you have to, but get out. Lots of good folks have already disappeared. They saw what's coming."

"Where did they go?"

"No one seems to know, and I can't say as I blame 'em for keepin' quiet. But get out—that's what's important. Once they turn you, you're one of them. Then you might as well consider yourself dead. 'Cause that's what *they* are."

124

# Chapter 15

A gentle nudge.

Kyle sat up and squinted at the darkness. The loud snoring from the other side of the large area told him where he was.

The strong scent of lavender snapped him fully awake. The hall light forming a rectangular haze in the open doorway outlined her slim dark form.

"What's up?" he asked groggily.

"Where were you earlier?" Allie whispered.

"When?"

"Around seven, seven-thirty. I came over from Dispatch to see if you wanted to go out."

"I went for a walk. What time is it?"

"A little after eleven."

"Isn't it kinda late for—"

"Wanna go out now?"

His cheeks flushed. Was this for real? "Now? Really? You and me? Right now?"

"Don't have a heart attack, Sonnet. My place, all right?"

"Your place?"

"My apartment. What's so hard to understand about that?"

"For a minute I thought I was just dreaming."

"You were. But now you aren't. You want to or not?"

"I'd be an idiot not to."

"Get dressed, then."

\*\*\*

One block from the Station, the fifteen-story brick building covered nearly one square block.

125

Despite the trimmed shrubbery and spruce trees lining the property, garbage lay everywhere. Barking dogs shattered the silence. Across the street, dark figures huddled in doorways, raising crumpled paper bags to their faces.

Allie's garden apartment was small and warm. The living room walls were light-blue, the furniture sparse but attractive. Flowers filled white ceramic bowls; a colorful arrangement adorned a metal pot near the front door. A large print of a bowl of fruit accented the space above the couch.

"Make yourself comfortable," she said, deadbolting the door. Then she disappeared down the hall.

A small-screened TV sat on a table against the far wall. Kyle lowered himself onto the couch and picked up the remote from the cocktail table. CNN showed a raincoat-covered newsman huddled in front of a burning building. Kyle quickly changed the station. Other channels revealed an infomercial about liposuction, a special featuring hair implants, one about hair removal, another probing breast enlargement and a show about a woman whose entire life changed when she discovered the right nasal spray.

On a local station, a program called "Who Should I Date?" showed a good-looking, half-naked dude around twenty years old sitting on a couch with three beautiful, bikini-clad women about the same age.

The bosomy blonde said, "What did you like about me on our date?"

He replied, "Like, you're a good kisser, but your tongue stud kinda got in the way. Maybe if you had it moved an inch or so back…"

"My kiss wasn't no good?"

"The stud—ya know?" He shrugged.

"What about my boobs?" she asked, cupping them with her hands.

"Little hard."

"They *look* hard," agreed the brunette. "Mine have that *soft* look." She covered hers with her palms. "Maybe if you had yours redone…"

The dude said, "I'd definitely go out with you again if you had the stud moved back, maybe your boobs redone—know what I'm sayin'?"

The blonde nodded. "Peachy. My daddy's a Congressman. We got *oodles* of medical coverage. Might even get that nipple ring I've had my eye on. Whaddya think of nipple rings, Brad?"

He shrugged. "Have to wait, see how yours is done." To the redhead he said, "Donna, you're a great kisser. That collagen job you had done? Really turns me on. Like, when do ya plan on havin' them injected again?"

"Next year. Why?"

"I'd have the collagen guy concentrate more on your right side," the brunette threw in. "Smidge lopsided from this angle."

Donna's slim painted brows pushed together. "Ya know, I caught that in the mirror the other day…"

Kyle switched to a laser surgery infomercial, muted the sound and sat back.

Allie came in wearing a pink bra and semi-transparent black panties. She was holding two glasses. Her bottom had a nice fullness to it. The tiny heart-shaped mole showed just above her left breast. Two more decorated her right thigh, halfway from the knee to the hip.

"You like brandy?"

"Never had any."

"Didn't you ever get to do anything?"

"Some guys smuggled in a bottle of *sake* once, but by the time it got to me, there was only a splash left." He sipped the warm liqueur.

She drank some of her own and set her glass on the table.

Kyle was already beginning to feel better. With a few of these in his system, things might turn out just fine. Brandy sure was a neat idea. Whoever invented it definitely knew what he was doing.

Allie reached for his belt buckle. "C'mon, Sonnet. Get naked."

"Why the rush?"

"Why the questions?"

Kyle pushed down his trousers and squirmed out of his tee shirt. Allie wrestled him down and kissed him. As cold and distant as she was when he first saw her, she was totally different now. Iceberg. That sure was a joke.

"I guess you really do like me," he said.

Allie shook her head sadly. "Now whatever gave you *that* idea?"

He shrugged. "The way you were at the Station—"

"That was *work*, silly. Monitors? People everywhere? Remember?"

"But—"

"Didn't I tell you at the Tech Novel I thought you were a nice guy? Didn't that tell you anything?"

"I'm not really experienced when it comes to girls, sex—stuff like that."

"Am I your first?" Her face was close. Her lavender scent mixed with the brandy on her breath.

"We weren't allowed to socialize much."

"That doesn't answer my question."

"There was one girl, but we didn't get much done."

"Tell me about it."

"Whaddya want to know?"

She shrugged. "What *did* you get done?"

"We messed around a couple of times behind the bleachers in the gym."

"So…how far did you get?"

"Just some kissing and touching."

Her eyes grew. "So I *am* your first."

"I guess you are…"

*\*\*\**

"What are your plans, Sonnet?" Allie lay on her side on the bed, propped up by an elbow.

"Going on back to the barracks before Stoner gets on the p.a. and—"

"I mean about the job, silly."

"I really haven't thought too much about—"

"C'mon, Sonnet—"

"My brain…just went blank."

"I don't buy that."

The only light, a faint haze from the hall, filtered in and showed a small flicker in her eyes. He couldn't even see the mole on her breast. But as much as he wanted to see that, reading her expression seemed more important right now.

"You don't like your work," Allie said.

"I'll get used to it." He saw no reason to tell her anything else. They'd just made love, but he still didn't know her very well.

"You think so?"

"It's not really *that* bad, I guess." He figured it wouldn't be bad at all once he learned to zone out like he used to at the Home.

"Wait till you get your first bank statement. That's when it'll all seem worthwhile."

He didn't like where she might be going with this.

"Why would that matter?"

She shrugged. "You'll be able to get your own place. You don't want to stay at the barracks forever, do you?"

"Not really…"

"And later on, after you've been there a while, you could put in for a transfer."

"A transfer?" That sounded promising.

"After you've put in six months you could be promoted, or transferred to clerical duties."

"No fooling?"

"I've seen several transfers in my five years there. Can you do clerical stuff, Sonnet? You seem pretty bright."

"I was good at math, and did fairly well in a basic bookkeeping class they offered us seniors last year."

"Good. Maybe you can consider that later on."

"What about you? You staying in Dispatch?"

"For a few more years. I've got some money saved. I'd like to buy a small farm in the country. One of those condemned places the Government took over and doesn't do anything with."

"And raise cows?" The image of Allie in a tee shirt and tight jeans squatting on a stool, milking a cow, would be cool for a sexy calendar, but not very realistic otherwise.

"Vegetables."

"Seriously?"

"My parents were farmers—that is, until they lost their place."

"What happened?"

"The State took it and sold it to a developer for a strip mall. We had to move into the city. One of those neighborhoods jammed with multi-dwellings. There were four other families living in our house with us. It really sucked. Daddy was so devastated about losing his place, he was never the same. He just sat in his chair in the living room and wasted away. He wouldn't even look out the window because of the buildings across the street. We had a painting of a farm sitting on the mantle. He stared at it every single day. The State gave us a good price for the farm, so at least Daddy never had to work anymore. But that wasn't the problem. They'd taken away his livelihood and he just stopped caring about things. When he died, Mom died a few months later. It was really very sad."

"A huge bummer."

"They left me some money. I've been investing it the last five years. I figure in five more years I'll have enough to buy a couple of acres and a small house up north. I'd like to buy a horse one day. Daddy had one. I learned to ride when I was little. But when they re-zoned the area, we weren't allowed to keep her anymore. So we had to sell her."

"Another bummer."

She sighed. "I loved that horse."

"Whatever happened with that strip mall?"

"The anchor store that was supposed to bring in all the business cancelled out at the last minute. The property's been deserted ever since."

"That *really* sucks."

"It's so sad... And stupid that it happened in the first place. But since the Government made it illegal to own parcels of land larger than three acres, we knew it was only a matter of time."

He wanted to tell her about Elden. Maybe he could take her to see him on his next visit. She'd probably enjoy meeting the old man. The three of them could talk about all sorts of things. Elden no doubt knew about farming. He probably also knew about horses, maybe even rode when he was young. Elden probably did just about everything when he was young. It was a different world back then. People probably rode horses all over the place.

Elden might have even grown up on a farm. He had that down-to-earth quality you never see in city people. His laid-back friendly attitude contrasted sharply with the intense hatred Kyle had witnessed so much the last two days. When he talked, you could actually sense a childlike innocence flowing from him. Country living might have instilled it in him.

Kyle wondered if he was right. He promised himself that the next time he saw Elden, he'd definitely find out.

Allie planted a warm kiss on his ear and all his thoughts of Elden vanished. "Wanna fool around some more?"

"Sounds like a nifty plan to me."

# Chapter 16

The last of the early morning fog a memory, Kyle hoped this first call of the day wouldn't be another Nathaniel Johnson fiasco. An accidental shooting, Falworth said on the radio. The police would be there shortly.

Less than fifty feet from the curb, the aged condominium reluctantly faced the new day. Its shingled roof showed large black patches of neglect. Its gutters, rusty and faded, sagged from the weight of too many seasons without maintenance. Its windows, filmy with dirt and grime, could barely see the man sprawled in the dew-soaked grass, clutching his left shoulder.

Buster rushed over, lugging his black bag. "How bad you hurt?"

"I'll be all right." His hand and much of his shirt were smeared with blood. Ribbons of it streaked his arm, gathering in a darkened pool on the ground. "Damn kid of mine, found my twenty-two rifle, didn't know it was loaded. Next thing I knew, he was pointing the damn thing at me." He smiled thinly. "Then *bam!*"

Buster examined the wound. "Firearms are illegal," he said, opening his bag.

"A damn *target rifle*, for God sake."

"Target rifles are classified as an illegal firearm, my friend. All calibers, including .177 pellet guns." Buster dabbed at the blood. "Got to be confiscated."

"No way!" The man struggled to get up.

Buster pushed him down easily. "If I were you—"

"Rifle's been in my family a hundred years. My old man's grandfather left it to him. My old man left it to me when he died."

Kyle kept glancing at the ambulance. Stoner was checking on something with Falworth. Good. For the time being, this dude was reasonably safe.

"Should've had it altered," Buster told the wounded man.

"You mean take out the firing pin, solder the barrel shut and turn it into a fucking *toy?*"

"Listen…since firing ranges now cater only to law enforcement officials, and private land is restricted to Government use, there's nowhere you can go to fire it anyway." Buster dropped the bloody swab into a plastic pouch and removed a fresh packet from his bag.

"Rifle's an antique, man. Be a crime to mess with it."

"It's a crime to keep it the way it is. Non-firing replica guns are the only firearms permitted for legal private ownership. That law went into effect ten years ago. Everyone was given a full year to surrender personal firearms and ammunition to the nearest police station in exchange for food stamps, gasoline coupons, Lottery tickets and other purchase tokens based on fair buy-back value. It was shown on all the TV stations and received global coverage for months. Where were you?"

"Listen, man…"

"No. *You* listen." Buster was finding it difficult to keep calm. "The replica gun law is the only piece of legislation that enables a private citizen to own a firearm. Ignorance is no excuse."

"Bullshit. Nothing but bullshit." The man made another pathetic effort to get up.

"Problem here?" Stoner had taken a printout from the ambulance and stood behind Buster, staring down at the bleeding man.

"Gunshot wound, Chief. Target rifle. Twenty-two."

"Who shot you, Mister"—Stoner referred to the printout—"McAfee?"

"My son. Stupid accident. Rifle's been in my family—"

"Illegal firearm."

"I was trying to remind Mr. McAfee of the replica gun law, Chief." Buster wasn't as agitated. Stoner's presence had taken the burden off his shoulders. "He doesn't want to take the law seriously."

A woman appeared at the screen door, fragile and tiny in her fluffy pink housecoat. Both hands covered her mouth. Her wide-open eyes were wet. Kyle wanted to go to her and force her to turn away.

Stoner grunted. "Illegal firearm. Punishable by substantial fines, imprisonment, or both. Where's your son?"

"In the house." The man began shaking. "Probably *still* scared shitless for what he did."

"How old is he, Mr. McAfee?"

"Teddy's nine." The man's eyes filled. "Whaddya gonna do? Arrest a nine-year-old? Put him in prison? Didn't even know the damn thing was loaded, for God sake."

"Did he know the rifle wasn't a replica gun, Mr. McAfee?"

136

"Listen—"

"*Did* he?"

"He's just a *kid*…"

"Where's your health card, Mr. McAfee?" Stoner pocketed his pen.

"Don't…have one."

"Where do you work?"

"I'm…unemployed." He looked down at his lap.

The woman at the door trembled.

"When did you last work?"

"Few months. What the hell's this got to—"

"Where?"

"Home computer business. We—my wife and me—we filled out insurance claims. Then…it sort of fizzled out when we…started having problems. I got this alcohol issue, and…well, I went nuts one day and threw the computer out in the street and—"

"Why aren't you in a relief barracks, Mr. McAfee?"

"The wife works."

"Where?"

"Takes in wash, does hair and nails. Listen, can't you do anything for us? Don't you have any feelings? Son's nine years old. Doesn't know what he did. I didn't even remember the gun was loaded."

"Did you have a health card when you were filling out insurance claims?"

"Yeah…"

"When did it expire?"

"A few months ago."

"Got any money? Savings?"

137

McAfee shook his head. "I've...been looking for another job."

"How badly do you estimate the damage here?" Stoner continued watching McAfee.

Buster irrigated the wound. He checked carefully behind the man's shoulder. "Slug's still inside, Chief. I see classic signs of fragmentation in the tissues."

Stoner nodded grimly. "What kind of round was it, Mr. McAfee?"

"Doesn't matter."

"What was in the rifle?"

"I don't see what this—"

"What kind, McAfee?"

"Fucking hollow point. What else you wanna know?"

Stoner and Buster exchanged gloomy glances.

The woman sobbed loudly.

"Hollow points do serious injury, McAfee—I'm sure you're aware of that. There's damage to your shoulder—lots of it. You've got no money, no health card. Your injuries will be expensive." Stoner shrugged. "Sorry, but we've got no choice."

"You mean...you're gonna *kill* me?" McAfee's voice had become a shrill gasp. He tried standing and fell back down. "You're gonna just *kill* me?"

The woman let out an ear-splitting wail and dropped to her knees.

"Listen, McAfee—"

"You can't put out a guy's lights just because he can't pay for a stupid accident. You just can't!"

"Mr. McAfee." Stoner lowered his voice. "You know what our policy is, and I'm sure you're aware

138

how this country's healthcare system operates. Since you've no visible means of medical reimbursement, we've got no alternative but to act in accordance with State regulations."

"You're gonna kill me!" McAfee squirmed in the grass.

Front doors eased open across the street. Two middle-aged women in housecoats hid behind a wooden privacy fence. A small boy watched from behind bushes in the yard next door.

Irritated, Stoner put his hands on his hips. "Let's hurry this up. People are watching. There're at least six idiots down the block holding goddamn cameras." For a moment Kyle wondered if Stoner would pull out his automatic and shoot all six of them.

Stoner kept his hands on his hips. "Sonnet, hold him down. Falworth, shut him up."

Kyle remembered the poor old man lying in the grass outside the burning building. *Pin him down. It's a game—nothing more.*

"Dammit, Sonnet!"

Taking a deep breath, Kyle dropped to his knees and pushed Mr. McAfee down. The man's arms were stiff tubes of ice.

Falworth removed a chloroform packet from his bag and approached from behind. Mr. McAfee struggled violently, his arms and legs flailing. A knee caught Kyle in the midsection, forcing a gasp from his throat. Mr. McAfee's struggles ceased shortly after Falworth's packet covered his mouth and nose. He slumped quietly in the grass.

Stoner closely watched the neighborhood activity. Two more guys in their early twenties entered the scene with cameras. Without taking his eyes from them Stoner said, "Euthanize this bastard so we can get the hell out of here. I'll conduct a search to confiscate that rifle."

"What about the kid, Chief?"

"We'll file a report to the State. Let those assholes sort this out. Last thing I want to deal with right now is some idiot kid. Where the hell are those damned cops?"

***

While Stoner and three cops searched the McAfee house for additional firearms and ammunition, Kyle sat tensely in the wagon.

Kyle was grateful Stoner hadn't ordered him to tag along. He didn't want to be near Mrs. McAfee to witness her agony. He also didn't want to be in the same room when Stoner questioned her. Stoner wasn't known for his sensitivity skills.

Kyle could only imagine how difficult it was for her to stand there helplessly while four uniformed men ravaged her house only moments after they'd euthanized her husband. How horrible to watch cold-faced strangers methodically pulling out dresser drawers, checking closets, rummaging through the clothes hamper and inspecting private belongings.

But that's what the law said. According to Stoner, "Anyone in possession of an illegal firearm is subject by the State to immediate search and seizure of any and all property, and will be arrested if strict compliance with the law is not observed."

Two little girls peeked at Kyle behind a porch rail. A man leaned against the doorway of the house directly across the street, smoking a cigarette. Three boys around five or six years old watched him behind a van parked in a driveway.

*Zone out,* his mind ordered. *You've done it before. You can do it now. Blur them out. Turn the street into the woods. A stream. A cluster of pine trees.*

The heavy thumping of Stoner's boots on the wagon steps jarred Kyle alert. Stoner pulled the door shut, sat with a grunt and reached for the log.

Buster's voice crackled from the dash unit as the ambulance pulled away. "Something just came in, Chief. Not far from the Station. Some sort of domestic accident."

"Lead the way. We'll be right behind." Stoner scribbled the coordinates onto his clipboard.

# Chapter 17

The hauntingly-familiar street made Kyle cringe behind the wheel.

His head spinning, he double-parked and applied the emergency brake with a shaky hand that quickly went numb.

The small two-story shuddered in fear, the blinds in its windows ominously drawn.

A heavy tingling crawled up Kyle's spine. *No. This isn't even the same street. It can't be. I'm just gun-shy. Overly sensitive.*

Stoner and Buster huddled behind the ambulance, waiting for Falworth to complete his call to headquarters. Kyle forced himself to believe he was worrying over nothing. These streets all looked the same. No reason to think the worst.

Falworth slipped out of the passenger seat. Hauling his bag, Buster circled the ambulance and squeezed through the battered wooden gate.

No. This wasn't happening. Lots of houses had similar gates.

When Buster shifted to the left, the image straight ahead sent a knife plunging through Kyle's heart.

Elden lay on the walk at the foot of the porch steps.

"*Elden!*" Kyle dashed through the gate and dropped to his knees.

The old man, obviously in great pain, smiled faintly. "Kyle. How…are ya, boy?"

"What…happened?"

The old man coughed wetly. "Seems I had a difference of opinion with a step, and the dang critter won."

The damned step...

The knife shoved farther in, causing an intense ache and a sense of helplessness he'd never known before.

The step was wobbly. He'd seen it and avoided it. But he hadn't thought much about it at the time. *You're young. You're also tall, with long legs. Just step over it. No problem. You don't want problems, do you? You work with Stoner; you should be adapting.*

He'd been so surprised someone had actually invited him into their home that he'd focused on the friendly old gent smiling at him behind ringlets of pipe smoke.

If only he'd done something about the step...

How long would it have taken? Five minutes with a hammer and a couple of nails? Ten, tops?

Just ten minutes of his time and Elden wouldn't have tripped or stumbled.

"Outa the way, Sonnet." The man of stone, his frozen face grim behind his visor, rapped him on the shoulder. "Things to do, remember?"

"Sir..." Kyle's mind turned blank. The words were out there, flickering like stars on a clear night. But like the stars, they were much too far away. Barely recognizable. With conscious effort he forced them into definite shapes, using all his concentration to bring them back. But when he opened his mouth, he realized that they

*(please don't do this)*

143

wouldn't budge, that they were

(*please don't kill this nice old man*)

lodged in his throat.

His words wouldn't work here. Stoner wouldn't be able to comprehend them. Kyle had already told Stoner he had no friends. And dead bodies didn't bother him.

But that was before he'd met Elden.

Buster sat beside Elden on the step. Off to the right, Falworth was talking to someone with his earpiece.

Kyle stared at Stoner, hoping to penetrate the rocklike skull just this once. "Please, sir…"

"What's the situation, Buster?" Stoner asked.

Buster used his penlight to check the old man for a concussion. "The leg's broken and the ankle's pretty bad, judging by the swelling. Man's much too old to be going through major surgery. Cutoff age for surgery these days is seventy-eight. And since this boy's obviously *way* beyond that, we've got no choice—"

"No!" Kyle tried pushing Buster away.

"What the hell?" Stoner grabbed Kyle by the arm and yanked him backward.

Kyle spun around. His face was on fire. He saw double. *Two* Stoners—a real bummer. Enough to drive *anyone* crazy. "You *can't* kill this man, sir! I won't *let* you!"

"Sonnet, get back in the wagon."

"Listen, sir—"

"The wagon, Sonnet."

"But—"

"The wagon *this instant!*"

"Captain Stoner—"

"*Goddammit, Sonnet!*" Stoner took two deliberate steps toward Kyle. Their helmets bumped together.

Kyle could no longer see the smoldering-eyed, rock-faced man in the yellow suit. Only Elden existed. Elden. His friend. The only person who'd ever asked Kyle to spend time with him. To sit down and talk a spell. The only person who'd ever shown him any sort of kindness.

Stoner's voice lowered to just above a whisper, but pure venom dripped from each word. "If you don't get back in that wagon right this instant, I'll take my automatic out of my pocket and blow your fucking head right off your shoulders."

Kyle shifted his weight and looked beyond Stoner. Elden lay on his back, his head propped up by the bottom step. With great effort the old man brought up a crooked index finger.

Kyle slipped past Stoner. He didn't even care if Stoner decided to pull out his automatic and shoot him. Kyle was going to share one last moment with his one and only friend.

He dropped to his knees beside the sweet old man. "What is it, Elden?"

"Reckon I won't be seein' Hell after all, young fella. Guess I'm luckier than I thought."

"I guess so," Kyle said softly. *One of us is*, he wanted to add. But he could only bite his lower lip and hold back the anger and the tears.

"Remember what I said about getting' out?"

"I sure do."

"Find 'em, son. They're out there. Somewhere."

The old man tried to hold out his hand, but his arm dropped quietly to the pavement.

\*\*\*

His eyes focused on the road ahead, Kyle drove in numb silence.

His hands tightly gripping the wheel, he forced himself not to think of Elden's body lying in the compartment next to Mr. McAfee.

*He was my friend and I let him die.*

Kyle had known about the step but hadn't done anything about it.

Stoner, staring straight ahead, hadn't uttered a word. Kyle knew he was in serious trouble. Insubordination, no doubt. Kyle had pushed Buster away and pulled away from Stoner. Stoner would consider that assault. It was a miracle Stoner hadn't shot him.

Kyle wondered if he should tell Stoner the reason for his actions. Maybe he'd understand. It wasn't insubordination, it was panic, hysteria. The sight of his friend lying broken on the ground had been too much.

"Sir?"

No response.

"Sir, I need to tell you—"

"Sonnet, don't talk or remind me in any way that you're anything but the mechanism maneuvering this vehicle. You pulled a major boner back there, and it'll be a month of Sundays before any of us forgets that. I don't mind a question every once in a while, even a stupid one. But one thing I *won't* tolerate is

146

insubordination. Do you happen to know the penalty for insubordination, Sonnet?"

"Sir—"

"The penalty for insubordination is death. Remember that. So shut up and drive, and maybe you'll get through the day without being shot. Is that clear?"

# Chapter 18

Oblivious of the snoring in the room, Kyle, in shorts and tee shirt, hunched forward on the edge of his bed, staring into the heavy darkness.

You couldn't go back, no matter how much you wanted to. Even at his tender age he knew the only direction in life was forward.

And 'forward' meant a future without a sweet old man who might have easily become Kyle's best friend. A man with whom Kyle could share his secret dreams. His fears and disappointments.

His grief a throbbing ache settling heavily in his gut, Kyle buried his face in his hands. He'd never felt so sad. So alone.

But he'd always chosen to be alone. By wandering off, he could immerse himself in the quiet natural beauty of the woods and almost convince himself that the world wasn't nearly as bleak. The woods comforted him, made him feel safe. He'd never felt this way among people.

Except with Elden. He had finally found an older version of himself. Someone he could communicate with on common ground. The feeling was new and exciting—like opening a package, or stumbling upon a five-dollar-bill someone had dropped in the street.

He didn't know if Allie could ever become this same sort of counterpart. He liked her and enjoyed her company but knew he couldn't talk to her as he could to Elden. That same sense of trust just wasn't there. Maybe it was because Allie was connected with Stoner—or because she seemed too content with the way things were.

The compact figure filling the open doorway made him cringe.

Stoner stood there in his khakis, his face hidden by the darkness of the hall. His voice, barely louder than a whisper, dripped as much venom as it had outside Elden's house. "Sonnet, in my office in fifteen minutes."

Then he was gone.

And there it was. His personal summoning to the gallows.

***

The wide-open doorway of Stoner's office resembled the mouth of some horrible monster waiting to swallow him whole.

Kyle's feet grew heavier as he neared it. Then they quickly turned to mush. He tried moving them but they wouldn't function. The urge to run away had swiftly become overwhelming.

Stoner must have sensed his presence. His "Sonnet, get the hell in here!" sliced through Kyle like a machete.

Despite his useless feet and limbs, Kyle managed to clear the doorway.

Stoner, standing smartly in front of his desk, stabbed a rigid index finger at the chair next to him. "Close that door and cover this chair seat with your pitiful ass *right now.*"

Humbly, Kyle did as he was told.

Stoner's small black eyes sizzled. "What you pulled yesterday has been festering in my craw. I figured I'd let you sleep on it so maybe now you'll realize the trouble you're in."

Kyle sat stiffly, terrified to move.

"Before I make any decision involving your future, I'd like to know if you've got anything to say. You hear me, Sonnet?"

"Yes, sir."

"Good. Good. For a moment I thought you might be deaf as well as dumb."

Deaf? Dumb? Apparently he was neither. Otherwise he could cope better. Things would be much simpler. But he couldn't pick and choose what to ignore and what not to. He recently ignored something he'd considered trivial. Because of it, a kindly old man was dead.

Stoner's clean-shaven face moved closer. An intense miasma proceeded him, brushing Kyle's face and making it difficult to breathe. "Anything to say?"

"I'd...seen the old man before, sir," he managed.

*"There's* a news flash. And what's *that* have to do with anything?"

"I...liked him, sir."

*"Another* news flash. Sonnet, you should be on CNN."

"He was a nice man, sir. He was a musician a long time ago. We had a nice long talk. He told me how things used to be—"

"Everyone dies." Stoner sounded tired. "Life is slow death. We're all given death sentences the day we're born. And I don't care what or who that old man was, he was much too old to be tended to."

150

"Do you…have family, sir?" Kyle immediately bit his lip. *Oh boy. Why did I just say such a stupid thing?*

Stoner stiffened. "What do you *mean*, do I have *family*?"

"Family, relatives, friends. A wife somewhere?"

"What are you getting at, boy?"

"Isn't there someone you care about, sir? Someone you'd grieve for when they died?"

Stoner forced a hand briskly over his brush cut. "I told you to make sense, dammit. We haven't got all morning."

"Sir, the old man was the closest I ever got to knowing someone. I was walking by the other day and he invited me to sit with him—"

"Sonnet, stay the hell out of that neighborhood."

"Sir?"

"It's a high-crime area. Multiple families and colonies of dumbass kids crawling all over the place like roaches. We're called there at least twice a week. Stay away from there."

"Elden told me how things used to be. He told me other things, too. I wanted to see him again so I could learn more about the old days."

"Why do you wanna learn about the old days?"

*I was born at the wrong time. All the things I'm interested in are dead and forgotten, and I'd like to know about how they used to be. Since I can't get out to the woods any more, thinking about these things can be my new happy place.*

"I just don't think life should be this way, sir."

"Sonnet, you're a moron."

Kyle realized the man must be right. Anyone who saw fault with the way things were was definitely a moron.

"If it's not how we do things, why should you care? You don't live years ago, you live right now. And if you're not where you are, you're nowhere."

"But—"

"Forget about yesterday. It's dead. So is Jeffries."

"Jeffries, sir?"

"Old man's name was Jeffries. Elden Jeffries." Stoner blinked. "I thought you were his friend."

"I...didn't know his last name, sir."

"Whatever. But getting back to what I was saying, live in the here and now. When you start worrying about what happened yesterday, you're in big trouble. You already are." He clasped his hands together behind his back. "Do you see any reason why we shouldn't stick you in the cooler to help you think things over?"

"The cooler?" Kyle had never heard of such a thing, but could tell by Stoner's tone that it was something he didn't want to learn about.

Stoner's face relaxed. This was obviously something that excited him. "It was designed for troublemakers and confused idiots who need quality time by themselves. It's in the basement. Want to see it?"

"Maybe later, sir."

"Then shape up and do your job. You know the policy. If I determine that you aren't working out, I'll slap your ass in a relief barracks so fast, your head will spin. Do you remember me telling you that, Sonnet?"

Kyle nodded.

"And didn't you tell me you didn't *want* to be sent to a relief barracks?"

"Yes, sir. I don't."

"You know what this all means, then."

Turning a blind eye and a deaf ear. Not causing a problem.

"It means you've got to start making the best of the situation. Understand?"

"Yes, sir."

"Now stop this nonsense, wake up, and grow some balls." Stoner straightened. "Don't you realize you're costing us money?"

"No, sir…"

"We have an ongoing lottery between Sectors. Sector Eight's constantly beating the shit out of us. They've been beating everyone for months now, and I'll do practically anything to see Marshall take it in the ass. Sonnet, are you telling me *you'll* be the reason we lose this month's lottery?"

A lottery. How lame.

He didn't even want to imagine what it was. But he figured he should at least express an interest.

"What *is* it, sir?"

"Our monthly tallies. One thousand wins automatically. This means we've got to take in roughly thirty-five a day to the plant. That's around twelve per shift. No one's ever done it."

Stoner circled his desk. "Last month we broke eight hundred. The month before that, seven-fifty. When you cause problems, you cost us time. That

153

nonsense you pulled yesterday, for example. We were at Jeffries's house nearly *half an hour*, Sonnet. It should have been no more than five minutes. A simple injection, bagging, and loading. If another call had come in, we would have been late getting there. Luckily for you, nothing came in, but your shenanigans still cost us precious time. And when you cost us precious time, you make things more difficult. Any idea how much money we stand to win if we break a thousand?"

"No, sir."

"There are twenty-five sectors in this part of the state. Each one of us has been contributing ten bucks a week, every week. That's forty bucks per month per man. Considering there're at least twenty participants in each sector, you're talking serious cash. How's *that* make you feel?"

*Really and truly bummed out.*

Kyle wanted to grieve over Elden while all Stoner cared about was hauling enough bodies out to the plant to win money.

"Make you want to get out there and kick ass?"

Kicking ass sounded good—especially since Kyle knew whose ass he wanted to kick.

"Yes, sir," he said flatly. "Kick some serious ass."

"Good!" Stoner rubbed his palms together. "I guess we'll have no more problems? No more nonsense about friends and relatives? How things used to be? That kind of thinking will put your head on wrong, and a head on wrong means time in the cooler. I don't think you'd like the cooler. No one has. Get it?"

"Yes, sir." The room had been growing warmer, foul-smelling. Kyle needed to breathe in some different air. Soon. *Very* soon.

"Let's get with the program. I'll forget about yesterday if you promise you'll try harder. Do you promise you'll try harder, Sonnet?"

"Yes, sir." *Oh, for some fresh air…*

Stoner nodded. "Good. Let's get it going, then. Our workday waits for no one."

# Chapter 19

Overturned cars and smashed pickup trucks cluttered the eight-lane highway. Glass, metal and plastic blocked several lanes. Two cops carefully rerouted traffic while two others placed orange cones in strategic areas.

A male victim in his late twenties, his face and neck covered with blood, squirmed on the macadam. A heavyset woman, her arms, elbows, and legs bejeweled in broken glass, crawled away as the ambulance approached. Two teenage girls, their tee shirts and jeans streaked with garlands of blood, huddled behind one of the wrecked vehicles.

Stoner swung open the wagon door. "This should burn off some breakfast calories. Get out your running shoes, Sonnet. Be prepared for some crawling and scrambling. Assholes are half-dead and wanna play hide'n seek."

Kyle said nothing as he applied the emergency brake.

"No questions this time, Sonnet?" Stoner seemed surprised.

Kyle remained silent. This one was pretty self-explanatory. And disgusting.

Even in their final agonizing moments, the victims struggled to get away.

*Hell's coming.*

Elden's words never rang truer.

"No questions, sir," he said softly.

"Good. Very good. Let's hustle, then. Chop! Chop!"

\*\*\*

The one-story brick home bore unmistakable signs of savagery. The deafening sounds of TV, exploding from every room, ricocheted off the walls.

A man and woman around forty sprawled on the floor in the hall, both victims of multiple stab wounds. Blood streaked the kitchen floor and portions of the table and refrigerator. Half a dozen blood-smeared steak knives lay scattered in the room. Rubble from tossed dishes and cups littered the floor and sink counter. A coffeepot sat on its side on the linoleum, its contents a dark pool beneath the table.

A teen boy and girl crouched in their own blood, crying and mumbling. A small white terrier spattered in red droplets huddled in a corner, shivering.

Stoner stopped in the middle of the living room and surveyed the ruins. Buster slipped into the kitchen to tend to the two teens while Falworth checked the two in the hall.

"Sonnet, turn off those fucking TV's! I can't hear myself think!"

Kyle killed the set in the living room. Five other units blared away in other rooms, each programmed to a different channel. After he'd switched off the last set, the crying and whimpering from the kitchen filled his ears, making him want to turn it back on to drown it out. He stayed in the room and sat on the bed, covering his ears and hoping the sounds would end soon.

*What's happening to me?* he wondered, his gut tightening. *Do I want everyone dead because the sounds of their agony are hurting my ears?*

Maybe he was no better than Stoner after all.

*No. Not possible. Stoner wants death. All I want is peace and quiet.*

Down the hall Stoner was saying, "See that? No sense taking guns out of the equation. Idiots will *always* find some other way to kill one another."

"I've been wondering about that," Falworth said.

"About what?"

"Taking guns out of the picture when there are too many people. As long as they're killing each other, the numbers stay down."

"Somewhat. But it's gotta be done right. Otherwise we end up looking like savages."

"Good point."

"At least that's how the politicians see it. Sonnet, what the hell are you *doing* down there?"

"Coming, sir."

"You're young, dammit. How long does it take to turn off a couple of television sets?"

Kyle went out into the hall. The whimpering had ceased; Buster had euthanized the two in the kitchen.

The heavy silence made Kyle hate himself.

"Sonnet, go on out there and get the bags ready. Don't take all day. We've got to stay on schedule."

\*\*\*

Allie sat by herself in the cafeteria, eating her tuna casserole. Her usual deadpan expression softened when Kyle sat down facing her.

"Heard you guys had a busy morning," she said.

"Ten already." He tried keeping the disgust out of his voice but immediately realized how impossible that was. "A traffic accident and a domestic. The domestic was bloodier than the accident. It looked like a serial killer stopped by to have a little fun."

"I've heard some really awful things about family squabbles," she said.

"'Awful' doesn't quite cut it."

"Pretty bad, huh?"

"There was even a dog that got in the way."

"Whose?"

"Guess."

Allie shook her head.

"The mutt had been stabbed, and when it hobbled over and got a little too close to Stoner's spit-shined boots, he sent it flying."

Allie's forehead bunched up. She looked like she wanted to get mad, but shrugged it off. "The Stone's really fussy about his appearance. His old Marine days have never left him."

"Shame the dog didn't know that."

Allie drank some coffee. Kyle could tell she wanted to say something to defend their boss but didn't know how to go about it. "He gets carried away," she said finally.

"Do we get points for a dog?"

"Points?"

"I was given the lottery talk this morning."

"It's the Stone's way of trying to develop a team feeling for everyone. He's not exactly a rah-

159

rah kind of guy, so he does it the only way he knows how."

"I don't give a rat's ass about that stupid lottery."

"Sonnet—"

"All that means—to me, anyway—is that Stoner's obsessed about the number of bodies—"

*"Sshhh!"* Allie mashed an index finger against his lips. There was no sign of Stoner, but others sat eating, chatting with their neighbors or watching CNN on the big wall-mounted screen.

However, the black box mounted over the camera heard everything.

"Tell me something, Sonnet. Did Stoner happen to mention the cooler?"

"Yeah, I heard all about the famous cooler."

"Don't take this lightly. It's nothing to mess with." Fear filled her eyes.

He wondered if he could get her to tell him more.

"What is it? Thumb screws? Chinese water torture?"

"It's worse," she whispered.

"Really? Tell me about it."

"From what I've been told, it's like…a vertical coffin."

"You're not serious."

"It's a four-by-four concrete room, with no windows or ventilation. But there's more to it than just its confined space."

Kyle had a slug of orange juice and tried to envision what else could be involved. It didn't sound

160

much worse than when the nuns had locked him in a closet for disobeying them. "Go on."

"They keep you locked in there until you tell them what they want to hear. There's no chair, no bed, nothing to eat. Just a jug of water, a hole in the floor and a roll of toilet paper. No light at all."

"Sounds like a brick shithouse."

"It's no laughing matter."

"So it's small and confined and there's nothing to do in there but drink water and pee."

"It's much worse than it sounds."

"Why?"

"I don't know. No one ever talks about it."

"Has anyone ever been in it?"

"Just a couple of guys. A long time ago, before I got here."

"So you don't know what they said about it after they got out?"

"No one saw them after that." Allie leaned closer. "Everyone says they all went crazy in that little room."

"Wow. A haunted brick shithouse."

"Sonnet, *please* don't make fun of this."

"All right." He figured he'd better watch it. She might lose it if he kept joking around. "I'm cool." He put on the same serious expression he'd used when the nuns let him out of the closet. "How's this?"

"I guess that'll have to do for now."

# Chapter 20

That night, Kyle and Allie strolled down the overgrown path spanning the large pond behind her apartment building.

The moon broke up the surface of the water with wavy rivulets of sparkling orange. Birds screeched from the trees in the tiny section of woods that hadn't yet been torn down. Shrill sirens cut into the stillness.

High-rises towered above the trees on the other side of the hill, their lights sparkling like diamonds behind the branches.

Kyle wondered what this place looked like before the land was carved into and stripped bare to build these concrete monstrosities. He suspected it was beautiful and serene—much like the woods behind the Home.

This was the sort of place where a young Elden could come after work. He'd bring his saxophone and sit on the grassy hill overlooking the water. Squirrels, birds and raccoons became his audience, the woods his auditorium.

"You're awfully quiet tonight, Sonnet. How'd things go this afternoon?"

"I don't want to talk about my day. Right now I'm thinking of something else."

"What are you thinking?"

He didn't want to talk about it. His memory of Elden remained close to his heart. It had been a very brief but special friendship. He wanted to preserve it.

"Please tell me, Sonnet."

He wondered if Elden would want her to know about him. Elden might have liked her, too. He would have said similar things to Allie

*("you like what you do?")*

that he'd said to Kyle. He wasn't giving her enough credit. Allie was a country girl and would want to know about Elden. If things had turned out differently, the two of them might have become friends.

"An old man we euthanized yesterday. His name was Elden. He lived a couple of blocks from the Station. I met him when I was taking a walk the other day."

She blinked. "So *that's* where you were when I came to the Station, looking for you?"

"Elden invited me over and we talked."

"What about?"

He was glad she'd asked that question. Allie wasn't like Stoner. She shared some of Stoner's opinions, but only out of necessity. Allie was raised on a farm. She'd appreciate the simpler things in life.

"We talked about music and art. Elden played the saxophone a long time ago, before sound systems, electronics and synthesizers changed music and everything else. He said people no longer cared about one another, and he blamed it on computers. He also said the world was going to hell, and there was nothing we could do to stop it."

"The ravings of an old man."

Had he heard her correctly? Had the word *ravings* actually come out of that pretty mouth?

"You...didn't know him. If you had—"

163

"Anyone who says something like that must have a few screws loose."

Why would she say such things about someone she'd never met? Elden was special. Anyone who made you feel good, who made you laugh, was special. Elden would have made her feel good, too. His smile alone could make anyone feel good.

"He was right and I believe him."

"Why?"

"He was over ninety years old. He was there. He saw things we can't even begin to understand or visualize. He—"

"He probably imagined them."

A tremor passed through his limbs. No matter what he said, Allie turned it into a negative. He couldn't understand it. He expected this kind of talk from Stoner. Stoner didn't care about Elden. All Stoner cared about was hauling enough bodies to the plant to win the stupid lottery.

But Allie was different.

So why was she taking the other side?

"How can you say that?" he asked.

"He was probably suffering from Alzheimer's. The stats say nearly ninety percent of everyone over thirty has some form of it these days. Your friend was three times that age, so I'll bet his brain was eaten up with it."

"I read an article in a science journal that said you can get Alzheimer's by not using your brain." He was happy he'd learned something that could be used to defend Elden. "Elden obviously needed a lot of brainpower for his music and art and all that other creative stuff everyone n o w seems to think is just a big joke. Elden probably had more on the ball than anyone else I know."

"Sonnet—"

"There's no music, no art. Creativity is dead. You need a big portion of your brain to create. Elden said everyone expects their computers to do their thinking for them. I learned a lot from that domestic call this morning. TVs sat in every single room. Each set was fixed to a different channel, and the volumes were on full."

"What's that prove? They liked watching TV."

"It added to the chaos. You couldn't hear yourself think in that place."

"You're reading it all wrong. One of them was probably watching something when the argument started. He turned up the volume to drown out the argument, and it undoubtedly escalated from there."

"There are no accomplishments anymore. Elden told me—"

"Forget Elden. He's dead."

Kyle took a breath. "Now you sound like Stoner."

She approached him and stood very close. Her lavender perfume was strong in the gentle breeze. Her hands, clasped behind her, made her appear smaller and vulnerable. But something dark and disturbing in her dark eyes took away any hint of helplessness. Her eyes betrayed her. There was no softness in them, no tenderness. They were the eyes of a stranger.

"Sometimes Stoner makes a lot of sense," she said softly.

"I wish you hadn't said that."

"It's the truth."

Birds skittered across the pond surface. One of them snatched up a tiny fish and disappeared into the woods. More sirens cut through the peacefulness.

"I've got to put up with the man all day, but on my own time I don't want to hear what he has to say."

"Sonnet—"

"You're the only friend I've got. I was hoping you'd agree with me once in a while. Like before."

"Whaddya mean?"

"You told me about your family, their farm. You told me you loved horses."

"It was the truth."

"Was it?"

"Of course it was."

"But now you're arguing with me when I tell you about a nice old guy I met the other day. You would have liked him—I know you would have."

"Sonnet, the old man's dead. I'm alive. And I'm your friend—like you just said. So don't fight me when I tell you the things you really need to worry about."

"I just don't believe in them."

"But you have to. The things that matter are the only things you have to worry about. Don't waste your time on intangibles—those senseless dreams folks cared about so many years ago. They're all dead now—the artists, their work, and their dreams. What matters now is survival. Do your job. Stoner will be good to you. You'll have a much better time, and in turn, *we* can have a much better time."

"How?"

166

"When you're on his good side, he'll give you more time off. Wouldn't you like having a couple of days off? We could get in my car and leave the city. We could rent a bungalow and walk in the woods. That's almost as good as your music and art, isn't it? You've been telling me how much you love the woods. Well, this could be exactly what you've been needing. We could breathe in some clean air, watch the birds and have fun with one another." She wrapped her arms around his neck. "How's that sound? It sounds pretty good to me."

His heart sank. The world was crumbling faster than either of them could possibly imagine and all she cared about was getting time off so they could romp in the woods.

"Do you like my idea?"

"Yes," he lied. If anyone was deaf and dumb, it was Allie. But he was too tired and disgusted to argue.

"Good." She kissed him. "How about if we stop fighting and get to the good stuff?"

"What good stuff?"

She gave him another kiss. "The making-up part."

"Right here?"

"It's as good a place as any."

"What if someone comes along and sees us?"

"No one comes out here anymore."

"No joggers?"

"There's a curfew for jogging in the city after six P.M. Too many muggings. The cameras hooked up to the high-rises see everything. They've got infrared now."

"Makes me feel much safer," he said resignedly.

They sat down on the grass facing the pond.

A large vehicle screeched to a halt on the private road behind them.

The wagon.

The side door shot open. Younger sat behind the wheel, staring down at them.

Bummer. What was it this time? Another fire? A domestic shoot-out?

Stoner hopped down the steps and stood smart and proud in his khaki uniform, a cold smile

*(khakis?)*

on his chiseled features.

What was he doing in khakis?

"Get in, Sonnet."

Something was very wrong here. This had nothing to do with a job—not when he wasn't wearing his yellow uniform.

The tight grin on Stoner's face told him this wasn't a work call.

"Wh-Where're we going, sir?"

"*I'm* not going anywhere. *You're* going to the cooler for twenty-four hours."

Kyle scrambled to his feet. "But—"

"C'mon, Sonnet. No more bullshit. Readjustment time. We all saw how you dragged your ass at that domestic today. You're in a rut, obviously. No doubt over your stupid old man. It's my job to snap you out of it. Climb aboard."

"But sir—"

"If you don't haul your ass up into this wagon this instant, I'll be forced to zap you with the tranquilizer gun."

# Chapter 21

The heavy metal door clanged shut behind him.

The surrounding blackness was as thick and as heavy as molasses. Kyle couldn't see his hand in front of his face.

The cooler.

He didn't want to say it aloud for fear of frightening himself.

It was funny how quickly things changed. He'd been so brave and cocky when Allie was trying to tell him about this place. In the span of a few seconds he'd become paralyzed by fear.

With a shaky hand he reached out into the darkness. The concrete scraped his fingertips like icy coral. He turned and reached out again. More icy coral. Behind him, the impenetrable mass of the heavy black door provided the same bleak permanence as a tomb. Only the fragile string of flickering orange haze spanning its bottom whispered the presence of an outside world.

Squatting, he investigated the slab floor with his fingertips. The overhead light in the outside hall hadn't permitted him to glimpse the inside of the cooler. And since Stoner had slammed the door shut as soon as Kyle entered the

(*vertical coffin*)

tiny room, there wasn't time to see anything before the heavy blackness encased him.

A metal vent covered the corner, with a thick metal lever to grab onto. He pulled it; a strong fecal stench rushed upward. He quickly released the lever. It slammed shut so loudly, the floor vibrated.

A roll of toilet paper sat in the opposite corner, a jug with liquid in the small triangular space next to the door. It was odorless. Water, no doubt. It made him wonder how long it had been sitting here.

They wanted him to forget Elden. They wanted him to forget Elden and become one of them.

A strong sense of *deja vu* picked at his senses. Darkness. Isolation.

Just like the old days, when he was locked in the closet as punishment for his "irritating habit of wandering off" by himself. "Mix, Kyle Sonnet!" Sister Maria Francesca constantly barked at him, her heavy bulldog face frozen in its perpetual scowl above its short, thick base of soft chins. "You must learn to mix. Otherwise, you'll never succeed. If you don't succeed, you'll never amount to anything."

But nothing they said or did could change anything. It just wasn't in his makeup to become part of the crowd. A smile flickered across his face in the darkness. The nuns were many things, but perceptive wasn't among their stronger qualities.

He'd spent many hours sitting cross-legged on the floor in the dark, imagining himself the hero in some audio book he'd listened to in the library. He became Captain Ahab and Fletcher Christian and Wild Bill Hickok and Henry Stanley and Sherlock Holmes and Superman and James Bond—every single hero he could remember. In his isolation he'd tracked down the giant white sperm whale…battled the incorrigible Captain Bligh…taken on six gunfighters single-handedly…trudged through darkest Africa, in search of the elusive Dr.

171

Livingstone...outwitted the nefarious Professor James Moriarity...pitted his wits against Auric Goldfinger...or Ernst Stavro Blofeld...or Emilio Largo.

They'd expected him to crack, to climb the walls.

Instead, he'd enjoyed his hours of solitude. And when their quiet padded footsteps woke him hours later he grinned inwardly, knowing they'd failed once again.

Now he was a grown man, and they were still trying to break him.

*Come to your senses. Don't be a problem. You're costing us money.*

*Mix. Become one of us.*

*Turn, Sonnet, turn.*

One of them. As good as dead.

He wondered if Allie had any part in this. Their lunch conversation was somewhat tense, but he'd been upset, and needed to vent his feelings. Both the Interstate mess and the domestic bloodfest were horrendous—he didn't think he was wrong in telling her about it.

*Was* he?

Some of the things he'd told her were pretty strong. The more he thought of it, the more he realized that he'd been stupid for saying them. But he'd seen a lot of violence that day—wouldn't he want to vent?

Allie had undoubtedly considered his comments offensive. She'd been with the Department for five years—ten bodies surely wouldn't be enough to keep her awake at night. But since Kyle hadn't been

172

doing this very long, his reactions would naturally be more negative.

But hadn't she tried to warn him? Hadn't she tried to tell him in her own subtle way to keep his mouth shut?

Would she warn him if she was planning to tell Stoner what he said? Why not just listen to his ravings and report to Stoner afterward? Why tell him to keep his voice down so the black box wouldn't pick up anything else?

Unless she was playing a part.

He tried to recall her reaction at the pond. Had she shown astonishment? Surprise? Had she tried disappearing in the grass?

He couldn't remember. His focus was on Stoner. The starched khaki suit. The image of power. The evil grin. He couldn't blame her for doing nothing. Offering resistance during an arrest would not be very bright.

Besides, she was probably scared and embarrassed.

On the ride over, all Kyle could think of was what Allie had said earlier.

"The only thing that matters now is survival."

Now he lay on his side, curled up in a ball on the cold concrete floor. Maybe she was right after all.

Survival. Winning.

Making your enemy think he'd won... Using your enemy's shortcomings...

Of course.

This would be the perfect opportunity to work on a new strategy. His experience with the nuns clearly demonstrated that he had a fighting spirit. It would be foolish not to use his talents for this latest challenge.

Stoner would expect him to be soft and pliable when he was released. To do whatever they said.

Kyle had the advantage because they'd never done a psychological profile on him. They didn't know how much he actually *enjoyed* being alone.

*Go along with their plan. Make them think they'd won.*

If they thought they'd changed him, they'd leave him alone.

But if they suspected he *hadn't* changed, the battle would continue.

Kyle closed his eyes.

*Rest. Recharge. Use this silent time to get your nerves back to where they were before you became part of this madness.*

*This was actually a good thing. You've wanted a break from the violence, the blood. Here's the perfect opportunity to take advantage of this sudden forced isolation. In just a few minutes, peace will be your constant companion for the next twenty-four hours, and you can finally relax and drift off into a deep—*

A loud metallic voice tore brutally into the heavy silence, making the walls vibrate.

\*\*\*

"Our world is shrinking."

The computer-generated voice erupted from a large speaker built into the ceiling, its loud, irritating monotone filling the small room and making the walls vibrate.

"As our population grows, our natural resources gradually become extinct."

Kyle mashed his palms to his ears.

"Human population reached one billion in the year 1804. The number hit two billion in 1927, three billion in 1959, four billion in 1974, and five billion in 1986."

Kyle lay on his back, his knees drawn up, using his forearms to help block out the loud, piercing voice.

"On October twelfth, 1999, six billion humans inhabited this planet. In the year 2010 the population increased to seven billion. Eight billion in 2020, nine billion in 2030, ten billion in 2039."

*Don't fight the voice—let your imagination remove it from your fantasy world.*

"If this dangerous, indiscriminate growth trend continues…"

*Think of Wild Bill Hickok. Don't worry about the voice in the background. It's no different from the p.a. system the nuns used to announce classes and activities.*

*The only thing that matters is what's going on in your head.*

"…society will be adding…"

The darkness smothering him turned into gray smoke, then dust.

"…another billion in population…"

The dust shifted, moving away from the spinning current caused by the stagecoach hustling down the dirt path.

"…every five years…"

*Deadwood, South Dakota. He climbed down from the coach. A crowd of starry-eyed townsfolk whisked him away, pulled him into the bar and brought him drinks. The place was filled. The piano player—a skinny guy with short curly black hair greased down and shining in the light—sat in a corner, his nimble fingers dancing vivaciously over the ivories. The room grew thick with smells of booze, sweat, cigarette smoke and perfume.*

"...and the earth's population will exceed eighteen billion by the end of the Twenty-First century."

*The cheery ambience was suddenly shattered by a booming voice calling from the street.*

*"Wild Bill Hickok! Get your sorry back-shootin' ass out here!"*

*He leaned against the bar and finished his whiskey.*

*"He's a fast one, Bill," the sullen-faced, mustachioed barman said. "He's killed ten men in the last week. Hell, he might even be faster than you."*

"Last year, the population of this country reached eight hundred million."

*"Counting to ten, Hickok..."*

"The state of California alone..."

*"If I have to, I'll drag your yellow ass outside."*

"...boasts more than one hundred and twenty million, the state of Florida..."

*He put down his empty glass*

"...forty million."

*and approached the swinging doors. Everyone stood rigidly*

"New York's population..."

*in front of the bar, gaping at him.*

"This is something I gotta do, folks," he told them. "When you're a gunman, you have to expect it."

"...totaled eighty million, more than half this number..."

*Silence. The eyes of the saloon girls*

"...in New York City alone."

*grew as large as silver dollars, watching him leave. He knew he could easily outdraw and kill the best of those after him. The asshole yelling at him didn't know it, but soon would.*

*He pushed open the doors.*

"Every second of every day, ten babies are born."

*Dressed in black leather, the gunman stood tall and proud in the middle of the street. His silver six-guns*

"In the beginning of the Twenty-First Century, fifty acres of the rainforest..."

*glittered in the afternoon sunlight.*

"...were cut down..."

"You're no good, Hickok," the gunman said. "You ain't nothin' but a stupid son of a bitch, and now you're gonna be dead as well."

*He stepped outside.*

"...every minute of every day...and since rainforests maintain weather patterns and the Earth's limited supply of fresh water..."

*The gunman kept his hands at his sides.*

"...the future of Man..."

*His fingertips dangled inches from the ivory grips.*

177

"...is in immediate peril."

*The sneer on his face said he considered himself superior.*

"Sixty years ago, more than half the rainforest was burned, bulldozed and obliterated..."

*Wild Bill nearly laughed at the man's expression. This is my dream, he wanted to say. You're toast.*

"Due to modern ecological efforts, this savage deforestation has been slowed down temporarily..."

*He descended the single wooden step.*

"...but scientists have determined that nearly all tropical rainforest ecosystems..."

*"You ain't nothin', Hickok."*

"...have been destroyed, causing global warming, which in turn has increased violent climatic activity..."

*"A back-shooter and a coward."*

"...which will quickly escalate."

*"You haven't the guts to shoot someone face-on."*

"The number of hurricanes, earthquakes, and tornadoes has doubled in the last ten years..."

*"You got somethin' to say before I stick your ass in the ground?" the gunman asked.*

"...and will triple in the next ten."

*"I'm a god-fearing man. Just because I'm gonna kill you don't mean I ain't religious."*

"The state of Florida, the victim of the major droughts and hurricanes crippling the East Coast..."

*"What don't you just shut up and draw?" Wild Bill said. "I'm gonna kill you because—"*

"...have reached epidemic proportions..."

"—you've got a big mouth and because you interrupted my party."

"…wildfires flaring up due to the lack of sufficient moisture caused by deforestation…"

*The gunman's hands slapped the grips of his pistols. His fingers curled around them, pulling them rapidly from their holsters.*

"…nearly fifty percent of the state…"

*Wild Bill's monogrammed 1851 .44 caliber Dragoon shot out like lightning, its hammer cocked a split second before the long barrel leveled perfectly at the gunman's square forehead.*

"…vast wasteland…"

*The roar of Wild Bill's gun echoed up and down the deserted street.*

*A large hole appeared in the center of the gunman's forehead. He stood there silently, his mouth open, his jaw dangling, both guns dropping at his feet. Then he fell quietly to the ground.*

Kyle dozed peacefully, a smile of contentment on his face.

# Chapter 22

The deafening bang of deadbolts slamming into metal jerked Kyle awake.

The door groaned open; a thickening bar of hazy orange seeped into the blackness.

A slim upright shadow broke up the bar of light. Stoner, neat and proud in his pressed khakis, filled the doorway. His cheap aftershave immediately penetrated the confines of the tiny room.

"Hungry, Sonnet?"

*Survival. Winning.*

*Making your enemy think he'd won…*

"Yes, sir!" Ignoring the protests of stiff joints, Kyle scrambled to attention.

The trace of a smile touched the corners of the bloodless slash beneath Stoner's nose. He sniffed. "You need a shower, boy."

"Yes, sir."

"You can do that later. For now, the cafeteria's first on our list." Stoner's eyes roamed all over Kyle, inspecting everything. "I told them in the kitchen that you'd be hungry enough for three men. *Are* you hungry enough for three men, Sonnet?"

"Yes, sir!"

"You feel differently about things?"

"Yes, sir!"

"No more nonsense about the job? The lottery? Grieving over an old man?"

Allie.

She *had* talked to Stoner.

*Make them think they've won…*

"No, sir!"

"Good. Good." Stoner's cheeks and jaw relaxed only an instant before growing taut again. "Let's fill up that gut, then. Evening's menu is roast beef, mashed potatoes, string bean casserole, and fresh apple pie for dessert. Sound good to you, boy?"

"Yes, *sir!*"

***

As he devoured his dinner, tiny glittering lights from neighboring buildings penetrated the heavy slab of darkness pressing against the cafeteria windows. The mixed aromas of cooked food had made his mouth water while he'd loaded his tray. The food was no longer steaming hot. It was ten-thirty—hours since the evening shift had finished supper. But Kyle was so hungry that every morsel melted in his mouth.

But even as he gulped down everything on his plate, his thoughts had settled on more important matters.

Allie was his main concern.

Since she'd been working for the Department for so long, she'd quite naturally want to adapt the same attitude as everyone else. Changing jobs wasn't easy; she was probably just as stuck in Dispatch as Kyle was as a driver. What she had told him about her childhood was probably the truth, but after five years working with Stoner, it was only natural that she'd do a complete turnabout.

It angered him that she'd let society change her, but he understood. A quiet, sensitive person could not survive long in this atmosphere. Her attitude changed, obviously, to blend in. Childhood hopes

181

and dreams had fallen by the wayside. Her appreciation for the simple things had metamorphosed into some silly notion she'd once entertained in another life.

Was there a chance he could help her find her way back?

Was it possible to bring the original Allie back from the dead?

"Are you okay?" she asked, sitting down beside him. She wore a loose-fitting red tee shirt, tan corduroys and tennis shoes. Her lavender smell was stronger than usual. And her hair was soft and full.

Despite this, her presence made him angry. He found himself stewing over the incident the night before. But he forced himself to think rationally. Survival. Winning. It meant many things. And one of them involved choosing your words wisely— especially among those you could no longer trust.

"I'm fine."

"I thought of you after they took you away, when I was trying to fall asleep. Did you think of me?"

"Yes." He was glad he could give her *some* truth without fear of being betrayed again. "As a matter of fact, I did."

She smiled.

"How'd you know I'd be here right now?" he asked, suddenly curious.

She shrugged. "Word gets around."

He said nothing. Her answer made his blood run cold.

She rested her hand on his. It was small, like a child's, and cold. "Do you feel differently about things now?"

Stoner's words again.

The more she spoke, the less he trusted her.

He fought down the unexpected burst of heat. He wanted to curse her for abandoning the feelings she'd possessed as a child. The fact that she'd killed the Allie he could have fallen in love with made him want to turn away from her forever. But there were more important issues to address, and after reminding himself

(*soft and pliable*)

what had to be done, he ignored his pent-up resentment—for the time being.

"I was stupid for thinking as I did." He forced out a laugh. "Can you imagine anyone wanting to change his entire outlook on life just because of one conversation with a senile old man?"

"Don't blame yourself, Sonnet. You want to change things, make them better. Isn't that basically how you felt?"

"Exactly."

"And how do you feel now?"

"I realize just how lame that sort of thinking is. As Captain Stoner told me, live in the here and now. If you're not where you are, you're nowhere."

Allie squeezed his hand.

# Chapter 23

Kyle experienced a strange euphoria when he awoke early, showered and dressed, and made his bed.

The barracks smelled differently. Normally heavy with the mixture of sweat, bath soap, and aftershave from his roommates, the area now emanated with an odd freshness.

But that wasn't the only difference. The water in the shower stall, always thick with a sulphur reek, now smelled sweet. The stall itself didn't appear as dirty, the tile floor less gritty.

The cafeteria buzzed with uniformed police officers, hospital staffers, and ambulance workers and drivers from the other shifts, but didn't exude its usual quiet chaos. Everyone appeared less grim.

Survival. It put a fresh light on everything.

Stoner was screwing his cap firmly onto his skull when Kyle entered the locker room. "Good to see you're up and at 'em this morning. No ill effects from your day in the cooler, I hope?"

"No, sir." Kyle, standing tall and proud, was pleased to discover that the taller he stood, the more he dwarfed Stoner. It gave him a strange sense of power—one which made this new day even sweeter. "I needed that day in the cooler, sir."

"Good. We've already got three to pick up this morning. Idiots tried robbing a 7-Eleven. There was a uniformed cop in there at the same time. Go figure. You ready for business?"

"Yes, sir!"

Stoner did another quick probe.

Kyle decided to let him sniff. What could he possibly pick up? Kyle's hatred for him? For the wagon? The job? His suspicion of Allie? His plans for escape? Stoner couldn't possibly sense any of that. The man was intimidating but not a mind-reader. Kyle's plans, still in their infancy, hadn't been worked out yet. At the moment, they were amoebic tadpoles floating around in his consciousness, hungering to grow, to develop.

Seeking freedom.

Satisfied with his evaluation, Stoner said, "Let's go, then. Chop! Chop!"

\*\*\*

A man sprawled on the ground amongst discarded candy wrappers and cigarette butts. Blood pulsed from two gaping wounds in his left thigh, streaking his faded jeans and painting dark patterns on the grass.

"Got him low." The tall, square man in the starched blue uniform kept his automatic trained on the wounded man's head. "Was making a run, so I clipped him. He tried to get off a round but wasn't fast enough." He grunted. "Cameras everywhere, as well as sensors and chips. Registers only have enough cash to handle the small percentage of customers who don't wanna deal with swipe cards. Safe holds less than forty bucks, key to the cigarette cabinet's locked up tight—and these losers *still* wanna rob the place." He shook his head. "Guess I'll never understand human nature."

Kneeling, Buster was careful to keep away from the spurting blood. "Looks like you nicked an artery."

The cop gave an indifferent shrug.

185

"Guess I'll have to clamp it."

Stoner grunted. "What the hell for? Bleeding'll stop once you give him the shot. And when he's bagged, everything'll be contained. Why waste your equipment on a corpse?"

The man sobbed loudly.

"Sorry, sport," Stoner said with an indifferent shrug. "You should know the rules by now. You're caught robbing a place? That's ten to twenty. You're caught robbing a place with an illegal firearm? That's the needle. Life sentences were done away with seven years ago due to lack of funding and space. They also did away with stays of execution, as I recall. Didn't they, Officer Reardon?" Stoner gave the man's name tag a quick scan.

Reardon nodded. "'Bout a year before the penal code was redone. Best thing they ever did was follow Britain's lead. Do away with degrees of murder. Murder's murder, no matter how you slice it. Too many damn killers were getting off. This new system makes our jobs *much* easier."

"So even if you *did* have a prayer otherwise," Stoner said to the man on the ground, "you shouldn't waste your time hoping for a break. And don't forget, you ran from a cop. When you run from a cop, he's legally entitled to use any method he deems necessary to stop you."

*"Please* don't kill me!*"*

"Buster, get this done. Idiot's playing havoc with my eardrums." Stoner sniffed twice. "And I do believe he's soiled his undies. Sonnet, fetch three bags and make sure the one for this boy's double-strength."

Kyle opened the front compartment and removed the bags. Best ignore Stoner. Think about the Plan. Surviving. Winning.

Buster administered the injection. The wounded man made a feeble effort to scream. The chemicals began working right away, catching the sound before it could gain the momentum necessary to expel from the lungs. He shuddered and lay still.

"What about the other two?" Stoner asked.

"Toast." The policeman beamed with pride. "Got 'em right in the tickers. One had his piece aimed at me." He shrugged. "Couldn't do much else."

"How about the cashier?"

A balding middle-aged man sat on the concrete stoop in front of the store, holding a large bandage against his forehead.

"Just a bad bang. Seen worse."

"I'll have one of my paramedics fix him up." Stoner jabbed a thumb. "Falworth? See to the clerk. Check for possible concussion."

"Yes, Chief."

"What happened?" Stoner asked the cop.

"Said one of 'em got him with a gun barrel, but it was just a glancing blow."

"No severe damage?"

"Just a goose egg. He'll carry around a bruise for a little while. Seemed fine when we talked. At least he was making sense."

"Good." Stoner nodded. "Bugs the hell outa me when we've got to euthanize the cashier along with the damned perps because of serious injury. Just *hate* when that happens."

On the way back from the rendering plant, the loud hum of the engine the only sound shattering the silence, Kyle once again distanced himself from his surroundings and concentrated on his plan.

It was imperative to learn everything he could about the area. A successful getaway required a thorough knowledge of his whereabouts.

This more than anything else concerned him. The State Home, situated on thirty acres of wooded pasture land a hundred miles north, wasn't far from the State Capital. Kyle had spent the first eighteen years of his life there. His knowledge of the state was limited to Internet sites, satellite scans, and compact discs. This hadn't registered until he'd acquired the laundry job and found himself constantly at the mercy of the van's GPS for delivery and pickup addresses for his daily route. Since he'd had the job only a short while, he hadn't had sufficient time to acquire much knowledge of the city.

Success demanded that he find different ways to leave the area without detection. But how could he leave if he had no idea where to go?

He promised himself he'd find a way.

While coaxing the wagon into its stall, Kyle could once again feel his nerves loosening. He was back again, safe and sound. As long as he was back here, he wasn't taking bodies to the plant.

"You did well this morning, Sonnet." Stoner carefully tore off the top sheet of the morning log and hung the board from its hook over the glove box. "You're taking orders like a champ."

"Thank you, sir."

"You keep this up and we'll be winning that lottery before you know it."

"I hope so, sir."

"Count on it." Stoner read his watch. "It's now one-oh-eight. Take an hour for lunch. I'll let you know when something comes up."

"Thank you, sir."

# Chapter 24

Situated in front of the window in the cafeteria, the afternoon sunlight streaking her hair, Allie slipped a steaming forkful of chicken potpie into her mouth.

"Busy morning?"

"Not bad." Kyle sat. "I just got a compliment from Captain Stoner."

"Consider yourself lucky. He doesn't hand those out very often."

"I've noticed."

"The Stone's a hard man to please. You more than anyone should know that." Darkness filled her eyes.

He suspected he was still on thin ice from his day in the cooler and didn't want to rock the boat—especially now.

"You're right," he said. "And I appreciate any encouragement he gives me."

"He'll be glad to hear that." Her smile convinced him Stoner would learn about this conversation very shortly.

Allie definitely needed to get away. Everything Stoner did or said was okay in her eyes. Everything had a purpose, a sense of value.

He wondered how things would be if they could have some time to themselves. If he could get her to revert back to the way she once was. A different setting might shock her into remembering how wonderful the world was outside the city. Her childhood might come back—her dreams, her

190

values. Then she'd see that what they were doing was wrong.

But he was nervous at the prospect of bringing it out into the open. What if it didn't work? What if Allie had already irrevocably changed? Elden's words

("*once they turn you*")

came back, louder than ever before.

He wanted Allie to be as she once was. Together they could find out where the others had gone.

That was something else that had been nagging at him. The "others" Elden had mentioned. Had some people actually escaped? If they had, where had they gone?

Or was Allie right about Elden all along?

No. He refused to believe Elden's mind had gone. Elden was sharp and as alert as anyone; he knew what was going on. Hell was indeed on its way; you could see it in everyone's eyes.

"I've been thinking," he said.

"I can tell something's on your mind."

He hesitated. Now that he had her attention, he wasn't quite sure how to get it all out.

"Go ahead. Don't be shy."

*Tell her. What have you got to lose?*

"I've been thinking of getting away."

"Whaddya mean?"

"We could take a ride in the country this weekend. That is, if we can both get the time off. What we were talking about before made me really miss it. How about it? Wouldn't you like to get away for a couple of days?"

She sat silently, her eyes dead steady on him.

His skin instantly grew cold. Was she suspicious? Maybe Stoner *had* picked his brain that morning in the locker room and warned her to be on her guard.

"Something wrong?" he asked.

"It sounds wonderful." Her deep sigh eased his tension. "Have you seen the schedule?"

"I don't even know where it is."

"It's posted outside your barracks door, silly. You really need to check it once in a while, you know."

"I'll get right on it after lunch, okay?"

"*Not* okay." She slid out of her seat. "I like to find things out as soon as possible."

* * *

A minute later Allie lumbered back, head down.

"I guess I'm working." Kyle suspected something would stand in his way.

A nod.

"Both days?"

Another nod. She sat down heavily and, thumping her elbows on the table surface, cupped her chin in her hands.

"Sorry."

She stared lifelessly at the table. Apparently she needed to get away, too. Maybe she didn't like what she'd become any more than he did.

If this was the case, he needed to give her more of a nudge. It would prove once and for all if he was right.

"I was really looking forward to being in the woods with you," he said. "It would have been cool, taking in the clean air, lying around in the grass. Maybe even doing some fishing. I've never had a chance to do crazy things before. I just thought it would be great to do them with you."

"Crazy things? Like what?"

Kyle lowered his voice. "Taking you out in the woods and ripping your clothes off. Fooling around in the water. I always thought that would be awesome—especially if others were nearby. That would make it dangerous. Or doing it in a canoe, or in the grass—"

"There's got to be *some*thing we can do about this." Allie jumped up and ran out of the room.

Higgins and Montgomery sat at a table near the doorway, eating their lunch as Allie rushed past. Higgins shook his head. "Hey, kid…looks like you might need a little help when it comes to romancing the ladies!"

Montgomery nearly choked on his food.

Farther down, Younger nibbled hungrily on a sandwich. "I been wanting the old lady to split for two years, Sonnet. Ten bucks in it for you if you come over to my place and do what you just did with Parsons."

The room echoed with sudden laughter.

Kyle sat in tense silence, trying to visualize what was going to happen when Allie confronted Stoner.

Could she actually succeed in getting Stoner to change the schedule? If so, that would be sufficient proof that she could manipulate Stoner. Stoner was tough and inflexible. Allie was just as tough, but in a different way. The fire inside her burned intensely; he saw it in her eyes every time she looked at him.

If he couldn't get off this weekend, he'd have to settle for the next one available. He'd have more time to refine his plan but would also be forced to put in additional hours with Stoner. The idea nauseated him. The more time he spent with the man, the worse he felt. It wouldn't be long before he gave himself away.

And he certainly didn't want to risk giving them more time to try changing him.

Allie came back and sat down. Her eyes sparkled. He could tell something was different.

"Any luck?" he asked.

"We're both off Saturday and Sunday," she said.

He sat silently in total amazement. It took her just two minutes to get Stoner to change the schedule. He didn't know if he should be pleased or frightened.

But at least she'd done what he'd wanted her to do.

She'd put his plan in motion.

# PART 2 - GOING HOME

# Chapter 25

Someone nudged Kyle awake.

Allie squatted beside his bed, tapping his arm.

It was fairly dark in the room, but he could tell she was dressed up. A heavy cloud of lavender floated toward him.

"Hurry up, get ready," she whispered. "I'll be outside in the parking lot." She whisked out of the room, leaving a swirl of her scent in her wake.

Kyle got out of bed, grabbed his leather bag from the top shelf of his locker and hurried to the bathroom.

Tracy, in flip-flops and baggy white boxers, staggered in as Kyle leaned over the sink, brushing his teeth. Younger, naked except for a light-blue bath towel wrapped around his waist, slouched in the doorway, wiping sleep from his eyes. Behind him, Higgins stifled a yawn.

"Methinks Sonnet's gonna be hidin' the banana out there in the woods with the Iceberg this afternoon." Tracy swatted Kyle on the butt while clomping over to the urinals.

"C'mon, Tracer man," Younger said. "Ease up."

Tracy positioned himself in front of the urinal. "Get a whiff of that?" He hawked loudly into the bowl. "Chick's out for bear."

Higgins placed his gear in a neat row on the wooden shelf above the sink. "Parsons sure is one hot babe," he said.

"When was the last time we saw her all done up like that?" Tracy said. "Take a gander out there, chick's bubblin' over. I mean Mount Vesuvius. Bet she spent all morning on that hair. Never seen it look *that* good." He poked Kyle in the ribs on his way back to the barracks. "You got it, kid. Whatever it is, you got it."

Kyle knew that when guys were jealous, they went overboard with their digs. It was no different at the Home in the locker room after a game—the winners puffing up, the losers struggling to melt into their gym bags.

A sliver of cold fear poked him between the shoulder blades when he realized how these guys would react if they discovered his ultimate plan.

\*\*\*

Allie kept the cruise control set at a steady eighty-five. The cool morning wind slapped their faces as her white convertible zipped down the multi-lane interstate highway.

Traffic was heavy even at that early hour. The fog had already lifted. Minivans, utility vehicles, pickup trucks and compacts propelled their passengers through the city.

Allie shoved a hand through her windblown hair. "Ever been out this way?"

"Never."

"No field trips?"

"The Home didn't have much bread for fun stuff."

Deserted fields and pastures drifted by. Abandoned farms and ranches, desolate in the morning haze, covered the overgrown pastureland. Dilapidated outbuildings and fractured fences peppered the hillside. A huge wooden barn loomed near the top of a hill, its tin roof dangling over the side.

A CNN special Kyle had seen reported that many of the larger industrial farms had gone bankrupt because of the huge influx of Asian immigrants landing on California shores twenty years earlier. The unrest in China led to a major revolution, causing nearly twenty-five thousand of its people to hit American soil daily in what proved to be the largest flotilla in history. The invasion lasted more than a year. By its end, nine million Asians demanded American citizenship.

The Government relocated the new immigrants to alleviate the overcrowding in California, giving them grants and placing them in work programs. Fishermen received boats, farmers land. The struggling American farmer and fisherman, shoved once again in the background, were hit hard. Denied the subsidies that once kept their businesses thriving, they were forced into bankruptcy.

Using their handouts, the Asian farmers bought up neighboring land. Diligently keeping in touch with their fatherland, these new Americans gave aid to their brothers by cooperating with Asian corporations in desperate need of chemical dump sites.

This practice eventually put ninety percent of American ranchers out of business. Their livestock died from grazing on poisoned land. Government Aid, exhausted by the Asian Grant Program, had become non-existent. And despite several marches in Washington, D.C. by outraged American farmers and ranchers, the problem was ignored by politicians seeking the Asian vote, which, by the year 2050, exceeded two hundred million.

"All this vacant land's a result of that flotilla, isn't it?" he asked.

"Actually, the Collapse started it. Vets quit tending large animals when they discovered they could make more money in the hospitals. They could work indoors and no longer had to travel constantly. Because of the physician shortage, a large number of vets filled these jobs, abandoning veterinary medicine entirely."

"A farmer can't keep livestock if he can't find vet care," Kyle said. "He's in more of a pickle when neighboring land is contaminated and his stock graze near it."

"That's only part of it, Sonnet. Because of the new Imminent Domain laws, the Government confiscated eighty percent of raw land for strip malls, condominiums, dump sites and shopping centers. Now the only people permitted to own large parcels are the handful of farmers and ranchers—mostly Asian—subsidized by the Government, and doctors running euthanasia compounds."

"Euthanasia compounds?"

"They figured they could earn a ton of money by eliminating sick people living in the country."

"And they just go out looking for victims?"

"People bring them in. Usually there's a reward. Last I heard it was a thousand bucks a head, or a month's worth of food coupons."

Despite the heavy wall of cold air pounding his face, a bubble of heat erupted within him. Not only were they killing people in the cities, they'd branched out into the country to work their evil. "This keeps getting worse," he said, trying to keep the resentment out of his voice.

"You really were isolated at that place, weren't you?"

"Sometimes I think it's better, not knowing things."

"It's life, Sonnet. Everyone needs to know how things are."

Stoner's words again—something he didn't want to hear right now.

"Getting back to the contaminated land," he said. "How are the chemicals brought over?"

"Corruption's so high up, no one bothers any more. Stuff just keeps coming in. The Bureau of Customs and Border Protection downsized years ago due to global integration. It makes imports even easier."

"You mean illegal containers?"

"During that terrorism problem we had, Customs developed the Container Security Initiative. They kept a sharp eye on containerized cargo getting into the wrong hands. But when the chip program eliminated the terrorism issue, the Government disbanded CSI. We still have agricultural inspections, but it's not much. I don't even think they use dogs anymore."

"So what's being done with all this farmland?"

"Not much. That's why you see all those FOR SALE signs out here. If you look closely you'll see a Government contact number. You can still buy land in small parcels of two- and three-acres, but they aren't good for anything."

"The land must be dirt cheap."

"Pennies an acre. Who wants to buy land bordering toxic soil? What's so awful about all this is that we've been contaminating land in other countries for more than a century—which the Government figured was okay. But when these countries turn around and do the same thing to us, we're shocked and angry."

They passed a sprawling ranch overrun by weeds and bushes. A deserted mansion reigned at the crest of the hill. Fences and paddocks surrounding the place lay in fractured sections. A large weathered FOR SALE sign marked the dirt path.

"The dumps aren't the only reason the land isn't selling, Sonnet. The gangs out here have scared everyone back into the cities."

"Roving gangs," he said, and the back of his head tingled. "I heard about them on CNN."

"They set traps to disable cars, then rob the occupants. They're really nasty. Many of them torture their victims to death, then take the bodies to local rendering plants for the reward money."

The "others." This couldn't possibly be what Elden was talking about.

"What about chips?" he asked. "Can't they hunt them down that way and—"

"Gang members dig them out with switch blades."

Kyle felt another tingle. "Hopefully, we won't get to meet any of these guys."

"Don't worry, I brought along my earpiece. It's in my bag."

"What'll *that* do?"

"Working with the DPC has given us a Class double-B rating, Sonnet."

"What's *that*? You're not gonna tell me we're allowed to *shoot* anyone, are you?"

"With that rating, we can get any law enforcement officer at our location within five minutes."

*Which won't make that much of a difference if the car's disabled and a gang shows up in two*, he thought grimly.

But he knew better than say anything.

# Chapter 26

Half an hour later, Allie took them down an exit ramp. A large block building with *ANTIQUES* painted sloppily on a sign bolted to its metal roof appeared about half a mile down the two-lane road. An abandoned filling station was its only neighbor. The asphalt wasteland fronting both buildings served as a battlefield of cracks and gouges. Weeds reached out in jagged clusters. The wind swept up from the valley, spewing food wrappers and fallen leaves across the two-lane road.

Inside, an old woman sat behind the cash register, frowning at a crossword puzzle. Smoke rose from the burning cigarette in the dented tin ashtray near her wrinkled elbow. The cluttered room smelled of smoke, varnish and mildew. "Lemme know if ya need help." She didn't look up.

A maze of slim aisles crammed with old furniture stacked with knickknacks extended to the length of the big building. Allie picked up a small ceramic horse. It was dapple-gray; a chunk of its right ear was missing. "It's an Arab." She examined the piece carefully. "Nearly seventy years old. It's really well-done. Look at all the detail—especially the face."

"How much?" he asked.

She turned it upside-down. Beside the initials *LY* and the date *'96,* a small white sticker marked the price in ink. She gasped, then replaced the piece very gently.

"That much?"

"More."

Down another chaotic aisle, a tarnished silver trumpet stood proudly on the chipped counter of an antique cabinet. *Stradivarius Model 37* was engraved in elegant lettering on its smudged pink bell, with *Vincent Bach* carved in similar script underneath.

"Isn't that a musical instrument?" Allie rested her cheek against his shoulder.

"A trumpet." It felt cool and light in his hands. He could easily imagine Elden standing beside him. *Try her out, Kyle, she won't bite.*

"How much is it?"

The tag dangling from a string attached to the spit valve displayed the price. "Twenty dollars."

"That's not very much."

"I think they sold for a lot more when they were new."

"Close to two grand." The old woman had snuck up behind them. Standing about five feet tall and weighing no more than ninety pounds, she gripped an aluminum cane in one arthritic hand. The cigarette smoke wreathed her leathery face in lively blue circles. "Fifty, sixty years ago." She shrugged. "Now they're only worth as much as a gallon of gas."

"Why?"

A shrug. "Nobody plays no more."

"I don't think they're *all* gone," Kyle said, a twinge of hopelessness gripping him.

The old woman hobbled silently back to the cash register.

"Try playing it." Allie nudged him.

"I don't know…"

"Don't you just blow into that little silver thingy on the skinny end?"

"They let me try one at the Home but I didn't do very well. I wanted to take lessons, but the music teacher quit coming around when the Home dropped the program so they'd have enough funding for sports."

"Try anyway."

Kyle wiped off the mouthpiece with his shirtsleeve. Then, taking a deep breath and setting his lips in a firm straight line, he forced a column of vibrated air into the tiny silver mouthpiece.

A sound similar to the mating call of a hysterical moose erupted from the bell.

Allie covered her ears and spun around. "Put it back!"

The old woman was cackling and coughing as Kyle and Allie retreated outside.

\*\*\*

Five miles from the antique store, a bumpy one-lane country road led them to a secluded glen. A wooden sign nailed to a post that said

*COTTAGES AHEAD INQUIRE*

pierced the ground. The sweet scent of fresh grass, azaleas and honeysuckle brought a smile to Kyle's face. To him, the familiar bouquet proved as appetizing as fresh homemade apple pie. The cold sourness of the city had vanished.

Pine trees bordered the dirt road. Sprinklings of wildflowers, daffodils and daisies collected in generous patches in the lush grass, adding to the richness in the air.

At the foot of the hill, a *FISHING* sign spiked the ground near a dock overlooking a lake. Half a dozen people hunched in canoes, their lines submerged.

Behind a cluster of pines, a row of log bungalows lined the grassy slope. A minivan and two small pickups sat in the dirt lot. A sleeveless white blouse and lime-green swim trunks hung from a clothesline strung across the front porch.

"Is this place Government-owned?" Kyle asked.

"When I was here last," Allie said, "they told me it was family-

owned, passed down long before the Domain Statute did away with private land. The grandfather law for private land covers fifty years. This place, I believe, was started up right after the New Millennium."

"When were you here before?"

"About a year ago I came with a friend."

"Boyfriend?"

She nodded.

"What happened?"

"We broke up."

Kyle couldn't help smiling.

"Why is that funny?" A spark of anger flickered in her dark eyes.

"It's not."

"You were smiling."

He didn't know much about women, but from what he'd learned, there were always eggshells to tiptoe across. He'd also learned that a well-chosen line was all that was needed to keep out of trouble. And if you sounded sincere, you were usually safe.

"If you hadn't broken up with him, I wouldn't be here with you."

She thought that over for a few moments. "That's one way of looking at it."

A small gray shingled building marked *Office* stood by itself down the road from the bungalows. Inside, a tall bony man, probably in his late sixties, hunched over the counter, squinting at a newspaper. He wore a stained white tank top, suspenders and jeans. Reading glasses were balanced on the tip of his large red nose. A strong whiff of b. o. and a reek of whiskey hovered over the counter.

Allie scribbled her signature in the book and dropped her card on top of it. The manager picked it up awkwardly, his knotted fingers moving stiffly. He swiped it through the reader beside the register and handed it back. He selected a key dangling from a hook on the wall and dropped it on the counter.

"Bungalow twelve," he said. "Checkout's eleven sharp." He thumped his bony elbows on the counter, lowered his head and went back to his paper.

"He looks pretty bad," Kyle whispered outside.

Allie made no comment.

"I'll bet he's got arthritis and something serious going on in his hips. And it looks like it's been quite a while since he's seen a dentist."

"Why should *you* care?"

He'd hoped being out here would make her feel better. But she'd become defensive, ready for a fight.

"I just don't like to see people hurting," he said.

"You really need to get with the program, Sonnet. You're all grown up now, so stop acting like you were just chipped out of a glacier." She jabbed a thumb toward the office. "Out here you'll be seeing more folks like that old man—and the old lady at the antique place."

Kyle couldn't help wondering if this was what Elden had been talking about. Where the others had gone. A bunch of crippled old men and women living out the rest of their frail lives hobbling around behind a check-in desk, or antique counter.

He remembered what Allie had said about euthanasia clinics. The way things were going, it wouldn't be long before people over fifty would all be gone. Then forty. Then no one with ailments of any kind would be spared.

Elden was wrong—Hell was already here.

"There aren't any doctors out here," Allie said. "Other than those running the clinics. Every once in a while the Government sends a group of men out here under the guise of conducting a survey, but they're really snooping around. Their cars are easy to spot, so word gets around and people scatter. If a Government man sees someone hurting, he'll report it. Some of these guys will come out here for a little fresh air, then look the other way if they see something that's bound to cause a lot of paperwork. The country's the last chance for these people.

They're old and can't afford health cards. They're living out their lives the only way they can."

"Why don't *you* report him?" Kyle asked.

"If that man wants to live that much, that's his business. Who am I to cause trouble? Besides, it's not my job."

"That's the way you see it?"

"What other way is there?"

A burning sensation flared deep in his gut. It occurred to him now even more than ever that Allie may not have already turned, but wasn't far from it.

It made him more determined than ever to save her.

# Chapter 27

That night, they made love in one of the canoes tied to the dock on the far edge of the lake.

Allie lay beside him on a bunched-up blanket, her contented smile reflected in the moonlight. She said how much fun she was having and how badly she felt for her attitude earlier. He told her that the important thing was that they were enjoying each other's company and shouldn't worry about anything else. She obviously liked that because she kissed him, and they made love again.

After pizza and beer they picked up from the country market down the road, they returned to their bungalow and made love again on the double bed beneath the shuttered window. Her face had softened. Her eyes appeared much warmer, her cheeks rosier, the perpetual pout in her lips gone.

As she lay beside him, she asked if he'd ever wanted to see the mountains, the ocean. If he'd ever wanted to marry, have kids. He told her he'd never really thought about it because he didn't know if he'd be a good father. She said he'd be a great father because he cared about people—and when you cared about people, bringing kids into the world seemed the natural thing to do.

She then grew quiet as she lay beside him, her eyes closed.

He thought about the trumpet in the antique store. How it would shine and glitter with the tarnish removed, the silver buffed to a high gloss. The valves stuck, but a heavy dose of oil would get them moving again. He had already learned about all that from his one and only lesson. Oil for the valves, Vaseline for the slides. A long coiled brush called a snake would clean out the horn, and a tiny, pine-tree-shaped brush would break up the crud gathering in the throat of the mouthpiece.

Had things been different, he could have brought the horn over to show Elden. The old man's blue eyes would have lit up. It would have brought back a slew of memories.

But Elden was dead, and the memories were no longer important. The old man had told him to get out.

A burst of reality tore into his thoughts. He *had* gotten out—at least, for the time being. He'd managed to coax Allie away from the city and bring her out here, where they could be free.

And why shouldn't he feel free? He and Allie were miles from Stoner, from the Station. Now all he had to do was confide in Allie, tell her his plan.

But what if something went wrong? What if she *had* turned after all?

Just because she'd melted somewhat didn't mean everything was okay. All it meant was that she'd needed time away, too. There was her dark philosophy of life to think about, her association with Stoner. You couldn't work with such a man for five years without his worst parts rubbing off. Kyle had seen several examples of it. She thought Stoner made sense, agreed with his spit-and-polish attitude, his unbending ways. Worse of all, she condoned what they did.

But Kyle was still confident he could get her sweet old self back. She had already softened—one night out here might be all it took to help her see what the world had become.

"Why so pensive?" She lay on her right side propped up on an elbow. Her hair covered her cheek like black velvet.

"I was thinking of you."

"What about me?"

"How beautiful you are."

"What else?"

"And how lucky I am to be here with you."

"Keep going, Sonnet, you're on a roll."

"I'd like to take advantage of you again."

"Really? When?"

"The sooner, the better."

"Then what're you waiting for? An invitation?"

"That'd be nice…"

"All right, Sonnet. Please…help yourself."

# Chapter 28

Beneath the bright, cloudless morning sky, Kyle and Allie strolled through the woods.

"I'm really enjoying myself, Sonnet." The breeze whispered through Allie's hair. "I'm having more fun with you than I had with—than I ever had."

He had never seen her so happy or carefree. Her hair gleamed, her eyes glittered. She moved free and easy in her blue shorts and red blouse, taking in the mixed smells of the country and its scenery. Looking at everything as if for the very first time.

"When Mark and I came here last year, we argued constantly. Every little thing that had gone wrong in our relationship came out."

"Then the trip was worth it."

"How?"

"You both found out how things were."

She thought this over. "You know, that place where you grew up didn't teach you much, but in a lot of ways you're very wise. I think you learned the really important stuff on your own."

"I thought about things all the time. The nuns don't really know about most of the stuff that happens in life. They're too wrapped up in their own little world."

"That's because they don't have to live in the real world."

"You're probably right."

He wanted to know more about how she felt about life. Before long, they'd be driving back to the city. His plan had to be presented in this setting and in this mood. For it to work, every aspect of it must be perfect.

But everything was. The sky was clear, the air pure and sweet. The birds sang from the trees. Allie was happy and content. The perfect time to hit her with his plan was now.

"Are you really having fun?" he asked.

"I just said I was. Why?"

"Are you happy because you're out here? Or because you're out here with me?"

"What are you getting at, Sonnet?"

She was watching him closely and would pick up on everything he said. He knew he had to be careful.

"There's another reason why I wanted to come here."

"I wish you'd say what you mean."

"I wanted to—"

Rustling behind them. A twig snapped. A loud clicking sound pierced the silence behind the trees.

A tense voice barked, "Don't move!"

Kyle and Allie exchanged shocked looks.

"Got money?"

The color drained from Allie's face. "Just c-cards."

"No *cash* money?"

She shook her head.

"How 'bout you, Stretch?"

Kyle shrugged. "Some singles. Maybe three or four—"

"Shut up, Sonnet."

"*You* shut up, bitch!"

She bit her lip.

"How 'bout it, Stretch? Got cash money?"

"A few bucks."

"Let's have it."

Kyle dug into his pocket, found the bills and pulled them out.

"Drop 'em right there on the ground in front of ya."

He did as ordered.

"Now get out. *Both* of you. I mean *haul ass!*"

***

In their bungalow, Allie, shaking and out of breath, snatched up her bag from the bed, opened it and dumped its contents onto the wrinkled sheet. She groped for the small black earpiece.

Kyle crouched in the doorway, catching his breath. A flare went off inside him as he watched her fit the pinkie-sized plastic crescent-shaped cylinder into her ear. "Who're you calling?"

She picked up the slim plastic dialer pad and flipped it open. "The Stone—who else?"

His temples blazed. "*Why?*"

"We were just *robbed*, Sonnet. Or couldn't you figure that out?"

"But…why Stoner?"

"We're part of his team. He's not one to let something like this go. You should know that by now."

"This isn't even his jurisdiction." The panic inside him struggled to take over. The idea of Stoner entering the picture made Kyle's limbs tremble.

"He's got connections. He's a high-ranking officer. And if he knows we were just robbed—"

214

"All that dude wanted was a little cash."

"You didn't see his gun?"

What was she talking about?

"He didn't have a gun…"

"You're sure?"

"He didn't want us to look at him. I didn't see *you* turn—"

"What about that click we both heard?"

"Lots of things click. That doesn't mean it was a gun."

"What do you think it was?"

"Sounded like one of those old Zippo lighters to me."

"We were robbed at gunpoint, Sonnet." Her searing glare told him the little girl he'd spent the last twenty-four hours with had gone. "It was a gun—not a silly lighter. Something has to be done. This place should take

better care of its visitors."

He had to think of a way to stop Allie from alerting Stoner. Their escape plan would be ruined.

"The dude needed money. Once he got it—"

"So? I need money. You need money. Didn't you want to buy that stupid trumpet at the antique place?"

The word "stupid" made the back of his head hot.

"You didn't pull out a gun and rob the old woman, did you?"

He stared at her, trying to figure out what was going on in that pretty little head. Her kind of thinking didn't even make sense.

"I just don't think he had a gun."

"No. It was a lighter. The jerk's robbing us so he pulls out a cigarette while he's doing it. Next you'll be saying it was a camera. He took our picture because he had no family and wanted us to be in his personal album. It would give him one special Kodak moment he could always look fondly on."

"Hope not. I really don't photograph well."

"This is far from amusing, Sonnet."

"I just don't think it was a—"

"It was a gun. Just because you think it was something else doesn't make it so."

"I don't know what it was. Neither of us saw it, remember? It didn't sound like a gun—not to me."

"Sonnet, how much experience have you had with guns?"

He remembered what happened to Nathaniel Johnson as well as Logan. And Mr. McAfee. "Not much—fortunately."

"Not any, maybe?"

"I know what they do when you point them at someone and pull the trigger."

"The jerk had a gun, Sonnet. Trust me."

This was going nowhere. She was hell-bent on bringing Stoner into this and he couldn't see a way of preventing it.

His plan was shot. She'd switched back to the cold, detached Allie in the blink of an eye. The little girl he wanted so much to be with was nowhere to be seen. He wondered if she would ever come back.

She sank on the edge of the bed and sat stiffly, looking past him, at the open doorway. Her eyes were glazed over in her anger. "Captain Stoner, please."

"Allie—"

"Hush... Captain Stoner?" Her eyes quickly brightened. "This is Allie. That's right. Sonnet and I are out here at Lake Monroe, and you'll never guess what just happened..."

# Chapter 29

The police cruiser slammed to an abrupt stop just twenty feet from the bungalows.

The passenger and driver doors swung open simultaneously. A tall uniformed dude slid out of the passenger's side, straightened, and carefully adjusted his service cap. His eyes took in everything. His attitude clearly said he was in charge and wasn't the type to take any shit.

The skinny uniformed driver silently followed the other man. The driver held something black and square in his hands. It looked like a camera, or tape recorder. Spotting Kyle, the first dude approached in long strides, stopping an arm's length away. The shiny black plastic tag on his blue shirt pocket flap said Mitchell. The silver bars glinting from each square shoulder said Captain. The method in which the piercing black eyes

settled on Kyle said trouble.

"Kyle Sonnet?" Mitchell asked in a loud baritone.

Kyle considered lying but knew he wouldn't get away with it—not with Allie so close by. "That's me."

A quick scowl. "You're the robbery victim?"

He nodded.

"Your complaint states that the perpetrator was armed."

Kyle took in a breath. "I'm really not sure about that."

"Someone said he was armed." Mitchell's black brows mashed together.

"He *was* armed." Allie slipped through the doorway and walked right over. "I know the sound an automatic makes when you jack one into the chamber."

Mitchell regarded her slowly. "See the gun, Miss?"

"Just before we ran away I saw something flickering in the sunlight."

"He was behind us." Kyle couldn't believe how easily her lie came out. She couldn't possibly have seen anything. He figured she was saying this so she wouldn't look stupid. There was no other reason. "She didn't—"

"Let her talk." Mitchell kept his attention on Allie. "Go ahead, Miss."

"I turned and saw a glint. He was bent over, picking up Sonnet's money, holding something in his other hand. Far as I know, it was a gun. Silver."

Without turning his head Mitchell said, "Get all that, Packard?"

"Yes, sir." The driver kept the recorder held out.

Mitchell sized up Allie's shorts and blouse. "So you saw the man."

"As I said, we were running, and I was at least ten yards away. I remember dark hair and some facial hair, maybe a mustache. Couldn't judge his size— he was bent over."

Mitchell jabbed a thumb at their car. Packard jogged over to it, pocketing the recorder.

"We'll do a scan of the area. We come up with something, we'll work up a composite." He nodded politely before marching away.

Kyle kept staring at Allie. She'd turned away—probably out of guilt or embarrassment. She couldn't possibly have seen anything. Like him, she was running for her life. And she reached their bungalow long before him even though he was nearly a head taller, with longer legs. Not once had she turned around. If so, she would have lost her balance and landed flat on her ass.

"Why did you lie?"

"What?"

"You were running away. I didn't see you turn around."

"I *did* turn around. What's wrong with you? Don't you want them to catch this jerk? It was *your* money he stole."

"I don't want them going after some poor schmuck just because you don't want to look stupid."

Her face flushed. "How can *I* look stupid? *You're* the one who didn't see anything..."

"At least I can admit it."

"We're not having this conversation." Her nose in the air, Allie trotted over to the squad car.

The heat rippled through Kyle's limbs.

\*\*\*

A small crowd had gathered in front of the lodge office. The old man who'd checked in Kyle and Allie leaned against the wooden railing on the front porch. A short squat woman wearing a yellow apron over her baggy plaid slacks stood beside him, puffing on a cigarette. Two men in their thirties and a redheaded woman in a tan bikini huddled near a van. A tall buxom woman in shorts and a loose-fitting

220

crop-top leaned against the front door of another bungalow, absentmindedly playing with her long blond hair.

Packard ripped several sheets of white printer paper from the machine mounted on the squad car dash and handed them to Mitchell. Mitchell leafed through them and gave them to Allie. "Pick out anyone who looks familiar, we'll bring 'em in. Packard, get the ambulance and the wagon out here. They should already be close."

"This is him." Allie held out one of the printouts. "He robbed us."

"You're certain?"

"Definitely."

"How about you?" Captain Mitchell shoved the printout in Kyle's face.

"I didn't *see* anyone."

Mitchell lowered the paper. His smoldering black eyes came into view. "How come she saw him and you didn't?"

"I was running. Didn't have time to stop and turn around."

"But she did?"

Kyle was getting more and more irritated by all this. "Guess she's more coordinated than I am. Probably the long leg thing. Got me into all kinds of trouble in gym class, too."

Mitchell hadn't liked Kyle's answers, judging by the cracks forming around his eyes. Kyle had the feeling the man wanted to take him aside and threaten him as Stoner most certainly would have done.

"Take Callahan with you," Mitchell said to Packard. "Bring back this perp. Call, you need backup." To Allie: "I understand you both work for Bill Stoner at Sector Nine."

Allie nodded.

"Working there long?" Mitchell asked Kyle.

"Not very."

"Thought so."

Packard fired up the cruiser, slammed it into gear and scattered dirt. The spinning blue lights climbed up the dirt road and vanished on the other side of the hill.

Kyle massaged his temples. Five feet away, Allie was engaged in conversation with Mitchell. Both were smiling, nodding, and having a good time.

Kyle wanted to strangle her.

\*\*\*

The irritating whine of the ambulance shattered the peacefulness long before the vehicle appeared at the top of the hill.

Kyle knew what was about to happen. A big yellow bus would not be far behind. Allie had brought death to this peaceful setting, this place they'd come to have fun and to get away from the real world. He could never forgive her for bringing it here.

The two vehicles slammed to a rocking halt forty feet from the office building, where the crowd had gathered.

Kyle couldn't bring himself to look at the wagon. Since he'd taken Elden to the plant, he could no longer face the yellow monster without the cold

222

sliver of guilt stabbing him between the shoulder blades.

The ambulance driver, two attendants, and the wagon driver approached Captain Mitchell. The wagon driver, tall and broad and anonymous in his yellow suit, moved in the same manner as the ambulance driver and both attendants. They were all one. Every last one of them had been cut from the same mold. There wasn't a heart or soul to be found among any of them. They were all dead—just as Elden had told him.

The group formed a tight circle, talking softly. They sounded like a nest of bore beetles. Mitchell immediately straightened, looking around to make sure no one had crept up behind him.

Allie approached the group. One of the ambulance guys stepped to the side to let her squeeze in. The irritating humming resumed. Laughter broke out. Heads turned in Kyle's direction.

Kyle felt like he was back in the schoolyard, waiting to be picked for a game of baseball or tag.

The police cruiser appeared at the top of the hill, approaching quickly. Creating a chaotic cloud, it screeched to a halt behind the wagon.

Packard and Callahan got out. Callahan pulled open the rear door and hauled out a man fully shackled and handcuffed. Callahan forced the man to the hard dirt. The prisoner struggled to sit up but the shackles limited his movements.

Mitchell barked, "Over here, Sonnet! We need your I.D. *now!*"

The prisoner made another awkward attempt to sit up. Callahan raised a foot and pushed him back down. The prisoner tried rolling away. Both cops whipped out their automatics, pointing them at the man's face.

Kyle's stomach churned. He turned away.

"Over here, Sonnet!" Allie yelled. "Let's get this thing wrapped up!"

Kyle's blood turned cold. If he didn't know better, he would have guessed she was the one in charge. Reluctantly he drew nearer.

Mitchell held out the printouts. "Let's see his face."

Packard grasped the prisoner by the hair and yanked the man's face in their direction.

Mitchell nodded approvingly. "Looks like a positive." He handed Allie the printout.

"That's him," Allie said.

Mitchell held out the sheet to Kyle, who stared at it and felt his limbs go numb. They wanted him to compare the printout to the shackled man. No big deal for Kyle. But it meant death for the poor slob.

And if Kyle didn't do this, Stoner would eat him alive.

"How about it?" Mitchell consulted his watch. "Don't have all day."

"I already told you I didn't see the man."

Mitchell moved in Kyle's direction. They were about the same height, but the man's attitude, impatience, and the glittering bars on his broad shoulders made him appear larger. "Does this perp look like the man on the sheet?"

"But—"

"Kid, do you know Bill Stoner and I go back a long time?"

It didn't surprise him one bit. "I didn't know that."

"Stoner's a good man."

Of course. The very best. A true humanitarian. Stoner also likes dogs and kids—as long as they don't mess up his shoes.

"Don't you think Stoner's a good man?"

Kyle swallowed the bitterness climbing up his throat. "Yes, sir."

Mitchell's eyes bored into Kyle's. He was trying to determine if Kyle was being sarcastic. Kyle's impassiveness told him nothing.

"The man knows how to reward loyalty," Mitchell said. "He's one man you definitely want on your side. You know that, kid?"

"I've been told that before, sir."

Mitchell lowered his voice, but the tension in it remained. "Then ID this piece of trash so we can all get the hell outa this pigsty."

Kyle sighed.

"It's either you or him. It's got to be neat to stick. It doesn't stick, we look like shitheads. I'm in charge, and if I end up looking like a shithead, I'm gonna blame someone for slapping that on me. I seem the type who wants to be known as a shithead?"

He sounded just like Stoner. But that was no big surprise. They all talked the same because they were all the same. All dead. Stones. Icebergs. No hearts, no souls.

"No, sir."

"Then make this easy on all of us."

The prisoner squirmed clumsily on the ground.

"Please don't kill me! *Please!*"

Mitchell held out the sheet. In that same instant Kyle saw

(*"Mix, Kyle Sonnet"*)

Sister Maria Francesca facing him. The bulldog face. The nasty expression. *If you don't mix, you'll never amount to anything. Do what they do. Say what they say.*

But what would he amount to if he did what they ordered?

That was it. An order. Mitchell just said Kyle didn't have a choice. Just following orders. How many times had he heard that before?

*It's either the dude on the ground or me.*

*Mix. Turn a blind eye, a deaf ear.*

The key word, Kyle. Turn. Once you've turned, you're dead.

He blinked. The face of Sister Maria Francesca vanished. Mitchell was back. But the message remained.

He had to do what they said. This was just like Elden lying on the steps. *Turn away, Sonnet. Go back to the wagon.* But this was much worse. Worse, even, than hauling Elden's body to the plant. *Turn, Sonnet. ID this piece of trash. You're costing us time. Time is money. You want us to win the lottery, don't you? You don't want to go back to the cooler, do you? You're causing problems. Complications.*

"Th-That's him," he said, a flurry of icy tingles rushing up his back.

226

Mitchell tossed the printouts. "Give him the injection. I'll get the papers ready. And get this done quietly. We have too many gawkers as it is."

The prisoner screamed, scrambling in the dirt.

Mitchell jerked a thumb at Packard, who produced a small roll of duct tape from his side pocket. He tore off a six-inch strip and slapped it over the prisoner's mouth. The prisoner twisted and jerked on the ground. The shackles clinked loudly.

The ambulance driver removed a chloroform packet from his black bag and held it tightly against the prisoner's face. The man went slack. The paramedic moved in with the syringe.

Alert and excited, Mitchell watched closely. "Morons break the law and expect us to go easy. Bastard used an illegal firearm to rob innocent people on vacation, then resisted arrest. Good thing for these speedy trials nowadays. Otherwise we'd be up to our eyeballs in felons and their worthless defense attorneys. Like in the old days."

Packard and Callahan removed the dead man's shackles, opened the trunk of the cruiser and dumped them inside. They slammed the trunk lid while the wagon driver helped the ambulance men lower the corpse into the disposable bag.

The dead bagging the dead...

"Was there...a gun?" Kyle said, staring numbly at the trees beyond the parking lot.

"Didn't find it yet. But we've got another car in the area. They'll check out the perp's trailer, top to bottom. We'll find it."

After the corpse was placed in the wagon, the paramedics approached the front steps of the lodge office. The old man watched them curiously. When he saw the hypodermic, he shuffled toward the office door. A paramedic grabbed him by the wrist. The old man yelled, tried to jerk free. The old woman sobbed loudly and beat the other paramedic on the chest with her fists. Mitchell, oblivious to the scuffle on the front porch, hadn't taken his eyes from Kyle. "No need to worry, kid. We'll find that damn gun."

# Chapter 30

Kyle and Allie packed their bags in total silence. Kyle didn't want to do or say anything to prolong their stay. He suspected Allie felt the same. The place had become cold and dark, hardened by a horrible memory; he wanted to leave as quickly as possible.

Outside, Kyle put the two small bags into the tiny trunk of the car. Allie slid in behind the wheel, jammed the key into the ignition and began to shake.

"Are you all right?" he asked.

She shot him a glare. "What do *you* think?"

"I don't think you're all right."

"You know something, Sonnet? Sometimes you amaze me with your brilliance."

"You want me to drive?"

She was silent for a moment. Then she got out, circled the car, slid into the passenger seat and slammed the door.

"You're sure?"

"No, Sonnet. I always like doing a Chinese fire drill whenever I get bored or upset."

That sure was ironic, he thought. Allie was the one who'd brought death to this trip. She'd brought in Stoner, Mitchell, the wagon, and the man with the needle. She was the one who'd ruined their vacation. Kyle was the one who was robbed, who'd wanted only peace and quiet. And to get away from the city.

But Allie was the one who was upset.

It was just as well. He could concentrate on the road and wouldn't have to talk or look at her. Looking at her right now brought the anger back.

The first five miles passed in tense silence. Then, without warning: "What's wrong with you, Sonnet? You embarrassed me back there. And in front of the Stone's friends."

Kyle gripped the wheel tightly. He didn't want to speak, to tell her what was on his mind. Because of her, they'd actually turned him into one of them. And he'd let her do it.

And all she cared about was that he'd embarrassed her.

"Are you listening to me, Sonnet?"

He nodded.

"Then talk, for God's sake. Tell me why you acted like…why you were such a moron."

Some inner voice told him to take her side. To agree. Just as he'd done with Mitchell. When he agreed with people, they left him alone. If he agreed with Allie, she might calm down and shut up. He didn't want to waste his breath talking to the woman who'd turned him into a member of the walking dead.

"I didn't mean to embarrass you. I was just…scared."

"Of what?"

"Of sending an innocent man to his death."

"Sonnet, they found the three families living in the area. The first one didn't match at all—two old people living in a tiny clapboard shack. The second, a family of five, couldn't have done it. Mitchell said all five chips were more than a hundred miles away.

230

The last family was that jerk and his girlfriend living in a beat-up travel trailer in the woods behind the lake. They're squatters, they don't work, and they've been sponging off the State for three years." She sighed. "He robbed us, Sonnet. Case closed."

Kyle didn't speak.

"Can we please stop fighting now?"

It was over—the plan, his dream—and all she wanted was for them to stop fighting. The spirited little girl was dead. She came alive only when life was carefree and full of romance. But when reality intervened, her true character emerged, burying the little girl without warning. She could never leave Stoner or the city—it was in her blood. And her blood flowed cold.

In just a few years the scowl she enjoyed displaying so frequently would become permanent. The coldness in her eyes would be irreversibly enhanced with wrinkles and age lines. The body might still retain its shapeliness, but the face would reveal a heart made of stone.

She was responsible for everything unpleasant and negative in his life. She'd made him turn against himself and become cold just like her. And Stoner and Mitchell. And all the other walking dead.

He wanted—*needed*—to be far away from her and the rest of them. If he didn't get away soon, he wouldn't be able to breathe.

"We'll need to stop somewhere," Allie said. "Fighting always makes me want to pee."

\*\*\*

A green sign marked *Hadleyville* in white lettering protruded in the ground near the entrance ramp.

A burger place dominated the straight stretch a quarter of a mile down the road. Two service stations, two fast food places and a souvenir shop advertising boiled peanuts, fresh fruit, body piercing and imported cigars, filled the block across the street.

Kyle stopped near the side door of the burger place. The front lot was packed. Vacant spaces behind the building abounded. "Why don't you go in first?" he asked. "I'll park and meet you inside. I'm kind of hungry."

"Me, too."

"Give me a minute."

"Don't be long." Allie grabbed her bag, got out and trotted up the paved walk.

Kyle circled the building. For nearly two minutes he sat facing the road, his pulse racing, his head hot.

Should he or shouldn't he?

Just leave her out here, miles from the city? The Station? Her apartment?

Wouldn't that be cruel?

Yes. It would be very cruel.

But would it be crueler than what she'd just done back at the bungalow? Would leaving her here be crueler than having someone put to death just because she didn't want to look stupid? Or bringing Stoner into this? Or forcing Kyle to compromise himself?

232

No. It wasn't. But it was serious business, no matter how he looked at it. Leaving her stranded here would probably be the cruelest thing he'd ever done in his entire life. And if they caught him, it would be the end of the line.

But he hated what they'd done—to him, his plans, his dreams. And he could never forgive Allie for helping them do it. If he didn't act now, he might not ever have another chance.

Elden had said find a way, do whatever you have to do and get out.

Hell was indeed already here, and he had to make his decision right now, while he was still able to.

A chill sliced through him as he pulled out and headed back to the Interstate.

# Chapter 31

It took more than an hour for his nerves to settle down.

As Kyle drove, he remembered an article he'd read in one of his science classes, stating that stress forces your brain to shift into a state of sensual overload. A fight-or-flight situation causes your heart to pump at two or three times its normal speed. Capillaries shut down, sending your blood pressure soaring, enabling you to sustain a surface wound and not bleed to death. Your eyes dilate and you see clearer. Digestion stops; so does sexual function. Even your immune system is temporarily turned off. Your supercharged body is structured to help level the odds between you and the danger. You leap higher, run faster and think quicker than you could in normal circumstances. Only when the danger is over will your body revert to its former state. When this happens, exhaustion quickly follows.

Two years earlier, Kyle found some pot in the hall outside the shower room at the gym. Curious, he picked up the plastic bag and shoved it in his pocket. He hadn't yet tried it but had heard and read about its mellowing effects. He planned to experiment with it during one of his excursions. But when he turned the corner and found himself staring directly at Sister Maria Francesca, he realized how easily his world could disintegrate.

"You'll be late for class, Kyle Sonnet. What is your excuse?"

Kyle could feel her gaze drifting downward, settling on his side pocket, where he'd stuffed the grass. He knew then that his nervousness would give him away. The fight-or-flight mechanism had already started. He could actually hear the blood pumping inside him. His mind went crazy with images. He visualized her frisking him, finding the pot and dragging him to the office.

His mind wouldn't function properly. Every clear thought in his head had jumped ship. He could only focus on his punishment. It would be nose-to-nose with the blackboard, writing *I will never smoke pot,* or *I am an idiot* a thousand times while everyone else enjoyed dinner in the cafeteria. There would be detention, extra chores after class. He would be forever known as the moron who was caught with the grass.

But even though his mind had gone crazy, his thoughts instantly cleared. The stress had caused something to rise through the fog, telling him that only his own conscience could trip him.

His excuse came out calmly—trouble with the paper towel dispenser.

A heavy rush of relief washed through him when she barked, "Hurry to class, then." She swept past him, her robe brushing him, her rosary beads slapping the pocket hiding the grass.

Now as he drove, he realized that what he had just done was much more serious than stuffing a tablespoonful or two of pot down his pocket. That nightmare had only taken a couple of minutes. This one was just beginning. And it couldn't possibly be rectified by stammering out some impromptu excuse.

*Guess I forgot about her when I pulled out of the food place.*

*I was still upset over the mugging and wasn't thinking clearly.*

As the curtain of evening slipped gently over the hills in the distance, white flecks of moon twinkled through the branches of the trees lining the roadway.

A *Quick Stop* sign flashed beyond the next hill.

The gas pumps were deserted. Two compacts and a utility van sat on the other side of the building. Inside the store windows people milled around, buying chips, pop and cigarettes. A big guy wearing a dark sweatshirt and a lime green baseball cap read a newspaper near the magazine rack.

Kyle parked beside a pump and sat trembling, the overload coming back in waves.

He'd not only dumped Allie in a strange place, he'd stolen her car.

Stoner would be munching on an economy-sized box of carpet tacks over this.

Reckless endangerment.

Vehicular theft.

Desertion.

Not to mention quitting. Quitters made him look bad, made it seem as if Stoner had done something wrong.

*You're not doing anything wrong, Captain Stoner. Mitchell says you're a good man, and good men don't do anything wrong.*

One of the compacts pulled away from the store, crossed the lot, bounced in and out of a

236

pothole and eased onto the main road. A black sports car swung in, disappearing behind the building.

After studying the odometer and doing a rough calculation, he guessed he had come a hundred miles. The gas gauge still clung near half; Allie had obviously selected the compact for optimum mileage.

It would be wise to gas up just in case. He wanted to go inside for something to eat but didn't want to stay in any one spot too long. It wouldn't be bright for too many people to see him.

He swiped his card in the slot over the pump and waited anxiously while the transaction clicked and hummed through its changes.

Would it work? Or was it already blocked?

The overload threatened to return. Stoner coming. The wagon pulling into the lot. *Parsons, give him the needle, you've earned the right.*

The *Approved* entry flashed boldly on the display. He filled the tank and kept an eye on the building, half-expecting someone to mash their nose against the window. But only the big guy reading the paper remained visible.

He reminded himself once again that all this was necessary. He had done the right thing. Sure, he had abandoned Allie and stolen her car, but he had no choice. They were killing him.

It was bad enough they'd already killed Allie.

He replaced the nozzle. The paper receipt curled quietly out of its slot. The metallic *"thank...you...for...your...business"* buzzed from its tiny speaker. He ripped off the receipt, got back in the car and did some quick calculating.

Allie no doubt went straight to the ladies room, washed up and came back out in five minutes. Since her hair was windblown, she may have spent another minute or two forcing a comb through it. Her next move would be to look for him. It wouldn't be long before she realized both Kyle and her car weren't out there.

She'd try rationalizing things at first. Maybe Kyle spotted something at the souvenir shop. He felt so bad for what happened, he wanted to make up. A trinket, perhaps—or maybe some chocolate.

She might even step inside and look for him there. More time lost. When she saw no sign, she'd blank out for a few minutes, succumb to the anger and go through the denial stage. No way would he even *think* of abandoning her, of stealing her car. The anger would take over. She was still upset from the incident at the lodge; keeping calm might take longer than normal. When she finally figured it out, she'd call Stoner.

All this would take between fifteen and thirty minutes. Stoner would be busy making arrangements to get her back before setting the jackals loose. This would add another half-hour or so to the process. Once Allie was safe, Kyle would be Stoner's primary concern. Mitchell and an army of cops would be called in. The ambulance and wagon would be on the prowl in no time.

Grand theft auto. Reckless endangerment. Desertion. Above all, *quitting…*

*Stole Parsons' car, eh, Sonnet? Bad move, boy. Real bad.*

*Looks like you're gonna have to be put down.*

*C'mon. Chop! Chop! Hold out your arm. You know the drill.*

The sign at the exit said *Terrytown*. Below it, a smaller sign saying *"a nice little community"* was barely visible in the approaching dusk.

Suddenly the Interstate scared him. Its openness. Its isolation.

He might stand a much better chance in a town.

239

# Chapter 32

Terrytown sat on the crest of a winding hill four miles east of Hadleyville. Spanning just six square blocks, the business district gave clear evidence of neglect. Pothole-eroded streets fronted half-vacant, soot-covered buildings. Weeds and debris covering the railroad tracks suggested train activity had ceased long ago.

One mile east, a freshly-laid multi-lane highway cut through the heart of the town. Kyle guessed that like most other towns he'd seen, the new road led to a giant megaplex of stores, malls, golf courses, condos and apartment multiplexes—all contributing to the death of the downtown area.

The dim light of a motel office barely pierced the darkness. Its sign, *Rooms*, screamed for a fresh coat of paint. A strip of eight rooms connected by a breezeway and another section of eight rooms mirrored the same degree of squalor and neglect evidenced by its surroundings. The hilly woods directly behind the wing of rooms gave the motel a lost appearance. Its closest neighbor, a boarded-up filling station, completed the picture of isolated degradation.

Kyle parked in front of the motel office, sat back and rubbed his eyes. Exhaustion was already kicking in. Not from driving but from the stress. No point in lowering his guard. It would be disastrous to assume his pursuers were far behind.

The office stunk of mildew, cigarette smoke, and stale beer. A pudgy dude around thirty-five in a stained white tee shirt slouched behind the counter, sucking soda noisily from a straw. He obviously didn't want to be here. He was probably just killing time, waiting for the right upper management position to open up. "Room?"

"Yes," Kyle replied. "Just for the night."

The clerk belched, sending over a miasmic cloud of stale cigarette smoke and something sweet. "It's all we got." He shoved the book in Kyle's direction and kept a watchful eye on his soda.

Kyle scribbled something illegible and handed over his card. The dude took it in his chubby hand and slid it through the magnetic track.

The overload drifted back.

Kyle jerked his face toward the filmy front window, alert for headlights. The empty street revealed nothing but a couple of street lamps lighting the blackness with dusty orange halos.

This transaction was taking forever.

It was just nerves. When you were nervous, everything slowed down dramatically.

But what if there was something to worry about? What if the transaction had encountered a block? If the Department had frozen his funds, he was screwed. The clerk didn't appear to be on the ball, but Kyle knew a little about people. When authorities were involved, even the world's dumbest moron wised up immediately.

The display beeped softly. The clerk glanced nonchalantly at it. He bent over the machine, studied it a moment and scratched the back of his neck.

"Everything cool?" Kyle asked softly.

The clerk slurped pop, a little noisier than before, and scratched his double chin. "So where ya from?" he asked, playing with his straw.

"Not far."

"Just traveling through?"

"You could say that."

"Business?"

This was not only taking too long, it was getting slightly suspicious. This dude definitely hadn't appeared the chatty sort—so why the sudden questions?

"Business," Kyle finally said.

"Don't see much else around here—not since everybody moved outa town. You wanna know something? When they put in that new road—"

"Why's this taking so long?"

The clerk shrugged. The twitch on his right cheek was noticeable. "Technology, man. Sometimes it'll have a glitch—"

"Give me my card."

"You're all right, sport. Just hang in there a few minutes and—"

Kyle reached across the counter and yanked it out of its slot. The clerk made a move to block Kyle's hand but was too slow.

"Don't have to get all huffy—"

"Yeah. I do."

"Can't give ya a room unless—"

"Thanks. I'll find another place."

"This is the only motel in town—"

It was a short jaunt down the walk to the thruway in back, where the ice maker and food machines clicked, moaned, coughed and hummed.

The food machine caught his attention. It took coins, not cards. Tough luck; he'd given the mugger all his cash.

But even if he had the money, he didn't have the time. Unless he missed his guess, the clerk had been signaled about the card and was ordered to try and stall him.

Kyle scrambled up the hilly woods behind the motel.

Just one minute later, the blinking blue lights penetrated the darkness in front of the motel, where he'd left Allie's car.

# Chapter 33

Curled up in a bed of pine needles behind a thick tangle of bushes, Kyle opened his eyes.

The low position of the sun told him it was early in the morning. His stomach grumbled loudly, alerting him of a nagging urgency. He'd spotted a restaurant down the hill on the other side of the railroad tracks the night before. Since he could no longer use his card, he might be able to scrounge something from the garbage cans behind the building.

Since they had already found Allie's convertible, he needed to look for another vehicle. It was early enough to move about. The cops probably had scoured the town for him and decided that he'd stolen another car. They wouldn't think he'd still be close.

But he knew better than to make assumptions. Best go on what he knew as fact and forget about guesswork. The flashing lights he'd seen the night before told him he couldn't make any mistakes.

The main road was deserted, the hum of traffic on the other side of the hill barely audible. The road went up a slight incline. Around the bend, a three-way intersection littered with debris formed the major artery. A park bench across the street posted a bus schedule on the Plexiglas wall behind it, advertising the bus route and flyers from a local clinic offering special rates for breast enhancement, facelifts, liposuction, Botox, and discounted prescriptions for Aspirin, Benadryl, vitamins and Tylenol.

As soon as Kyle reached the sidewalk on the other side of the tracks, a uniformed cop appeared at the corner.

The overload came back, this time in a heavy cold swell.

No sudden moves. Make believe you've just seen Sister Maria Francesca only minutes after you found that stash of pot. This time, instead of concentrating on the contents in your pocket, dwell on something else. And by no means think about Allie's car...or Stoner coming after you...or getting jabbed with the needle.

It would be stupid to panic and run. The cop can't be sure who you are. Even if the word has already been put out, he has to get closer for a better look. He can't positively ID you at thirty yards unless he's sure. You've seen several cops since you left the Home—you know they're not very bright.

Kyle knew that if he decided to run, he'd make a mess of it. His legs had become stiff and heavy, his feet unsteady, like soft clay.

Food. Restaurant.

A leisurely walk. Breakfast.

It was senseless to panic. The cop might be on the lookout for someone else tall and slender. Lots of dudes on the run were tall and slender—many of the serial killers Kyle had read about were the same basic build.

While his feet performed their required task, Kyle took deep breaths to relax. When he felt more at ease, he glanced to his right.

The cop was moving in his direction.

*Keep your head.*

Maintain an abrupt but unhurried pace, face front, on the alert for any possible escape route. Tight alleys separating the buildings were out of the question; they might lead to locked doors or dead ends.

Indoors, he could lose the cop. Out in the open he was a sitting duck.

*He tells you to halt, you'll be forced to. That'll be it. If you don't stop, he's allowed to shoot you. Thanks to Stoner, the rules are imbedded in your brain.*

A shiny black Oldsmobile stopped in front of the eatery, parking along the curb. The driver's door swung open. A well-dressed fat man about fifty years old squeezed out of the seat, slammed the door shut and waddled toward the entrance.

Kyle increased his pace until he was directly behind the man. On impulse he snuck a peek behind him. Talking busily to his radio, the cop continued approaching.

The big man pulled open the door and disappeared inside. Kyle slipped through, letting the door ease shut behind him.

The heavy aroma of bacon, freshly brewed coffee and baked cinnamon rolls made Kyle's mouth water. A desk, cash register and two armchairs gave the small lobby a warm, comfortable feel. The sign *OFFICE* marked the center of the door on his left. A hallway with *Rest Rooms* painted over the archway came into view. A smudged window appeared on the right, showing the dirty brick building across the street.

Ignoring the succulent smells, Kyle hustled down the carpeted hall.

The men's room, good thing, was empty. There were two booths. Two urinals. A sink. A battered white garbage can. Another smudged window. Two crumpled paper towels sat on the dirty tile beneath the sink. Two crushed cigarette butts lay next to the garbage can.

The chipped windowsill, covered with layers of paint, rose reluctantly. Kyle heaved upward until the heavy wooden frame groaned open, stopping when the gap was large enough to accommodate his slim form.

Kyle squeezed through the open window and dropped to the hard ground. He stood there a moment, scanning the area. No one in sight. The narrow cobblestone street was deserted. So were the dark windows of the big brick building facing the restaurant. Using his body weight, he pulled the window shut.

At the curb he peered around the corner. No sign of the cop.

He was probably in the restaurant, asking questions.

Relieved but still famished, Kyle scrambled back up the hill, to the safety of the woods.

\*\*\*

Remnants of the dying sun, a dim orange ball submerged in a sea of charcoal gray, hung low on the horizon.

The brush grew thicker, his steps heavier. Kyle's legs had become concrete pillars.

247

Lightheaded, he searched for a secluded spot among the pines. Under a barricade of fallen branches and loose brush, he could rest. He needed to close his eyes and let his mind ease up. Forget about Stoner and Allie—at least for a little while.

*They can't find you out here. No one can find you out here.*

That was something—especially since he was so weak from hunger that he could collapse at any moment. The last meal he'd eaten was breakfast with Allie the day before.

He surrendered to sketchy gray patches of semi-consciousness interrupted by chirping birds, excited cicadas and the soft humming of remote traffic. Everything softened, blurred, grew distant...peacefully silent...

*** 

A high-pitched sound.

Overhead, the sun flashed slivers of blinding whiteness through the tree limbs.

Shielding his eyes, Kyle raised an arm. The air was warmer, fresher.

It was inconceivable that he had slept the entire night. He must have been more exhausted than he thought. All that walking, forcing his worn-out, starving body through the woods, hadn't helped.

Distant laughter forced him alert.

He lay still, listening to the birds while the wind pushed quietly up the valley...

The wind shifted, snaking through the trees and bringing the sounds closer. There were two distinct sounds: giggling and moaning, made by a male and a female.

His senses alert, Kyle crawled through the brush. The sounds became more distinct as he neared the crest of the hill. The breeze brought with it a faint whiff of perfume.

Allie?

His pulse hammered. That meant Stoner was close. And the wagon. And—

No. This fragrance wasn't lavender, it was minty.

Besides, Allie wasn't a giggler.

Twenty feet below the crest, a young guy and girl, both in their late teens, squirmed on a blanket spread out in the grass behind some bushes. Ten yards farther down, a small white pickup truck sat about ten feet from the curb.

The girl lay on her back, blouse open, brassiere pulled down. The boy straddled her, his pants pulled down, his face buried in her chest. Squealing, she grabbed fistfuls of his long red hair.

Mindful of the hidden grooves etched into the earth, Kyle edged down the hill. The foliage provided enough seclusion to conceal his approach. Anyway, they were too busy to notice.

It was time to use a tactic he'd read about, when the hero wanted to give the illusion that he was armed. It might work with these two. They were most likely skipping school. They'd already be paranoid, their imaginations in overload.

His right hand buried in his trouser pocket, Kyle emerged from the bushes. "Don't move!"

The boy jerked his face around. The girl's head lifted, her light-brown hair hanging over one bare shoulder. Her mouth fell open. A tiny whim- per trickled out of her throat.

"The keys to your truck. *Now!*"

The boy's numb expression made him appear dim-witted. He was either too frightened to move or couldn't remember where he'd put his keys.

"C'mon." Kyle risked a quick glance at the deserted road. "Don't have all day."

The boy suddenly realized his trousers were pulled down. His gaze returned to Kyle while he dug inside a pocket. Something jingled. The keys appeared. He tossed them clumsily at Kyle, who scooped them up with his free hand.

The boy's eyes grew. "You're...L-Lyle Sonnet! Cops are lookin' for you!"

The girl's face paled. "S-Sonnet?"

"God *damn*." The boy's eyes filled the sockets. The beginnings of a smile brushed his fine features. "Lyle Sonnet..."

Kyle gripped the keys. "It's *Kyle*, not *Lyle*."

The girl said, *"Pl-Please* don't hurt us, M-Mister Sonn—"

"Why aren't you two in school?"

The girl blinked. The guy continued smiling stupidly.

The girl lowered her voice. "You're not gonna do anything...bad...to us, are ya?"

"Don't do anything stupid and maybe I won't."

"You're not gonna...*rape* me?" She shivered.

All he needed right now—a crazy female.

"Sorry, don't have the time. Nothing personal." Kyle yanked open the door of the pickup.

"I'll do whatever you want." She turned, propping herself up on an elbow. Her hair slid off a shoulder, some of it covering a breast. She knew what she was doing. "Just don't hurt me...not too much, anyway..."

Kyle slid behind the wheel. "Now what fun would that be if I can't hurt you?"

"You can tie us up when...when you're finished..." A glazed look filled her eyes. "That way, you won't have to kill us."

"Girl, you've been watching way too much television."

She continued looking at him with that same glazed stare, her boyfriend nearly as zoned out as she was.

"I have an idea. Let *him* rape you. He's already dressed for the occasion—in a manner of speaking..." He fired up the ignition and jerked the pickup away from the bushes.

# Chapter 34

A ham and Swiss on rye sat amongst wads of crumpled wrappings in a small basket on the bench seat. The couple had apparently brought along lunch.

Ignoring the waves of dizziness, Kyle scarfed it down while driving. His stomach craved more—three more of those, some potato chips, and a slice or two of apple pie thrown in for good measure.

*Relax... We'll get something as soon as we can put more miles behind us.* Gas stations and fast-food places abounded; grabbing something wouldn't be a problem.

A sign—*Hadleyville, 2 mi.*—whizzed by.

The fastest way back to the Interstate was through Hadleyville. Then he could get on the same road he'd used the night before. The Interstate was only a few miles from there. He'd be long gone in minutes.

Hadleyville was set up like many other towns—two major roads making up the business district, with strings of shops and other businesses fanning out. Tattoo parlors, computer distributors, hardware stores, a body piercing place, a barber shop and a drugstore advertising cut-rate prescriptions lined the street.

*Take a left at the intersection, drive a few miles, and the Interstate's yours.*

Everything would be fine.

Except, of course, for the roadblock.

Five police cars blocked the intersection of Hadley Avenue and Main Street. The vehicles were arranged in pyramid fashion, the cruisers spaced about a yard from one another.

Six police officers lined up in front, riot guns gripped firmly. The ambulance and wagon sat behind the cruisers, doors wide open. The yellow uniforms waited patiently, anonymous and inhuman behind their visors.

A large square man in khakis fronted the six-man unit, his loudspeaker raised.

The crackling message shattered the silence.

"Kyle Sonnet! Stop your vehicle and get out! You are under arrest! Any resistance and you will be shot immediately! You are ordered to stop, get out of your vehicle and lie face-down on the pavement!"

Kyle slowed the pickup to a stop. His heart thrashed wildly, his mind whirling. This was it—the moment he'd been dreading.

To his right, a bank entrance encircled the building, looping back to the main stretch, where the roadblock was set up. Signs lined the brick drive in neat intervals. *Entrance. ATM. Drive-Thru. Deposits. Exit. Have A Nice Day.*

The roadblock prevented anything larger than a bicycle to squeeze through. Parked vehicles and crowds of shoppers made it impossible to swerve onto the sidewalk for a quick getaway.

A police car crept up behind him, easing to a stop about thirty feet from the pickup.

"Kyle Sonnet!" The man with the loudspeaker sounded agitated. "Get out of your vehicle now!"

Kyle slipped the gearshift into neutral but kept his hand gripped around its handle.

"Kyle Sonnet! You have ten seconds to get out of your vehicle!"

The man behind Kyle cracked open the door of his cruiser. The dark barrel of a gun protruded beyond the edge of the door.

"*Ten!*"

His right hand clutching the gearshift, Kyle eased open the door with his left.

"*Nine!*"

The man behind Kyle lowered one foot to the pavement.

"*Eight!*"

The cops at the roadblock swung their riot guns in his direction. It happened in unison—as if they'd practiced the move over and over. The man using the loudspeaker sidestepped out of harm's way.

"*Seven!*"

Harm's way. Escape.

The man behind him stood in their direct line of fire. To make things even better, a large group of bystanders had gathered in front of the hardware store in the middle of the block to watch the fireworks.

"*Six!*"

Kyle let his door yawn open. He lowered his left foot to the pavement.

"*Five!*"

Behind him, the officer turned his head. A radio crackled.

"*Four!*"

Kyle slammed the gearshift into reverse, jumped back inside and yanked the door shut. The pickup bucked and squealed on the pavement, smashing into the front bumper of the cruiser. A sickening *crunch!* resonated down the street. The sound of applause and whistling accompanied it.

Knocked to his knees, the officer gasped in pain. His gun clattered onto the pavement. The color drained from his face when the open door of the cruiser twitched dangerously close.

Kyle slammed the gearshift into drive, jerking the pickup into a severe U-turn. The truck groaned in protest, its tires shrieking loudly in a quartet of smoking rubber. The pickup roared past the cop as he rolled between two parked cars to get out of the way.

The roadblock crew fought for a clear shot. Onlookers screamed, bumping into one another as they fought to get back inside. A toddler waddled over to the curb. Its frantic mother dropped her grocery bag and took off after the child. Fresh-baked bread, bagels, a dozen eggs and three tubes of cinnamon rolls shot out into the street. A man with a camera wandered out among the chaos to take a picture of the retreating pickup. An exasperated police officer rushed out to him, snatching at the camera. The man yelled loudly, pulling himself and his camera free. The crew lowered their riot guns. The cop who'd rolled out of the way of the pickup dashed across the street and leaped into his squad car. He was about to slam the cruiser into reverse when three young women wandered out of Ye Olde Body Piercing Emporium, blocking his path.

Kyle made a sharp right, soaring down the residential district, the needle twitching close to seventy as he propelled the truck east.

***

Columns of towering pines loomed straight ahead.

Splotches of charcoal clouds drifted lazily past the full moon. Cicadas provided irritating background music.

When the country road deteriorated into a thick mesh of wild brush, Kyle inched the pickup into a cluster of scrubs, camouflaging it among low-hanging branches. The ham and Swiss long digested, hunger stabbed at

him again. His gut ached like an open wound. His thirst made things even worse. Later, perhaps, after some rest. He was no hunter. Even if he stumbled across some game, how could he catch it, prepare it?

Besides, he was in no shape for a struggle.

It was hard enough finding the strength to gather enough pine needles to make up a suitable bed in the back of the pickup. It took every last bit of energy he had left to climb into the bed. Not even nineteen and he already felt like a hundred.

Sleep came almost immediately.

# Chapter 35

The hooting of an owl woke him.

He sat up sharply and rubbed his eyes. Pine needles slid down his shirt.

The darkness had become a heavy, suffocating blanket. Only a few stars winked behind the pines. His back ached from the rough metal bed of the pickup.

*Need to keep moving. Can't stay in one place too long.*

The grassy hill leading to the main road blinked brightly against the night. A strange light played havoc with his vision– white sometimes, red others. Each time it blinked, a cluster of trees lit up behind it. He didn't think it was a traffic light.

*Why would they need light out here?*

The blinking came from a telephone pole— about twenty feet up, near the top. Since he couldn't see what it was, he backed down the pitch-black country road until its message became visible.

It was one of those screens used to display official messages, bulletins and alerts issued by the Police Department, informing people without computers or TV service of something of a highly sensitive nature.

A life-sized computer image filled the screen.

Kyle's driver's license picture…with something very different about it.

The eyes…

They weren't his eyes. They'd been altered in some way, probably with the help of computer imaging.

The dark, angry eyes flashing on the screen held something cold and venomous in them. But that wasn't all.

The image showed a man much older than Kyle, his ruthless expression deadly frightening.

A display of bold black print flashed below his chin.

*KYLE SONNET AGE: 27*
*HEIGHT: 6'3"*
*WEIGHT: 200 LBS.*
*HAIR: LIGHT BROWN*
*EYES: BROWN*
*WANTED GRAND THEFT AUTO, MULTIPLE COUNTS*
*ASSAULT WITH A DEADLY WEAPON*
*ASSAULT ON A POLICE OFFICER WITH INTENT TO KILL*
*INTERSTATE FLIGHT*
*WARNING: INDIVIDUAL IS ARMED & DANGEROUS, AND SHOULD NOT BE APPROACHED DIRECTLY.*
*CALL YOUR LOCAL POLICE DEPARTMENT*
*A REWARD WILL BE CONSIDERED*

Kyle gazed dumbly at the screen.

Age 27? Six-three? Two hundred pounds?

*You're six-one, tip the scales at one-fifty-five after a heavy meal, and won't be nineteen for months. How could they screw up so badly when they have your file and a copy of your driver's license?*

But that wasn't the only thing bothering him.

*Assault with a deadly weapon?*

The two horny teens had undoubtedly gone to the cops and told them they were robbed at gunpoint.

*That was what you wanted them to think, wasn't it? Why you stuck your hand in your pocket, acting like a smartass street punk and talking like someone who knew how to kick ass. Your plan was to sneak up on them and get them thinking that you actually had a gun. That way, you didn't have to fight for the keys to the truck.*

*Slick, weren't you? Didn't think there would be consequences. Thought they were impressed. Hell, the girl even wanted you to rape her. Good thing you used your brain for that. Otherwise, you'd be facing a rape charge. Bad enough they've got you for armed robbery.*

What about that other charge?

Assault on a police officer with intent to kill.

The chaos at the roadblock had embarrassed them. It was only natural they'd want to get even by exaggerating the facts.

This would explain the strange face reflected on the screen.

But why?

Obviously to make you appear more dangerous.

The age-change was also a no-brainer. Eighteen made him too young, too innocent. They'd never expect an eighteen-year-old to be dangerous, cunning or smart enough to elude the police.

And that other "minor" discrepancy… That one made no sense, either.

259

If he'd wanted to kill that cop, he would have run over him while he'd had the chance.

His face burned in anger.

But at least now he knew just how dirty they played.

*** 

Cold and exhausted, Kyle trudged unsteadily down the dirt road.

In the distance, long crooked strips of tree branches poked the violet sky. Straight ahead, the world turned as cold and as dark as the inside of a cave.

He wondered how close Allie and Stoner were. If they were driving the wagon. Or scouring the countryside in a cruiser. He could almost hear their conversation.

"I really don't think he can make it out here on foot, Chief."

"Don't underestimate Sonnet, Parsons. Look how easily he slipped away from you."

"It wasn't my fault. He tricked me."

"Immaterial. Let's find him, not waste time with needless drivel."

Sounds of barking dogs. Two, maybe three.

Not close, but when the wind shifted, they definitely sounded closer.

Great. The cops were using dogs.

*I'm a goner.*

The road ahead disappeared into a thick bar of darkness. It was impossible to see his hand in front of his face.

*Keep moving. Use short steps so the tips of your shoes can search for obstacles and breaks in the pavement. You can't relax now—not with dogs hot on your ass. Now you've got to find some place to hide while you wait for daylight.*

If only he'd been able to keep the truck...

But it was hot, and undoubtedly chipped. No matter how he looked at it, the vehicle was more trouble than it was worth.

It was much easier maneuvering on foot.

However, dogs could easily outrun a man...

Behind him, the quiet hum of an approaching vehicle drowned out the energetic chirping of the crickets.

261

# Chapter 36

He froze, listening.

The wagon? No, smaller.

A cruiser? Not loud enough.

A small car. Would Allie be out here by herself? No. Stoner wouldn't allow it.

But it didn't matter who was driving this vehicle. It might be Allie or Stoner, but it could also be a total stranger greedy enough to turn him in.

Kyle dove into the bushes and burrowed into the wild brush. Hopefully he wouldn't have to worry about sharing his space with snakes or other critters. If he did meet up with something, maybe it would sense he was just passing through, and would let him be.

The coolness of the ground proved strangely refreshing. Waves of dizziness flowed through him. Keeping flat, he began to crawl. The crunching sounds of the brush yielding beneath his weight made it almost impossible to hear anything else. But he was sufficiently concealed, and was sure he couldn't be seen from the road.

His right shoulder thumped into something solid.

A blast of brightness raced past his vision. He lay still, waiting for the painful moment to pass. Then he rolled over and opened his eyes.

The star-glittered sky extended just beyond the skeletal branches of the trees. He remained motionless, the tingling in his shoulder scurrying down his arm. Felt like someone was poking him with needles.

The pain ebbed, leaving only a light burning. Using the fingers of his left hand, Kyle traced the obstacle.

A deadfall.

He gently examined his shoulder. The sleeve wasn't torn; his arm was dry. No blood, just some tingling. Nothing to worry about. He'd bruise, but a bruise wouldn't kill you.

There were other more urgent things to consider. The passing car, for one thing. The barking of dogs, louder than before, drowned out the crickets and the cicadas.

What happened to the car? Had it gone? Or had the driver seen him and stopped?

Kyle lay still, the heat in his shoulder a dull ache. The nearby sound of a car door creaking open, then thumping shut, chilled his blood. He almost cried out. A cold, slimy bubble squirmed up his throat.

Hard shoes tapped the pavement.

Kyle took a deep breath and held it.

The shoes tapped a few more times, then stopped.

Had they stopped moving? Or had they reached the grass?

Kyle turned his head ever so slightly.

The penetrating haze of a flashlight leaped toward him. Kyle's body grew cold. His jaw clenched; his gut tightened. The deadfall would provide sufficient cover. It was much bigger than he was. If only he'd been able to reach its other side…

The light shifted, settling dangerously close to Kyle's face.

Choking back a cry, he pressed the back of his head into the thick brush, willing himself to flatten into the ground. He imagined himself a lump of dough thinning out after a long, brutal session with the rolling pin. For a frozen eternity he lay as still and as quiet as a dead man.

The beam of light stopped moving.

A man's soft voice. "Kyle Sonnet?"

Kyle bit his lower lip.

"That you, Kyle?" The voice was thin and high-pitched—nothing like the commanding voice of Stoner or Mitchell, or the Hadleyville cop. It was gentle, strangely comforting.

"Listen…I know you've got to be careful, but you can trust me. I'm a friend. I can't stand cops, either. Bastards killed my wife…my kids."

The sudden silence quickly became as heavy as a cloak of chain mail.

"I know you're on the run. I also know you're hungry, tired, and would like a shower and a place to rest. I live just a few miles down the road. You're welcome to sack out there. My place is small, but there's more than enough room. Got a couch, and you can have some food and stay there until you're ready to move on. How 'bout it?"

The man sounded sincere, but Kyle knew he had to be extremely careful. Lying was so easy nowadays. This man could be an ambulance driver…or another wagon driver. The promise of a reward could be the primary motive. Everyone went crazy over money nowadays.

"You can't stay here very long. There are gangs out here, they've got dogs, and they roam the woods

264

at night to see what they can find. During the day, squad cars patrol this road. In the early morning hours they look for people they can cart off to the plant. There's a plant just a few miles from here. Your only hope is with me. I don't care if you've got a gun. I'd like to help if I can."

The idling car was like music to his ears. He could knock the guy down, get in, and take off. The dude's voice was high-pitched and whiny—how many tough guys sounded like that? It was hard to tell how tough a guy was when you were lying in a clump of weeds and couldn't see him.

But when you had nothing to lose, not much mattered.

The man said, "You can even hold your gun on me until you're sure you can trust me."

"I don't trust anyone." It spewed hotly from his throat, making his limbs throb.

"Can't blame you, everyone lying, trying to trick one another, turn each other in for money." The man sounded bitter, angry.

"What's your game?" Kyle asked.

"My game?"

"Why help me at all?"

"Need a friend, don't you?"

The man did sound sincere. Besides, Kyle was too tired and too hungry to steal another vehicle. Starvation and exhaustion can make you seriously lethargic.

The barking grew closer.

"Gangs'll be here in a couple of minutes..."

The rumbling in his gut had become unbearable. If he was going to die, he might as well do it on a full stomach. Maybe after a decent meal he could steal this man's vehicle. He wouldn't hurt him, just tie him loosely, lock him in a closet and move on.

Kyle slowly got to his feet.

# Chapter 37

Its tiny engine whining, the small car bounced over the crumbling country road.

Kyle hunched down in the passenger's seat, trying to avoid bumping his head. The driver had no intention of slowing or swerving to miss the many potholes. He drove intently, frequently using his rearview and side mirrors even though Kyle saw nothing out there but total darkness. The man seemed scared. Kyle wondered if he was having second thoughts about picking up Kyle.

Or, like Kyle, was a wanted man himself...

"Those dogs I heard," Kyle said. "They sound pretty big."

"Shepherds and Pit Bulls. The gangs use them. They usually come out at night, looking for anyone wandering around. Anyone is fair game. You don't want to be caught out here after dark."

"Any idea who they are?"

"Kids, mostly. Punks. Usually around sixteen, seventeen years old."

"And they go out looking for people at night?"

"You get caught out here with a flat? Engine trouble? You'd better have your earpiece so you can get someone out here in a hurry. Otherwise, you're toast. These boys will slit your throat, toss you in the back of a pickup and cart you off to the plant before you even know what's going on."

"I've heard there's a reward for doing that."

"A thousand a pop's not bad these days. Especially if you're a punk kid with no home, no education, and no way to make an honest living.

These kids are bastards. When the Family Planning Act was implemented, hundreds of folks drove their surplus kids out into the woods and dropped them off."

"I guess I was lucky I was in a Home," Kyle said flatly.

"Not everyone's fond of being sterilized, Sonnet. Especially when you don't know what they're really doing while you're lying on the table."

*Like shoving a chip in your ankle "for the pain?"*

"I don't know *how* many kids I've seen scrounging for food out here on my way home from work," the man said. "It's really pathetic."

"You can't pick them up and take them anywhere, can you?"

"They're more dangerous than a dropped-off pet. Best thing is to call Population Control. They'll come out, but if the kid gives them trouble, they'll just shoot him. It's justified as far as they're concerned. Government owns all this vacant land. They have no qualms about shooting trespassers."

"You live out here?"

"I have a small place. Condemned land. I own about half an acre. Borders a toxic dump. But at least no one bothers you."

"What about the gangs?"

"They're not that bold. Not yet, anyway. Cops come out every once in a while for a spot check. They catch any of these punks hanging around, they'll shoot them on sight. Otherwise these kids would be hauling us out of our homes, slitting our throats and carting us all out to the plant. I hate cops, hate 'em with a passion…but sometimes even *they* have their uses."

"What happened…to your wife?" Kyle asked.

The man reached behind his glasses to wipe an eye. "Nancy was a head nurse a few years back, worked at Hadleyville General. About five years ago the place was going through a lot of changes—doctors leaving, nurses being fired, forcibly retired, the damned big shots running the hospitals all getting greedy, dipping into everything but healthcare. Nancy had a helluva time getting things done. State would send early release felons to replace her nurses and aides. She'd have to train them and at the same time keep a sharp eye on the drug cabinet. Black market drugs were bigger than ever—which made things even worse. Hell, back then you could buy someone's car, maybe even half a dozen sessions with his wife, for a c.c. or two of morphine. Aspirin went for twenty bucks a tab back then. Why bust your hump on a twelve-hour shift in the E.R. when an ounce of illegal codeine could earn you a thousand bucks?"

The man's laugh sounded like a grunt. "Ex-cons would raid the cabinets, take as much as they could cram in their pockets, then disappear. They'd earn enough money from just a couple of sales and wouldn't have to work for the rest of the year.

"Since Nancy was in charge, it was her fault whenever something went wrong. Her responsibilities grew and her hours expanded. She'd do three twelve's in a row, then four. Cons saw her shuffling around like a zombie, so it was easy to pull shit right under her nose. Drugs, medical equipment, and supplies came up missing."

The man took off his glasses and wiped both eyes. The car swerved onto the shoulder. Kyle's head thumped the side window.

"One day a cop car showed up in our driveway. I knew something was wrong because a wagon and an ambulance pulled in behind the cruiser. And you know what happens when *those* bastards show up."

Kyle knew all about them. But he said nothing.

"Cop ordered us outside. Nancy was to be euthanized...along with my kids."

"Why?"

"She'd given medication to some family without sufficient healthcare coverage. My two girls were also guilty—they were friends of the family's kids and had been instrumental in getting them to the hospital to see Nancy."

"What did she give them?"

"Vitamins."

"I don't understand."

"They're considered black market products, right up there with morphine, codeine—all the big guys."

"Vitamins aren't drugs. *Are* they?"

"Government says they are. Those fuckers always have the last word."

"But—"

"Vitamins *help* people, Sonnet. Keep 'em *healthy*. When people are healthy, they live longer. And you know how that irritates the shit out of our beloved Government when people are healthy, don't you?"

"There must be some other reason—"

"Healthy people live longer, and are happy. And they do all kinds of illegal things. Like having sex. When people have sex, babies are born. And when babies are born, the population increases. Can't have *that*, can we? We sure as hell can't have a bunch of happy, healthy people squirting out babies. Especially since they came up with their famous Family Planning edict, giving them the power to sterilize both parents so they wouldn't be able to make more than two. That's another one of those instances where everyone gets fucked because of the actions of dumbasses. The law originally went into effect because of the reckless actions of the minorities—those stupid, low-income, bed-hopping assholes that crank out kids and force the Government to fit the bill. But like everything else, this got into their feeble minds and festered, making them even more power-hungry."

As they went deeper into the country, the potholes grew larger and more plentiful. The car bounced over the road like a basketball.

Kyle couldn't understand even people like Stoner putting a woman and her two daughters to death because of vitamins. But it actually made sense. This man's wife was distributing black market products. She'd become an enemy of the State.

"I'm surprised they didn't give you the needle anyway," Kyle said. "They might have accused you of harboring a fugitive. Good thing you didn't try to fight them."

"I wanted to. God, *how* I wanted to! I wanted to take that jerk's gun and shoot the ambulance driver, the wagon driver—every one of them. Oh, I fussed a little, even pleaded with them to spare my family. But when it came right down to it, your friend here, the very *respectable* George T. Manlon, turned out to be nothing more than a giant bucket of chickenshit."

The main road ended. Manlon inched them down a twisted one-lane road, this one in a much greater state of deterioration.

Barely visible in the headlights, a small beat-up trailer sat nestled in a cluster of thick brush, everything around it overgrown and wild. A heavy layer of broken limbs and a thick tarp of pine needles covered the roof. Wild vines and limbs obscured the windows.

Manlon killed the ignition and doused his lights. "Let's get you something to eat."

# Chapter 38

In the dim kitchen lighting, George Manlon looked like he hadn't slept in ages. The dark circles beneath the nervous bloodshot eyes hiding behind the thick-framed glasses made them look lost and frightened. His waxen complexion suggested he'd returned from somewhere bad, but had brought back a lot of what he'd seen with him. His stained white shirt was unbuttoned and not tucked in, his baggy pants a size too large, his thinning black hair unkempt.

The trailer was a mess. Clothes and laundry had been tossed in heaps on the shabby couch and the plaid armchair. The few knickknacks sitting on shelves looked like they had been bought at the local five 'n dime.

The kitchen was small and cluttered, smelling of grease and burnt toast. The refrigerator was scratched and dented, the door partially covered with a two-year-old calendar and two awkward pictures done in crayon of a stick-figured family of four standing in front of a frame house.

Kyle devoured a plate of scrambled eggs, bacon, and toast while Manlon tried making coffee. Manlon's hands shook so much, he dropped too much into the pot, then had trouble scooping out the excess. The thick glasses perched over the bridge of his long pointed nose kept sliding down. The sheen of sweat covering his face glinted in the light.

"Tell me, Sonnet. Why're they after you?"

Kyle sat in tense silence. This was just like the time Elden had asked him a similar question. But

273

now there was even more of a reason to be silent. George Manlon's family had been slaughtered by the Department. The fact that his new visitor was a former wagon driver would push the man over the edge.

"I know what I read on the screen coming home." Manlon checked to make sure the coffeepot was plugged in properly; the cord was old and frayed. "But I also know how those bastards operate. How they lie, tell us what they want us to know." Manlon stared at Kyle. "You look much younger than your picture. Skinnier. Doctored it, didn't they? You probably didn't look mean enough."

"Not much of what I saw was accurate."

"They quit going after the truth long before I was born. They don't want people to know what's really happening." Manlon crossed the creaky floor. He placed a cracked white sugar bowl on the table. "Don't want to give you any sort of edge. They just tell you what they want you to know. If you don't like it, they stick the needle in your arm. Then they zip you up in one of their black bags and turn you into fertilizer."

*Complications. Problems. This one will be easy.*

"This isn't going to be good for you." It was time to let Manlon know how much trouble he could be in. "I'm a wanted man."

"Don't care. They come out here, I'll get away. If I don't, they might as well go ahead and put me out of my misery. I can think of a couple of hundred things I'd like much better than living like this."

274

"You're a sitting duck out here, aren't you? It's really isolated."

Manlon grinned for the first time, showing brown teeth. He pointed to the ventilation duct at his feet. "That cool air coming up from the floor?"

"Air conditioning?"

Manlon shook his head. "I bought this trailer from a guy they tried to nail six, maybe seven months back. Taylor was his name, hated the damned cops even worse than I do. Bastards killed his girlfriend, her brother and the family dog. Don't know why they euthanized the girlfriend and her brother, but they killed the dog when it tried defending its master. Taylor got away. They lost his trail because he knew how to slip away and cover his tracks. He'd go out late at night and set traps for the cops. When they came out to investigate, he shot 'em." Manlon chuckled. "Had a damn arsenal he'd collected over the years. Uzi's, revolvers, automatics. Some of his guns were a hundred and fifty years old. Got most of them from his grandfather, who was a hunter until the Government made criminals out of anyone owning a firearm. But Taylor didn't give a rat's ass what the Government called him. Kept his guns hidden away in safes, coffins and footlockers buried in garbage dumps all over the county. He claimed he had more than fifty thousand rounds of ammo stashed in a dozen different calibers."

"You can kill a lot of cops with that much firepower."

"Taylor killed nearly a dozen before they finally got him."

"Dead?"

"No doubt. You kill a cop? There's no place you can hide. They brought in the Feds, the National Force, even SWAT teams. I saw it on CNN. It showed him biting the big one. When they were finished shooting him, he was unrecognizable. Dinner entertainment."

"He must have been chipped if they found him."

"He got rid of the damned thing."

"Then how'd they find him?"

"Personally I think someone turned him in."

Kyle's curiosity flared up instantly. "How'd he get rid of the chip?"

"Dug it out."

"Himself?"

"You gonna get a damned *doctor* to do it for you? First of all, you gotta find one. And good luck, trying to get one of those self-absorbed pricks to do something like that. It's against the law, and you know how those wimps are when legalities are involved. They get bent all outa shape—like when people were slapping them with malpractice suits fifty years ago. But digging out a chip? They want money—lots of it—even before they agree to do the job. But it can be done, believe me. You're desperate enough? You'll dig out that damned chip."

"I guess Taylor was desperate enough."

"You shoot a dozen cops? Your ass had *better* be desperate."

Kyle could only guess how desperate you had to be to dig it out yourself. No matter how you did it, it was bound to hurt like the blazes. Finding an effective painkiller would be even harder than finding a willing doctor. But if Taylor could do it, it was possible.

If only he knew where the damned thing was...

Manlon lowered his fleshy butt into a cheap metal chair. It creaked beneath his weight. "Damned cops, those ambulances. It's a crime what we've turned civilization into." Manlon sat hunched over, his elbows on his thighs, his shirt tail a wrinkled V between his legs. He looked up at Kyle; his eyes were even more bloodshot close up. "Know what ambulances were originally used for?"

Kyle shrugged.

"They saved people's lives. *Saved* people, not put out their lights. Funny, don't you think?"

Saving people's lives. Had Elden known that? Of course. Had the old man lived, he would have told Kyle all about it. Elden would have eventually told Kyle everything.

"But they don't want things like that known. That's why they went on that big kick in Washington a few years back, rewriting all the books for the schools. They don't want people knowing what it was like in the old days. Don't want us knowing society used to care for people."

"How did you find out?"

"Nancy learned a lot of things in healthcare. She said as recently as twenty years ago, an ambulance would rush out to your home for any type of accident or medical emergency. They'd give you medical treatment, then haul you to the nearest hospital, where real doctors would take care of the rest."

Kyle sat in shocked silence, trying to understand. Remembering things he'd read in school that didn't make sense.

Now he knew why.

"Doesn't sound possible," Kyle said, almost to himself. "Everything changing so drastically in just a few years..."

"Society's twisted. You're young, you don't see it yet. Wait till you're older."

Elden had practically told him the same thing.

"They don't teach you what you should know anymore, Sonnet. That's why they did all that rewriting. Did you know euthanasia was once against the law?"

"They've been putting down animals for more than a century, haven't they?"

"It's okay to put animals down—especially in cases of indiscriminate breeding. People have always been stupid about breeding animals. They're stupid about breeding anything—even themselves, which is why we're all in such a pickle."

"How long ago did this happen? Euthanizing people?"

"Forty years or so. But twenty years before that, it was unheard of. A doctor tried doing it just before the Twenty-First Century. They crucified him for it."

"I don't understand."

"He tried helping people."

"By euthanizing them?"

"Only the most extreme cases. Terminal cancer victims in excruciating pain, with no cure in sight. AMA, as always, dragged its feet. Didn't know if they should approve effective FDA-regulated medication for serious diseases. This doctor tried helping people by giving them the option to put themselves to sleep. He said that if you couldn't stand the pain anymore and no longer wanted to live, you should have the right to die with dignity. The AMA and the Government didn't like what he was doing so they tossed him in prison."

Something else he hadn't read in school. Kyle wondered how much of all this was true. It was a shame Elden wasn't around to verify any of it.

"Like I said," Manlon added, "all the books have been rewritten, so you won't find that anywhere. Society doesn't know what it wants. When it changes its mind, all hell breaks loose."

"Now it wants to get rid of people," Kyle said.

"You never did say what you did to piss them off, did you?"

"No."

Manlon got up to pour the coffee. "It's all right if you don't want to tell me—I understand. What I read on the screen and heard on TV was their usual bullshit. You're too young to have done all they said. I'll bet you're not even twenty-seven, are you?"

"Nineteen in a few months."

"You probably pissed off the wrong big shot. You're obviously independent enough to have pissed off someone important." Manlon smiled tiredly. "Could that be it?"

"Just about." Kyle stared at the darkness filling the tiny kitchen window. It was hard to believe—society caring about people, then changing its mind and turning to the needle to keep the population down. "If ambulances were originally used to help people, what were wagons used for?" he asked.

"They had what they called meat wagons. Police used them to pick up dead bodies at crime or accident scenes. But following the ambulance and euthanizing people before hauling them away? That's a brand-new innovation—for want of a better term."

"What about dumps?"

"They were used for garbage, rendering plants for shit. And wagons were originally school buses." Manlon shook his head. "Life's a new breed of animal. If you were able to see it coming, you'd definitely bust your ass to get out of its way."

*Get out, Kyle...*

Kyle drank some coffee. It was hot and strong. He was beginning to feel much better. "Mr. Manlon—"

"George."

"Like I said, you're gonna be in a lot of trouble if—"

"And like *I* said, I really don't care. They took my family away and I stood there like an idiot and watched them do it." Manlon's eyes glittered behind his glasses. "You think this is quality living for me? I used to be a   fucking *lawyer*, for God's sake!"

Manlon's arm shook as if he had just been poked with a cattle prod. "Last time I set foot in a courtroom was just a few days after Nancy and the kids were gone. I dropped papers. I stuttered, forgot my summation, and ended up running to the men's room to throw up—in the middle of a case!"

Kyle had nothing to say.

"We had a mansion. Three cars. A swimming pool. My girls went to private schools. We had a condo near the lake. We'd go there every summer to fish and water ski. Now look at me. I sweep up the loading dock at the supermarket outside Hadleyville. It's the only thing I can handle without making a pathetic mess of things."

Kyle stared at his coffee cup.

"You know what they used to call lawyers in the old days?"

Kyle shook his head.

"Ambulance chasers." George Manlon's laughter sounded like a weak cough.

# Chapter 39

Stretched out on the musty-smelling couch, his ankles resting on its worn arm, Kyle stared up at the dark ceiling. The tiny porch light lit up a corner of the filmy window. Outside, moths scurried about in their narrow column of tawny haze.

Too many things were on his mind. What to do when morning came. Where to go. How to get rid of his chip. Manlon's food had filled him up, brought back alertness and energy, but Kyle's talk with the poor man had only made the situation hopeless.

It wasn't surprising. Manlon was a bitter shell of a man, shattered by grief and hatred. Nothing coming out of his mouth could be anything *but* hopeless.

But no matter how everything looked, certain things hadn't changed. Kyle needed wheels. And the only wheels available belonged to George Manlon. The little car sat in the bushes twenty feet away, a small triangle of its dusty roof reflecting the porch light like snow. It wouldn't be difficult taking the keys from the kitchen counter, where Manlon had dropped them.

*You should be ashamed of yourself.*

Manlon had endangered his own life by picking up Kyle and bringing him home. Taking anything from him would be something only a cold-blooded thief would do.

But what choice did he have? On foot, he might cover twenty miles before nightfall if he left early enough. He'd be in the same position he'd been hours earlier—vulnerable, unarmed, unable to move fast, and at the mercy of the gangs.

In a car he could do three or four hundred miles before running out of gas. By that time, he could be in the next state.

But there were cops everywhere, gangs everywhere. And when you crossed state lines, you had the Feds to contend with. With more charges tacked onto your file. And yet another stolen vehicle to answer for. The more charges, the bigger the reward. The bigger the reward, the more people would be looking for him.

He didn't know who he should fear more—the cops or the gangs. The longer you were on the run, the angrier the cops became. When the news boys entered the picture, the manhunt became a sensationalized odyssey. The story would be blown way out of proportion, turning him into a cult hero. And cops hated cult heroes.

Where would this all end?

What happened when they traced the car? Would they charge Manlon with harboring a dangerous fugitive? Would Manlon be able to lie? Tell them Kyle took his car at gunpoint? Or would Manlon break down and tell the truth? The man's nerves weren't exactly in mint condition. If he *did* tell them the truth, he'd be given the injection on the spot. Kyle would not only be guilty of stealing Manlon's car, he'd also be guilty of causing the man's death.

The ancient refrigerator kicked on, moaning through its worn-out machinery. Its vibrations chugged away like an overloaded freight train. It sounded almost as if it was outside as well. Manlon would soon have to replace it.

Outside, the moths circled one other, wings fluttering. Moths led such quiet, basic lives. People could learn from them.

People were too stupid and too greedy to keep everything quiet and basic. They stole things they didn't need, bought things they couldn't use. They had more than enough food, shelter, and all sorts of ways to keep the lights on—yet they always wanted more. Extras, as Stoner would say. Conveniences. Things you don't need. The whole world was upside-down and people still wanted more—

The living room window exploded with blinding white light.

A cold twinge jabbing him in the spine, Kyle twisted on the couch and slammed to the floor.

A booming metallic voice vibrated the walls of the trailer.

*"George Manlon! This is the police! You are under arrest for harboring the fugitive, Kyle Sonnet! Come out now!"*

Shaking in terror, Kyle pushed himself up from the floor. The vibrations he'd heard and felt earlier were cop cars creeping down the dirt road. Manlon's home was probably surrounded.

The trailer rocked. Manlon, his gut jiggling over the elastic waistband of his blue-and-white striped pajama bottoms, rushed into the living room. His face was bone-white in the harsh glare of the spotlight.

"They've found us, Sonnet! Oh God! They've found us!"

Kyle crawled over to the side of the couch and pulled the cord behind it. The blinds toppled down, dimming the spotlight's brilliance. Another cord closed the curtains over the blinds. The curtains were frayed and torn, but with the help of the blinds, weakened the glare.

"Sonnet." Manlon's voice was choked. He looked like he was about to throw up. "Maybe if you could just tell them—"

*"George Manlon! You must come outside* now!"

Manlon quivered. The air grew thick with a fresh ammoniac stench. The man's crotch turned dark. Manlon looked down at himself. "Oh God, *look* at me! Oh *God*!"

*"Manlon!"* boomed the loudspeaker.

"What can we do?" Manlon buried his hands in his thinning hair and ran down the hall. The trailer thumped and shook from his heavy footfalls. "What do we do? They're out there *again*! Oh God! They're out there *again*!"

*"George Manlon!"*

Kyle grabbed Manlon's shoulder before he could rush past. "There's something we can do about this. There's *got* to be."

*"This is your last chance, Manlon!"*

"They're going to kill me." Manlon's sobs were loud and pitiful. "I'm dead. Oh my God...I'm dead!"

*"George Manlon! You are harboring the fugitive, Kyle Sonnet, who is accused of several major felony crimes. If you don't come out this instant, you will be immediately euthanized!"*

Whimpering, Manlon ran around the room, bumping into the couch, the armchair, a small table. Knickknacks toppled from shelves and skipped onto the worn carpeting. "This is it. I'm gonna die. They're gonna kill me!"

Kyle grabbed the trembling man by both shoulders and shook him. "They killed your wife and your kids. Nancy and Tabitha and Beth. Killed them all, didn't they? Talk to me, George. Think. Don't let them win!"

"K-Killed Nancy." Manlon's lips moved awkwardly. He was looking in Kyle's direction, but his eyes had gone blank. "Killed my w-wife. Nancy. They k-killed Nancy."

"And Tabitha?"

"Yep. Tabitha. Killed her."

"And Beth."

"Yep. B-Beth. My baby. Killed my b-baby Beth!"

Kyle couldn't tell if he was getting through to the man. Manlon had a much better grasp of reality earlier, when he was angry. Right now he was terrified, and there wasn't time to snap him out of this.

But maybe if Kyle said the right thing...the right phrase. It just might register, get Manlon rationalizing again.

Taylor. The man had lived here. Had he possibly left anything of practical use?

"George, your only prayer right now is to fight back. What about Taylor? Did he leave any guns lying around?"

*"Manlon!"* boomed the loudspeaker. *"The criminal you are harboring tried to kill a police officer! He has stolen two vehicles and robbed innocent people at gunpoint! Sonnet is also wanted by the Department of Population Control for placing a fellow co-worker in extreme jeopardy. Sonnet is a former driver for the Department of Population Control—"*

"You son of a bitch…"

Swallowing a warm gooey lump, Kyle removed his hands from Manlon's shoulders.

"You're *one* of them…"

"Listen, George…"

"You *bastard*."

"Listen to me."

"You worthless pile of dogshit…"

"If you'll just let me explain—"

"I want you *out* of here."

"But—"

"Now! I want you out of here *now*!"

*"George Manlon! You have ten seconds to show yourself!"*

Manlon's wet, glaring eyes burned into Kyle.

*"Ten!"*

"Listen to me, George—"

"You son of a bitch…"

*"Nine!"*

"If you'll just *listen* to me…"

"You're one of them. You took my wife…my kids…to the *rendering plant*."

*"Eight!"*

287

George Manlon's face changed, a cold, glassy grin covering it. "I know what to do. I know *exactly* what to do."

*"Seven!"*

Manlon shuffled over to the front door, wrenched it open and stood in the doorway. He glared one last time at Kyle. His eyes were enormous. Slobber covered his mouth and chin. Triumph flickered in his eyes. Then he turned to face the front.

"He's here! Kyle Sonnet! Come get him! Come and—"

The explosions rocked the trailer, penetrating the night air. Semiautomatic gunfire ripped into George Manlon, slamming his body against the door frame and forcing him to perform a bizarre, jerky, marionette-like dance before his blood-drenched, mangled body dropped to the front steps.

The smell of cordite, burnt flesh, and released sphincter hung heavily in the air. Kyle buried his nose in the crook of his elbow.

*"Kyle Sonnet!"* boomed the loudspeaker. *"George Manlon can no longer help you. Come out now and face your punishment."*

Lying face-down on the trailer floor, Kyle fought hard to stay calm. He could rationalize about all this later, after he'd escaped. He had to think. Keep the panic out—it could only make things worse.

*"Come out now, Sonnet!"*

Escape.

Was there even a slight chance?

The ventilation duct.

His thoughts looping, Kyle crawled into the kitchen.

*"Kyle Sonnet! If you do not come out immediately, we will destroy George Manlon's trailer!"*

Kyle groped for the rusty metal vent. Luckily, no screws fastened it to the floor. Taylor had obviously designed it to be removed in a hurry.

While he forced his trembling hands to pry the vent loose, tongues of hungry flame sprayed through the open doorway, sweeping over the worn rug just five feet away.

# Chapter 40

George Manlon was right—the ventilation shaft had indeed been removed.

Kyle carefully squeezed his long, slim frame through the oversized opening, noting how easily he filled the hole. Taylor must have also been slim; he probably decided it best to keep things small. Although the shaft opening was cut six inches wider than normal, its hole would not accommodate anyone with an ample midsection. George Manlon would never have been able to fit through.

Something hot and loud shattered the front window, turning the living room into a heavy surge of golden flame.

*"Kyle Sonnet! If you come out immediately, we will stop using the flame-thrower! Otherwise there will be nothing left of George Manlon's trailer but ashes!"*

Kyle tensed himself in preparation for the drop, but when his chest scraped against the narrow opening, he stopped moving. His shoulders would not clear.

A cold sheet of panic sliced through him. He squirmed helplessly, a fish on a line, sucking in his breath, tensing himself, visualizing himself smaller and skinnier, twisting one side while forcing the other painfully through the sharp opening. Heavy dark smoke and toxic fumes from the melting carpet and sofa crept steadily toward the kitchen. Kyle willed himself not to breathe it in.

Black with flame, swirling tatters of the living room curtains dropped onto the smoldering couch.

After considerable struggling, Kyle's left shoulder finally cleared the obstruction.

As the murky smoke covered the opening overhead, he stumbled around beneath the trailer, bumping his head in the total blackness. Working by touch, he discovered stacks of magazines and newspapers, then wondered why the spotlight hadn't penetrated the underside of the trailer. After more investigating he guessed Taylor had fortified the skirting with weeds, pine needles and branches, making it impossible for anyone to see underneath the trailer.

But it didn't make any sense. The cops had the place surrounded.

Fumbling around amongst the garbage, Kyle accidentally knocked over a pile of old wooden milk cartons and magazines. His knee disappeared into the ground, forcing him on his side.

A hole.

Kyle shoved the trash aside and groped around. A definite slope in the dirt. It was a hole, all right. Judging by its diameter, it was large enough to hide in.

The noxious fumes drifting down the ventilation opening slithered along the underbelly of the trailer. In minutes the area would be engulfed. He had no choice but find out what Taylor had done. If he could hide, he might be able to wait them out.

If only there was enough air...

The hole, about waist-deep, was sliced clean with a sharp-edged object. The earth felt cool, untouched. Crouching, he carefully replaced the milk cartons. He then got down on all fours and instantly discovered a side of the hole was missing.

A tunnel?

The shaft seemed to be about three feet in diameter—large enough to enable him to move about freely. Judging by its angle, he guessed it would run somewhere southwest of the trailer, to the main road. He had no idea where the tunnel ended. He didn't even know how far Taylor had gotten. Taylor might have started the tunnel and abandoned it when it proved too much effort. Digging a tunnel single-handedly would undoubtedly be tough.

The tunnel air turned stuffy, the ground cool and damp. At least the toxic smoke hadn't penetrated the entrance.

Muffled yelling rang above his head. The cops were no doubt pissed and frustrated, desperate to capture him.

Something grazed the top of his head.

A plastic pipe protruded just beyond the tunnel roof. Undoubtedly a crude air hole stuck in the ground. Kyle put his ear close to it; a trickle of warm air brushed his earlobe. Where did its top extend? The grass, over- grown and wild, would hide a small pipe if it was concealed among bushes and stumps.

Another air pipe was stuck in the ground a few yards farther down. Kyle guessed that he'd come a quarter of the way to the dirt road. If he was lucky, the cops would be preoccupied with the trailer and wouldn't be aware of anything going on under their feet.

*Keep moving.*

He had no idea how many cops were out there, or their positions. The only thing that mattered was getting away. The dudes were bent out of shape over the Hadleyville mess and didn't want the same thing to happen here. This was no doubt why they'd blown George Manlon apart even while he surrendered.

Another air pipe brushed his head. Just above it, the loudspeaker crackled loudly.

*"You've got ten seconds, Sonnet!"*

*Here we go again.* The cops obviously loved the suspense factor.

*"Ten!"*

Another pipe. He tried remembering what the front yard looked like, but the images were patchy—pine needles and overgrown brush. He'd been too exhausted and hungry to notice much of anything when Manlon brought him here.

*"Nine!"*

More darkness.

His fears quickly took over. Had Taylor finished the tunnel? How far had he dug before he was forced to run?

*"Eight!"*

He forced himself to believe Taylor had completed his escape route. If he thought the worst, he was doomed. Taylor *had* to succeed. You don't kill twelve cops and sit around, playing with yourself while their buddies hunted you down.

*"Seven!"*

Another air pipe. How far this time? Thirty yards? Forty? How far to the dirt road was it?

Where the hell *was* he? Crawling around in circles? Why was the loudspeaker just as loud as before?

*"Six!"*

Panic thundered through him. Circles. Dead end. Plus the fact that this tunnel had been made by a crazy man.

He hadn't wanted to think about that at all. It was the one thing he hadn't considered during his talk with Manlon.

You don't kill cops if you have

*"Five!"*

the required number of brain cells buzzing around in your head. Taylor's family, like George Manlon's, had been slaughtered, and Manlon was as loony as a bedbug.

*"Four!"*

Something else occurred to him. Didn't Manlon say Taylor was caught? Or was the man killed?

Did it matter?

*"Three seconds, Sonnet!"*

Yes, it mattered—especially if Taylor was caught during his dig...

Voices, very clear and distinct. Three, maybe four. They were directly above his head.

"Why don't we just toast the damn trailer? Stupid fuck ain't got the stones to give it up."

"Gotta make it look good."

*"Two seconds!"*

"For who?"

"News hounds."

"Bastard kid *needs* wasting. Hell, he tried running over Stewart. Man's pension kicks in less than four years from now."

294

*"One second!"*

"Full benefits, Class A healthcare rating. Stewart ain't even fifty."

*"Kyle Sonnet, your time is up! You've given us no choice!"*

Kyle bumped against a solid wall. Cold earth. Roots.

Something made from burlap, grass, roots and pine needles covered the area above his head. He pushed, but it barely budged. He pushed harder, this time putting his shoulders into it, and it finally gave. It weighed at least twenty pounds and was obviously designed to blend in with the terrain. Kyle inched it up until a heavy cloud of tangy fumes assaulted his nostrils.

The flames of the trailer, the spotlight, and the flashlights jumping around in the woods came into view.

Kyle knelt in the midst of wild brush and scrubs on the other side of the dirt road, at least thirty yards away. Six cruisers sat in Manlon's front yard, about sixty feet from the trailer. Two parked right off the road blocked the drive. Two other squad cars were parked along the main road, on the other side of a thick grove of scrubs. The ambulance sat about ten feet behind George Manlon's car, the wagon directly behind the ambulance. A fire truck rested in the brush on the other side of the trailer. Three uniformed fire fighters stood out front, gripping fire hoses and dousing the pine trees at frequent intervals. A dozen cops surrounded the trailer, now just a blackened twisted shell of aluminum engulfed in flaming debris.

Down the road near the turnoff, a cruiser rested in the grass near some scrubs, its door slightly ajar.

No one stood within a hundred yards of it.

*** 

The tunnel cover rocked awkwardly to the side.

Kyle squirmed through the narrow opening and replaced the cover. Keeping his stomach on the ground, he crawled through the tall brush.

The four cops in front of the other two cruisers carefully watched the trailer. The cop with the loudspeaker stood smartly about ten feet to their right. Two uniforms patrolled the backyard on the right and two on the left, all four holding riot guns. Someone shouted, "Think I saw something in the woods!" They all disappeared, flashlights flickering.

A tall, broad-shouldered dude in a white uniform held the flamethrower firmly in both hands. His head was covered by a helmet, his face concealed by a black rubber mask. Two large tanks were strapped to his back.

The man clutching the loudspeaker jumped to attention. *"Kyle Sonnet, we are now going to destroy George Manlon's trailer!"* He turned to the man in white. "Go ahead, Carl, empty your tanks. Burn that sucker down."

Carl braced himself, took careful aim, and fired.

A thick column of blue-green flame splashed from the long, tapered barrel, fanning outward and becoming a blinding starburst.

The trailer windows exploded, turning the cool evening air hot and sour with fumes. Rough remnants of paneling and insulation fell from the bottom of the jagged opening that was once the window, hopping onto George Manlon's sizzling corpse and down the steps in flickering blue and green bubbles. The stench of burning plastic filled the air.

One man hawked into the grass. The dude with the flamethrower lowered his head and adjusted his mask. The loudspeaker was dropped on the grass as its owner bent over, braced his palms on his knees and hacked away.

Kyle reached the squad car. Everyone was coughing or throwing up, and totally unconcerned about anything else. He gently eased open the door.

Someone from the woods shouted, "Something's running around over there!"

Someone else yelled, "Firefighters! Spray that goddamn scrub before it torches!"

Three hoses aimed at the sparkling group of trees behind the trailer.

"Sully, turn that spot *this* way!"

"Blinding my ass, goddammit!"

The man coughing in the grass cleared his throat and picked up his loudspeaker. His voice was raspy. "Two more men get right out there, see what you can find! That's probably him out there. Sucker won't slip by us *this* time!"

No one noticed the cruiser moving slowly away, its headlights off.

# Chapter 41

His neck and armpits sheathed in cold sweat, Kyle fought to keep the cruiser at a steady eighty over the bumpy two-lane road.

Stealing Allie's car had unnerved him, made him jumpy and paranoid. The excitement returned when he stole the pickup, but the fear had not. He wondered if such fear, like everything else, dulled with repetition and experience.

Sneaking away from George Manlon's burning trailer in a stolen squad car quickly proved him wrong. The fear, bigger and more powerful, had returned.

In spite of everything, he struggled to stay calm and alert. To consider himself lucky. Above all, not to succumb to the panic.

The cooked remnants of George Manlon's trailer would occupy the cops for precious minutes. It would take some time for the firefighters to hose down the debris and the surrounding area. They might stick around and sift through the charred rubble to see what they could find. Maybe they'd discover the tunnel, maybe not. The site would be a mess. Newspapers, magazines, and trash would smolder for weeks.

Stoner would call to ask how the search was going. He'd want to know the details and would turn psychotic if the conversation didn't move in the right direction. He wouldn't want to hear the news that no body was found. He'd want to conduct a personal search.

To add to the chaos, the cops combing the woods would be trigger-happy. The sight of a deer or raccoon might turn into a guns-blazing frenzy.

Just ahead, the sign

*Interstate 3 miles*

issued a wash of warm relief throughout his tense limbs.

The luminous digital clock on the dash said four-fifteen. There would be no traffic this time of the morning. Judging by the gas gauge, he figured he could make at least a hundred miles before he was forced to ditch the cruiser.

But since he was chipped, he had no chance of slipping away. They'd monitor him on their map, knowing where he was, where he was heading. Catching him would be no challenge.

But where had they planted it?

He didn't even know if the chip was in his foot. He'd read something that said the foot was preferred, but this did not limit the implant to that location. Some people were injected in the arm, others on the back of their neck. The Government chose to vary site locations for its own purposes. If Kyle did manage to slice open his foot, there was no guarantee that he'd find the chip. It could be near his ankle, or lodged behind his heel. It might even be a couple of inches up from the ankle…or near his calf.

He'd twisted his right ankle during that one traumatic baseball game. Injecting the chip near the damage site would be easy. The foot was bandaged to protect the injury—who would notice a tiny incision that would already be healed when the bandages were removed?

But all this meant nothing. If Kyle chose the wrong foot, would he have enough remaining strength to slice open the other? Would he have the courage to try his heel? His ankle?

What if they *had* chosen his neck?

It didn't matter where it was—removing it was essential.

He'd stolen three vehicles and nearly run over a cop. What they'd done to George Manlon was solid proof that they wanted Kyle dead on sight.

*\*\*\**

"Sonnet? Kyle Sonnet?"

The strange metallic voice sputtered from the dash speakers, jerking him out of his numbness.

Keeping his eyes on the road ahead, he felt around for an on/off switch, or volume control. No such animal. It figured. Too bad he couldn't rip the damned thing right out of the dash. He suspected the voice wasn't going to shut up.

"We know where you are, son. Least you can do? Give us your side of the story."

*Son?*

*Your side of the story?*

"C'mon, boy, start talkin'. Don't have many options left, ya know. And you can't get very far. We know for a fact you're about twenty miles south of the State Capital, but you can't get off 'cause every turnoff's bein' watched. We also got the next four exits blocked off, both directions. Case you're interested, we also got a roadblock set up just a few miles outside the corporation limit, and this here's one you can't possibly get past."

Kyle couldn't help smiling. The bad vibes they were getting from the news made them look awfully stupid. He could see the headlines:

*Desperate Fugitive Slips By Cops AGAIN!*

Or:
*Orphan Escapes in Police Cruiser!*

The TV stations would even include shots of the State Home to emphasize Kyle's tender age, which might have already been corrected.

All this would no doubt force the cops to try a much softer approach.

"Yes, son. A roadblock. This one's got more than twenty police cruisers to it. You ain't in Hadleyville no more."

Why were they telling him this?

And why would they need to tell him anything when they obviously held all the aces?

Kyle set the odometer to 0. Twenty miles at ninety miles an hour meant, roughly, fifteen minutes. He noted the time on the dash clock.

"Son, my name's Captain Ted Dennings. Call me Teddy—everybody else does. I've been assigned your case, and if you wanna know the truth, it don't look too good for you right now. There's a stack of charges against you a mile long, you're hightailin' it in a stolen police vehicle, and we know exactly where you're headed. Tell me…this sound very bright to you?"

Maybe not, but it was his only option. If it hadn't been for Elden, Kyle wouldn't have known to do this in the first place. He would have gone on doing whatever they told him and would have ended up dead anyway.

He'd rather be stupid than dead.

"Like I said, don't look too good. Tell me…how far ya think you can get?"

When the odometer registered four miles, Kyle lifted his foot off the gas and eased onto the shoulder of the highway. There was no other car in sight. They'd undoubtedly rerouted traffic.

The riot gun propped up against the dash was secured with a metal clasp. He'd never liked guns, but this one made him feel a lot better right now. He found a small tapered catch on the underside of the receiver and depressed it. A single pump caused a red 12-gauge cartridge with a black stamp saying *double—00—buckshot* to drop into his lap. He repeated the action until the chamber was empty. Six cartridges were lodged in the gun. He reloaded them and snapped the weapon back into place.

A snub-nosed .38 Special revolver loaded with six full metal-jacketed cartridges rested in a buffed leather holster in the glove box. The barrel was clear of obstruction. The oily smell suggested the gun had recently been cleaned. A speed loader containing six more rounds sat between a small box of Kleenex and three tubes of vanilla-flavored lip balm. He could find no extra ammo for the shotgun.

"You get close enough to that roadblock, you'll be toast, son." Dennings spoke frankly, as if he were discussing the weather. *Keep on going, you're likely to meet up with some rain, might as well wait it out for a spell.* "Police have enough firepower to stand there shootin' at ya all day long. Don't ya think any of 'em'll be able to blow out your tires, turn this shindig into one humongous turkey shoot?"

A fully loaded teargas gun lay beneath the driver's seat. Kyle spent some time inspecting it.

"You haven't given us much choice, son. Haven't given yourself much, neither—not with what you been pullin' lately. Sure been one busy whippersnapper. Whatever in God's creation would possess you to try runnin' over a police officer?"

Kyle placed the revolver and the teargas gun beside him on the passenger seat. He checked the console for other ammo but found only notebooks, pens and pencils, a fingernail clipper, a spool of waxed dental floss, and a giant packet of French lubricated condoms.

"Reckon you just panicked, got that pickup goin' and didn't see Officer Stewart. That what happened, son? You never done anything that reckless before. Goin' by what your boss Bill Stoner told us, we're inclined to go along with his line of thinkin'. Wouldn't ya like to tell us your side? So we can get everything down just right?"

Stoner's name had brought chills to his spine. He could imagine the conversation.

*"Sonnet's a waste, Dennings. Didn't work out at all. Didn't like his job, couldn't keep his mouth shut. Had to stick him in the cooler after just a couple days in the field. Boy just won't listen to reason, won't obey orders. Won't put things in proper perspective. He's a menace, needs put out of our misery."*

"We know ya don't wanna do any more damage. Isn't that why you stopped the cruiser? Doing a little thinkin', are ya? Tryin' to sort it all out? C'mon, son, tell us your side. Do ya good."

*They want your side of the story. Those morons actually want to hear what made you go off the deep end. They want to know why it bugged you so much that Stoner and Buster and Falworth calmly euthanized your one and only friend and made you haul him to the dump. Then used Allie, someone you really wanted to trust, to make you another charter member of the walking dead.*

*Yes. They really want to know.*

*They're too stupid to figure it out on their own.*

# Chapter 42

A four-lane bridge appeared in the distance.

"We spent some time talkin' to your old boss, son," Dennings said. "Bill Stoner says you coulda been a good man."

The odometer registered twelve miles.

"Your boss seems to think you coulda been an asset to the Department. What went wrong? Tell us what turned your head around. Why you're dead-set on gettin' yourself splattered into the next county."

The image of Elden lying on the steps drifted back.

*Don't dwell on that. Think of other things, such as what you're going to do when you reach the roadblock.*

But at that moment he remembered something else just as painful as Elden's death.

Allie, talking and laughing with Mitchell, Packard, and the others. Standing twenty feet away, totally alien from him. The Allie who didn't care about human life, who'd rather condemn a man to death than embarrass herself.

She was more dangerous than Stoner could ever be.

The evil within her was safely concealed beneath an exterior of quiet beauty.

"Good thing you got that chip in ya, son. Otherwise we'd have a helluva time keepin' up with you. Good idea, that chip. Yes sir. Shoulda started that up fifty years sooner. Woulda made life a *whole* lot simpler for all of us."

Dennings had that good-buddy approach down pat. Someone you've gone drinking or fishing with in the old days. Kyle could ask him to fetch his rods and a couple of six-packs. They could meet at one of the local lakes and spend a quiet afternoon doing the macho thing.

Fifteen miles on the odometer...

Another bridge loomed in the distance. Some of the morning fog had lifted, revealing a hazy tree line on either side of the bridge.

Something began nagging at him.

Something Dennings had said about that chip...

What had Allie told him in the cafeteria?

Chipping a vehicle...

A police cruiser was chock-full of expensive weapons and gadgets. It would be disastrous if the vehicle fell into the wrong hands.

The police would want their cruisers outfitted with an internal chip. They'd want to know the instant something was stolen.

If they deactivated the cruiser, Kyle would be stuck in the middle of nowhere and would have to continue his escape on foot. They could just drive on out and pick him up at their leisure.

Kyle's foot twitched on the gas pedal. The speedometer needle dropped from 90 to 80.

For some reason, they wanted him to keep moving.

They wanted him to get closer to the roadblock...

They knew he was armed. They obviously didn't want to risk coming up behind him in the middle of nowhere. He wasn't a trained professional. If he got excited, he'd do something stupid.

By distracting him, he'd automatically drive closer to the roadblock. Twenty cruisers, thirty or forty cops, and probably a dozen snipers awaited him. Their firepower would be awesome.

And they could stop him wherever and whenever they wished.

*That* was why they were being so nice and chatty.

Kyle could imagine them discussing it in their squad room.

*Talk to the boy, coax him along, make him think we're all trying to help. Tell him about the roadblock. This way he'll think we really are on his side. When he finally sees us, it'll be too late. We'll have a couple of units patrolling the back roads. He'll be trapped, and the news boys will be there to tape everything. Sonnet can't outsmart twenty cops and a team of snipers. He'll have to surrender peacefully. This way we won't look like shitheads when we blow up a dangerous wanted man.*

Dennings was probably right there in the thick of it, ready to make headlines. He'd be a hero. The papers, CNN, and the Internet would have him primed for a medal—maybe even a high-ranking position in public office. Discussions for an autobiography and maybe a movie deal would pop up. Local and national talk shows would clamor for interviews.

Dennings would become an institution. He might even end up with his own talk show.

"Wish you'd try communicatin' with us, son. It would give us the idea you're sorry the way things turned out. We'd think you were tryin' to cooperate, make things right. Every little bit helps."

Just before the bridge, Kyle slammed on the brakes and coaxed the cruiser off the road, down the muddy ditch leading to the marshland below.

\*\*\*

"Communication's the name of the game, son." Dennings' voice was softer, gentler. He sounded like a priest in a Confessional booth. *Say three Our Fathers, four Hail Mary's and don't ever do that again, son...*

"Way it is now? We got no idea what's on your mind. We're in the dark, and we're not very partial to that place, you get my drift. You gotta sympathize with us. Someone's out there causin' all sorts of trouble and confusion. We'd like to know where he's comin' from, what's on his mind. Savvy?"

Kyle parked in some tall bushes in the ditch beneath the bridge and switched off the ignition. The riot gun remained within easy grasp. The handgun and teargas gun lay on the seat.

"Thinkin' it over, are ya, son? That why ya stopped again?"

They were probably waiting for him at the other end of the bridge. If they were hiding in the trees, they'd have the element of surprise on their side as well as tree cover for protection. It was a perfect spot for an  ambush. The three-foot-tall metal divider separating the lanes would make it impossible to turn around without getting blown away.

"Listen, son…we know you're thinkin' it over, maybe reconsiderin' things. That's real good. There's any way we can clean this up without a bunch of other folks gettin' hurt, we're two hundred percent for it. You cooperate? I guarantee we'll help ya out any way we can. How's that sound?"

The handgun would be his best bet. The riot gun was too big and cumbersome, and good only for close range. The teargas gun would be useless out in the woods.

Kyle picked up the .38 and held it in his hands. It wasn't that long ago that he was afraid of these dangerous chunks of cold metal. He'd wanted to jump right out of his skin the first time he'd seen Stoner's automatic. Now, as he held one in his hands, he discovered it had become his best friend, and might even save his life.

He pocketed the gun. It bulged but didn't limit his movements. Now he actually felt like the dangerous desperado the police had turned him into.

He got out of the cruiser and climbed the slope.

The gentle whine of an electric compact descending the bridge broke the silence.

# Chapter 43

The car stopped in the middle of the highway. The tinted window slid down slowly.

A woman about forty sat behind the wheel. Her flaming red hair hung loose, brushing her bare shoulders. A knotted blue-and-white striped scarf covered her neck. Her sleeveless white blouse was half-unbuttoned, revealing a freckled cleavage peppering the swell of a large bosom. Silver bracelets adorned both wrists. Her long fingernails were painted a rich red gloss.

The two-seater was much too small to accommodate someone hiding in back. The trunk was also tiny. The car wouldn't afford much speed. Electric cars were manufactured for economy, not luxury or an adrenaline rush. But it could be used to gain some much-needed distance from the roadblock if they didn't encounter any cruisers on the way.

"Which way you headed?"

"Hadleyville," he lied. No sense trusting anyone at this stage. Especially someone who just got through a giant roadblock.

"That's quite a ways." She reached up to fluff her hair. A heavy cloud of gardenias drifted toward his face. Really bad vibes here. Something wasn't right. She seemed nervous—squirming in her seat, fidgeting. He

wondered if she was sitting on a nest of fire ants.

Whatever was going on, he wanted no part of it. "It's all right. I'll get there." He waved.

"C'mon, get in. I'm headed there myself."

Yep, she was definitely worried about something. No, it was more than that. Panic showed in her eyes; they'd grown bigger the moment he'd waved. She probably knew who he was. He didn't know why she'd endanger herself.

Maybe she was the crazy type that liked danger. She obviously wanted the reward. The jewelry clinking on her wrists suggested she was the high-maintenance type that enjoyed money.

Kyle didn't have many choices left. The roadblock was only a couple of miles down the road. They'd probably monitor the motionless cruiser another minute or so before deciding he'd abandoned it. Even if they weren't watching for it, they'd notice his chip had moved away from the location. Either way they'd be out here shortly.

"C'mon. Get in. I don't bite."

What the hell... He could let her drive a few miles, then show her the gun and force her to pull over. He could tie her up with her scarf and belt and leave her in the bushes.

"Name's Trudi," she said. "With an 'i.'"

The thick gardenia scent filled the inside of the car. She shifted her legs, which were highly visible under her short black skirt. Even with his suspicions he still found himself taking his time with his examination, noting the slender ankles, the open-toed black pumps and the crescent-shaped white scar below her right knee.

She obviously wanted him to notice. Did she want him to try something? Maybe she was the type who liked making it with fugitives.

Or maybe it was just a ruse to play for more time. *Keep him busy, Miss. Distracted. You're a fine-looking gal. Let him see what you've got. Make him sniff at you for a while. We'll do the rest.*

"You're Kyle Sonnet, aren't you?" she asked.

He wanted to jump out even though the car was doing close to 40.

"They've got screens all over the place." She wrinkled her nose. "Not a very good likeness, though. You're much younger and better-looking in person. The picture they keep showing makes you look nasty."

Kyle watched the road while she drove. Still no traffic. His right hand rested on the revolver in his pocket. Another roadblock was probably set up not too far away.

He strongly suspected Trudi was taking him there.

"Actually I'm a friend. You don't know me, but I know you. And believe me, I hate those damned cops as much as you do."

Kyle wanted to laugh.

Everyone hated the damned cops.

But something was still off. She wasn't as angry as George Manlon.

You didn't have to be angry to go after a reward. Just greedy.

"You really drove for them? I mean, were you *really* a wagon driver?"

He nodded.

"You just don't look like one. I mean, they're all...older."

"I was a quick study," he said flatly.

She didn't catch the sarcasm. "No, it's something else. They all have that look in their eye."

"Look?"

"No sign of life. They even smell bad. How could a nice young guy like you even think of doing that for a living?"

"When they threaten to send you to a relief barracks, being a driver sounds pretty good."

"Yeah, they make you do what they want. And when you fuck up, they come after you. What did you do for them to be after you? By what they've been saying, everyone thinks you're a serial killer." She went silent, turning back to the road and sliding closer to the door.

"What's wrong?" he asked.

"You're not one of *them*, are you? A serial killer?"

He wasn't in the mood for this. He wanted to drop her off and take the car. "I did whatever they said."

Her eyes grew. "You actually *did* all that stuff?"

A line of pine trees—a wall of green-brown— whizzed by. He longed to be there instead of in this car with this chatty, gardenia-smelling bitch.

Trudi broke into shrill laughter. "I'll be damned. They're actually telling the truth for a change!"

"Tell me something."

"Sure thing, baby."

"How'd you get through the roadblock?"

Her right eye twitched. She reached up and tried covering it, camouflaging the motion by turning it into a hair-sweep thing. Then lowered her hand and smiled sheepishly. Kyle could tell she was about to say something stupid.

"Roadblock?"

"The one you had to get through to drive out here and pick me up."

"I...don't know what you mean."

"There was no roadblock?"

"Actually," she said after some thought, "there *were* some cops blocking part of the Interstate on the way into town, but they let me through."

"Just like that?"

"They were letting everyone through. They seemed more interested in the traffic coming in."

Letting everyone through... That would mean more traffic. If so, why was her car the only one he'd seen?

"They didn't stop you? Tell you anything?"

"Whaddya mean?"

"Any kind of instructions?"

"Instructions?"

"Didn't they tell you what to say when you found me?"

"What to say?"

He wanted to get her to stop the car. Then he wanted to slap her, kick her out and take the car. She was obviously stalling for time. Stalling or racking her brain for the right answer. Neither tactic would work here.

"Working for them, aren't you?" he asked harshly.

"Working for them? I don't know what you—"

"Pull over."

"What?"

He pressed the cold barrel of his revolver firmly against her temple.

She shrieked, slamming her side against the door. The car swerved.

"You heard me."

"Listen...Kyle..."

The loud clicking of the hammer made her jump. She lost control of the car again. He caught the wheel with his free hand and righted it.

"I've got nothing to lose, lady. Nothing. And if you don't pull over right now, I'm going to blow your pretty head off."

Shaking, she brought the car to an abrupt stop.

Kyle kept the barrel of the gun pressed against her head. He was surprised his hand was dead-steady. No doubt because of his anger. But that helped his situation. To her this meant he could kill her without breaking a sweat. "What did they promise you?" he asked.

"L-Listen—"

"What did they promise you, dammit?"

Her cheeks flushed; her eyes burned into his. "It so happens there's a reward for your ass." Her voice, no longer soft and flirtatious, had turned hard and cold. "Ten thousand bucks can pay my rent and keep me in groceries a lot longer than that stupid home computer business the State assigned for me. A girl's got to take care of herself these days, and a grand a month just doesn't cut it. A grand a month? C'mon now. I go through more than that in nail polish!"

"Ten thousand dollars?" Cool. They thought more of him than he figured.

"Yeah, and you know what? I deserve every damned bit of it. Those damn cops…you know what they did?" Her face twisted with hatred and anger, making her appear ten years older. He could only imagine what had happened to etch the wrinkles and the cracks into her milky white skin. The hatred and the anger had obviously been well-fed over the years.

This woman was Allie in just a few years.

"I'll bet you'd like to tell me all about it," he said. "But I really don't have the time to listen. Back up."

"What?"

The gun pressed against her head again. "Back up to the bridge. Do it right now or I'll shoot you. I tried to kill a cop. The only reason he isn't dead is because he rolled out of the way in time."

She used the mirror to guide the little car back where she'd picked him up. Kyle pushed open the door and jumped out.

She screamed at him, her voice growing hoarse in the wind sweeping across the highway. "You don't know what those bastards did! You don't know and don't care, do you? Well, I got one thing to say to you! They'll get you, and when they do, I'm gonna make damn sure I get what they promised me, because they screwed me before! They ain't gonna do it again, you hear me, Kyle Sonnet? They *ain't gonna do it again!*"

Kyle descended the hill beneath the bridge, where he'd dumped the squad car. When he could no longer hear the quiet hum of Trudi's car, he crossed the muddy stream. Beneath the elevated highway, a hilly terrain covered with wild underbrush extended well into the woods.

Concealed by the tall weeds, Kyle moved directly beneath the bridge, making for the pine forest half a mile straight ahead.

The screeching of approaching sirens penetrated the breeze slapping his face.

# Chapter 44

The cover of the bridge and wild brush shielded him from the sun and the highway, enabling him to reach the woods. The creek separating the path had dried up long ago—possibly the result of condominium development branching out from the city.

The sirens had passed over his head a few minutes earlier, diminishing into silence. The howling of the wind beneath the bridge didn't reveal any new dangers. A quarter of a mile behind him, the stolen cruiser sat in the bushes, barely distinguishable in the shadow of the bridge. With their equipment, it wouldn't be long before they found it.

The uneven terrain, brush, mud and exposed roots made each step difficult. Garbage dumped from the bridge littered the path with cigarette butts and food wrappings. Used condoms lay discarded on the greenery, dried up and filmy. A half-eaten roast beef sandwich, the meat green from decay, sat in the dirt. Flies feasted eagerly.

A burst of wind brought with it the hum of voices.

He hunkered down in the overgrown brush, listening, only the wind and the chattering of birds answering his fears.

Allie told him vicious gangs lived out here.

George Manlon said they were kids dropped off by their parents just as animals had been dropped off.

About a hundred yards farther down, he heard more voices. This time they sounded much closer.

High-pitched.

Women?

He got down on all fours and cautiously peered through the brush.

Two skinny boys around ten years old sat cross-legged on the ground in the clearing, sharing the remains of a rabbit carcass. The dark-haired boy wore tattered baggy black trousers much too large, a filthy white tank top and mud-caked tennies. His companion, about the same age, had dirty long blond hair. His face was smeared with dirt. Wearing faded jeans and no shirt, he eagerly picked his portion of raw rabbit clean.

A few feet behind them, an emaciated brown-haired boy no more than six sat hunched over on a deadfall. He wore filthy shorts and no shirt and stared toward the Interstate, his head tilted as if he were listening.

"Rabbit's too fuckin' small," the blonde said, licking what was left of the bone and tossing it in the bushes.

"Like, there's a fuckin' grocery store out here," the dark-haired kid said flatly.

"Jeez...seen bigger squirrels."

"Find one your *own* self, then."

"Can *shit* a bigger turd than that fuckin' rabbit..."

"Show me."

"Lie down, pucker up."

"Ain't falling for *that* one again."

"Thought you'd be dumb enough to."

"Get Mumbles for that. He's dumb enough."

"Mumbles wouldn't know what you were doin', you shat in his face."

319

"Hey, Mumbles! They here yet?"

Oblivious to his companions, the third boy kept staring toward the highway.

"Tell that dumb fuck his folks ain't comin' back."

"Told 'im before. Three or four times."

"Tell 'im again. Maybe he forgot."

"Hey, Mumbles! They ain't comin' back!"

The boy lowered his head and sobbed.

"Fucker can't even take a joke."

"Misses his folks."

"What the fuck for? Assholes dropped 'im off. Miss yours?"

"Don't remember."

"Me neither. Mumbles needs to be cool."

"Fucker's six. Don't *know* cool."

"Won't make seven, he don't get cool."

"Don't know no better. Was happy with his folks."

"Ain't right in the head. How can you be right when they bring ya out here and drop ya off?"

"Didn't know they'd do that."

"Knows it now."

"Still misses 'em. Don't know *what* they did."

"Needs to."

"We tried. Didn't believe us."

"Told ya, ain't right in the head."

"And *you* are?"

"See *me* waitin' for my ol' lady to come back?"

"Mumbles ain't you."

"Needs to get real. Forget his fuckin' folks and start thinkin' about the damn cops. They find us, we're dead meat."

"Mumbles don't give a rat's ass about no cops."

"Hasn't eaten five times since he hooked up with us. Folks dropped 'im off, what? Month ago?"

"All right, motherfucker," growled a voice directly behind Kyle and just a few feet away. "C'mon outa that fuckin' bush!"

***

The razor-sharp blade of a hunting knife glinted in the sun. Held dead-steady in an underhand grip, it remained less than six feet away, ready to strike.

Its owner, about sixteen years old and just as skinny as the other three, stood about an inch shorter than Kyle. He wore threadbare jeans, unlaced tennis shoes and a hunting shirt completely unbuttoned, revealing many ribs.

"What'd ya find, Moe?" the dark-haired boy said from the clearing.

"Fuckin' asshole." Moe's squinting eyes didn't stray from Kyle.

Kyle remained on one knee, half in the bushes, his left arm resting on his thigh, his right hand at his side. The other two joined Moe and stood off to the side, both holding tarnished steak knives in their small trembling fists. Mumbles was probably still sitting by himself, waiting for his parents to return for him.

"Wanna join?" Moe displayed a mouthful of uneven, decayed teeth. "Gotta share. Empty your pockets. Right now."

"Now?" Kyle asked.

"I wanna cut 'im!"

321

"Wait," said Moe. "Gotta see what he's got first. Might have cash money we can use. Empty the pockets, motherfucker."

"You sure about that?" Kyle asked.

"I wanna *cut* 'im!" The blonde shook so badly, he could barely hold on to his knife.

"You don't empty those pockets," Moe said, "I'm gonna let Eric cut you up. And when he's done—"

"All right. You win." Kyle slowly straightened, reached into his pocket, pulled out the .38 and aimed it directly at Moe's face. "This what you're interested in?"

"Mother*fuck*!"

"*Jeez*!"

"God*damn*!"

The boys backed up stiffly. Then, in a single burst of flailing limbs, they scattered loudly in the brush.

Pulse pounding, the gun soaked with his own sweat, Kyle moved shakily away from the brush.

His long, slender legs pumping furiously, he sprinted for the pine forest.

# Chapter 45

His happy place.

The woods always felt more alive than anything else he'd ever known. The trees giant sentinels guarding the outer perimeter, the birds scouts warning of intruders. And the traps devised by Nature to protect it— deadfalls, exposed roots, uneven ground, hidden vines, stumps—added to the vibrant picture of a kingdom diligently attempting to keep out Man and his implements of destruction.

It would provide seclusion and protection.

As Kyle proceeded, the marshland grew harder. Roots, stumps and deadfalls littered the path. Thick vegetation made mobility much more difficult.

More voices, closer this time, drifted toward him.

There were two, maybe three of them.

Those young drop-offs again?

They wouldn't dare track someone who was armed.

The shifting wind could be distorting things, turning an innocent gust into something frightening.

Keeping low, he scrambled up a hill littered with fallen limbs. The overgrowth and foliage would obscure him. As long as no one had brought along dogs, he'd be safe.

Scrubs and wild brush engulfed him. Low-hanging vines formed giant spider webs. Fallen limbs, moss and ensnared leaves provided excellent camouflage. Mountains of pine needles and leaves covered the ground.

An enormous oak tree stood proudly amidst the pines. Seventy feet tall and nearly two yards thick at its base, it dwarfed its neighbors in girth and mass, its long, outstretched limbs keeping the others at bay. It would serve as a handy watch tower. The branches, thick and as sturdy as steel cables, were capable of supporting much weight.

Branches poked and brushed against him during his climb. He paused and nudged them away. It was difficult staying close to the trunk, but he managed, knowing how easy he'd be spotted if he became careless.

Halfway up, he stopped climbing and peered around the massive trunk.

About a hundred yards in the distance, eight uniformed cops trudged through the weeds. Their guns drawn, they moved cautiously. One of them carried a loudspeaker. Six wore binoculars fastened by straps around their necks. One held his in front of his face, pointed at the woods. A jagged sliver of bouncing glare reflected the sun off it.

The cop with the loudspeaker yelled something. The others moved toward him and formed a small circle.

The man with the binoculars abruptly straightened, turning toward the woods.

The dancing glitter of the lens grew much brighter. Kyle flattened his body against the rough bark. His pulse thumping, he willed himself to become part of the trunk.

Tense moments passed. Their voices increased in volume. They were probably getting ready to use the loudspeaker. *Kyle Sonnet, you've got ten seconds to surrender before we set the woods on fire...*

He remained perched on his limb, as still and as quiet as the tree itself.

He heard nothing.

Had they surrounded the base of the tree? Were they grinning up at him, their guns pointed at his perch?

He imagined Stoner climbing the tree, the automatic clamped between his teeth, Allie waiting below, her eyes wide with fury. Behind her, Buster holding a hypodermic at the ready. Off to the side, a body bag had been spread out among the pine needles.

Certain he was sufficiently camouflaged, he cautiously shifted his weight, edging toward his right for another look.

They were walking away, back in the direction of the bridge.

Why hadn't they used the loudspeaker?

Why hadn't they ventured deeper into the woods?

He was a wanted man—why would they leave so abruptly? Why hadn't they brought their dogs? Why wouldn't they come out here with at least two or three dozen of their friends?

*Stop overanalyzing. You should be overjoyed that they're leaving. It doesn't matter if or when they'll be back—what matters is that they're leaving!*

Gunshots. Three of them in a steady cadence. A scream.

Pulse hammering, he clung tightly to his branch, held his breath and waited.

A brief silence.

Another gunshot, another scream.

More silence.

The cops probably found the drop-offs.

When he'd gathered up the courage to move and breathe again, he risked another look.

Lights flashing, three cruisers sat at the far end of the bridge. A gust of wind brought with it the unmistakable sounds of engines coming to life.

*\*\*\**

Deadfalls covered with pine needles and broken limbs crisscrossed the uneven paths ahead, making it nearly impossible to squeeze through the low branches poking at the ground.

Slipping through thorn bushes and duck-walking beneath vines and other dense growth quickly proved grueling. Worn-out, sore and hungry, Kyle forced himself to keep moving. It would be humiliating to be captured here. Submitting to Stoner and Allie, watching their faces light up when the needle was injected into his arm, would be horrible in this serene setting.

A massive deadfall blocked the path.

No problem—just step over it. He'd done it dozens of times before.

However, this time was different—probably because he sensed something wrong the instant he moved toward it. In that one terrible moment he knew he'd screwed up. He wasn't paying attention or watching what he was doing. He was still wondering why the cops hadn't bothered coming into the woods. That thought, as well as constantly glancing over his shoulder to make sure he wasn't being followed, had made him vulnerable.

Instead of calculating where to step to avoid the deadfall, he realized a split second too late that he'd messed up.

He placed his foot in a tangle of deteriorating branches but didn't notice soon enough that his ankle had turned. A chunk of dry branch broke off, jerking his foot sideways while trapping his ankle, forcing him off-balance and propelling him downward.

His ankle remained trapped, twisting his leg. The sound of a walnut cracking issued loudly beneath him, sending a blinding onslaught of red-hot pain racing up his leg.

His vision blurred, he collapsed on his side. With agonizing effort he rolled over, directing his body toward the deadfall. The scorching white ball that had once been his ankle screamed out, bringing tears to his eyes.

Using both hands, he gingerly freed his leg from the roots and vines, then lowered his burning foot carefully to the ground. His entire limb had become a pulsating blister, each movement producing a stab of nauseating brilliance.

This was just like the time he'd twisted his ankle at the Home. But this time no huge nurse hovered over him, telling him she'd give him something for the pain. Something for the pain. It sounded cool. He almost wished the nurse could be here with her stuff, getting ready to inject him with something to take the sting out.

Beyond the trees, the sky displayed a soft serenity. The songs of the birds hadn't changed in intensity or in volume. He was all alone. This place he'd always loved so much had suddenly become his enemy.

At the Home he'd been an innocent kid, craving fresh air and escape from civilization. Sensing this, the woods viewed him as a friend and had welcomed him.

But since he'd become a member of civilization, everything had turned upside-down. People hated him, dreaded his presence. Even without his yellow suit he saw himself as a symbol of death. Sensing this new dark presence, Nature had employed its natural defenses to repel him from its boundaries.

He was as good as dead. Miles from civilization, concealed by the heavy growth of the wilds.

They'd have no trouble catching him now. Stoner didn't even have to get out of his chair. The list of charges no longer mattered. A simple "He's hurt, has no health coverage" would suffice. This would absolve them of any public scrutiny. Their next step was to cart him off to the nearest facility.

He'd be lucky to manage a hundred yards in this condition. Maneuvering on one foot in this brush would be comparable to the miracle of the loaves and fishes the nuns always talked about.

The simple act of sitting up became a major effort. A brutal stabbing in his ankle forced him to remain frozen, teeth and fists clenched while waiting it out.

The throbbing storm finally ebbed into a distant hum. The heat diminished, becoming tolerable. Sensing the tight spring uncoiling inside him, he surveyed his surroundings.

He had no idea where he was. For all he knew, there could be a town just beyond the ridge.

But in which direction?

It didn't matter. Getting there would prove impossible. Dying from exhaustion, starvation, or infection before reaching civilization was inevitable. Civilization. The mere thought of it made him tremble. It represented everything he despised, everything that had gone wrong with the world. All it had given him was pain and grief. It would be horribly ironic

if he had to rely on it to survive.

He needed sleep.

He could use his shirt-sleeve to wrap his ankle. Once he'd found a secluded spot, he could grab some shuteye.

Rest. Recover.

Then he could search for food and hunt for another vehicle.

Right now, rest was important. He hadn't been able to relax for a long time. Not at George Manlon's, nor in the bungalow with Allie.

It was a very long time ago indeed. Not in actual weeks or months, but it seemed like a lifetime had passed since he'd left the Home.

A group of trees led to a slope, a creek cutting through ten yards farther down. A thick swell of pine needles at the base of the trunks reached heights of nearly two feet. It wouldn't be difficult to cover himself. He could wrap his ankle and sleep for a while. The needles would not only hide him, they'd provide a comfortable mattress.

But first things first.

Kyle rolled onto his stomach, grimacing when the gun mashed against his thigh. A discomfort, yes, but necessary. It had already saved his life. But now, since things had gotten drastically worse, he realized it might serve one last useful purpose.

With his knee bent, he pushed himself down the slope. Exhaustion beckoned by the time he reached the water. He forced it away while lowering his face to the cool, clear stream. The water, sweet and delicious, sent a comforting warmth throughout his exhausted body. Sated, he lay back and let the sun do a similar job on his skin.

The sensation relaxed him. He could stay here for hours. Just close his eyes and let the breeze massage his skin. Let Nature—

Reality.

Stoner. Cops. Gangs.

He sat up sharply and listened.

Nothing. They'd left, remember? Got in their cruisers and made tracks. They probably found Trudi, pulled her over and grilled her. *Where'd he go, Miss? Why didn't you hold him for us? Why didn't you use your womanly charms? You couldn't seduce an eighteen-year-old boy?*

His ankle had swollen to nearly twice its size. Broken blood blisters forming jagged bluish-red tattoos intermingled with the swelling. He had to wrap it, take his weight off it.

But first it had to be cooled off.

Gritting his teeth, he carefully unlaced the shoe and slid it, a fraction of an inch at a time, off his foot. Then the sock. He lowered his injured limb into the cool water, gasping at the sudden jolt, then relaxing as it quickly reduced the burning intensity within it.

For several wonderful minutes he kept his foot submerged. Then he pulled it out gently and rested it in the soft grass. He stuffed the sock in his shoe, tied the laces to his belt, and enjoyed one last refreshing drink.

At the top of the slope he tore off a sleeve of his soiled shirt and ripped it into strips. He carefully set his injured foot down flat on the pile of pine needles. The pain protested angrily, clouding his vision.

He examined his foot and tried not to be sick. Dried blood and misshapen purple bruises and blisters covered his ankle and instep. Most of the swelling had localized over the bone jutting out from the instep. He bandaged it as firmly and as carefully as he could while keeping the pressure minimal, then gingerly replaced the shoe, lacing it just enough to prevent him from tripping when he tried to get back on his feet.

Before lying down, he covered his feet and legs with pine needles. His vision grew worse—blurred, shadowy images, the trees hazy phantoms watching him.

*Just push the pile over you. But do it quickly because you're losing strength. The needles are as heavy as the bodies you and Stoner used to shove into the wagon.*

*Forget Stoner, he's a million miles away...*

*Forget them all. Everything happened in another life. You'll never see them again.*

The last thing he saw was the huge swaying pine branch ten feet above him, blocking out the afternoon sunlight.

# Chapter 46

The huge black phantom changed shape.

It was Allie at first, then Stoner. This strange transformation continued, becoming a frightening mask with large piercing black eyes and leathery skin. The ugly presence held out a cloaked arm, beckoning to him. But the phantom's fingers were not fingers at all, but long needles. The shape changed once again, developing into a black rectangular object sliding toward him and swallowing him.

He tried reaching out, but his arms were pinned to his sides. He was imprisoned in a small black room made of concrete. A foul smell erupted from the floor. The room grew smaller. He screamed. The vibrations of his scream made the room shake so violently, the floor wobbled. He had the sensation of falling.

He was lying on his back in the darkness. Once again he tried reaching out. When his palms touched the roof of his prison, he realized he was trapped in a metal

(*coffin?*)

box. A loud engine roared all around him, its sound chillingly familiar. His next discovery, the most frightening of all, turned his blood to ice.

*Oh my God, I'm in the wagon...*

*They're taking me to the rendering plant and I'm not even dead!*

"Sonnet..."

Who was that?

Allie?

A man's voice.

Stoner? No. Probably Falworth, since he'd be the one driving.

The metal box began shrinking. The weight on his chest was so heavy, he could hardly breathe. Pressure being applied to his right side. This pressure was sharp—not at all like the cold heaviness on his chest. More like a poking.

Someone prodding him in the ribs. Kyle's eyes snapped open.

*A dream I was dreaming...*

Darkness.

Someone had turned off the sun.

Not so long ago, it had been visible through the branches above his head. Jagged shards of brilliance beyond the pines. Now all he could see was darkness and a sliver of moon trapped within the branches of an oak tree.

"C'mon, Sonnet." The voice was gruff, the strong smell of cigarette smoke drifting over with it. "Get up."

Something prodded him again. The woods exploded in a kaleidoscope of bright light. Unlike the warm caress of the sun, harsh beams of nervous glow moved only a few feet away, all glaring directly at his face.

Flashlights.

"Get up, Sonnet. Time to go."

Kyle tried to shield his eyes but his arm weighed a ton. He'd forgotten the pine needles covering him. As he worked his arm free, more dropped on his face. He pulled his other arm free, then used it to wipe his face. His pulse raced; his blood thundered through his veins.

They'd found him.

Obviously a shitload of them, judging by the flashlights. And if they were greedy enough for the reward, they wouldn't let their guard down.

"I'll get up," he said, fighting to keep his head. "But get those damned flashlights out of my face. They're blinding me."

The lights lowered, creating a strange radiance at the foot of his makeshift bed.

Kyle waited for his night vision to adjust before struggling into a sitting position. Pine needles slid from his clothing; dead leaves dropped from his hair and cheeks. His ankle throbbed angrily. He must have been asleep quite a while; he could barely feel his limbs. He forced himself to his full height and grabbed a low branch to keep his weight off his bad foot. Once upright, he leaned against the trunk and brushed himself off. His right hand wandered over to his pocket.

The gun was gone.

Had they taken it? Or had it fallen? He tried spotting it in the dark pile, but their lights weren't focused on the right area. Dizziness waned; he fought it off. His entire body was stiff and sore.

The man facing him could have been Mitchell or Stoner. But the uniform was wrong. It looked almost like a hunting shirt. In the peripheral glow of the flashlights, the area above the shirt pocket was bare. No name tag. No ribbons. The pistol belt wrapped around the man's slender waist resembled one of those six-shooters Kyle had seen in history books.

The man had on a pair of thick, mud-caked knee boots. A baseball cap matching his shirt covered his head. Dark hair ballooned out from the confines of the cap, reaching his shoulders. A heavy beard concealed much of his face.

He'd never seen a beard on any of these Government assholes before. Stoner wouldn't tolerate a beard; neither would Mitchell. Everyone Kyle had ever worked with was clean-shaven.

But it wasn't the man's appearance that held Kyle's full attention. It was the double-barreled shotgun gripped firmly in front of him.

The riot guns the cops used were all single-barrel pumps. This weapon looked like a double-barrel coach gun used two hundred years ago in the Old West.

"Where we going?" Kyle asked, surprised his brain was able to function.

The man gestured to his right.

A trickle of ice sliding down his back, Kyle hopped awkwardly over the deadfall blocking the path.

# Chapter 47

A dark van waited at the foot of the slope.

Kyle heaved himself up into the middle seat. There were no interior lights; the inside of the van was as dark as the night.

The dude with the coach gun slid in next to the driver. A guy with long curly hair sticking out from under his cap sat on Kyle's left. On his right, a long-haired skinny young chick. A cap covered her head as well. Since it was so dark, he couldn't tell if everyone was armed. Judging by the ease with which they all moved, he assumed they knew what they were doing.

Behind Kyle sat two others. The one time he tried to turn around, the chick elbowed him in the ribs. No one said anything; everyone faced the front.

Without the aid of headlights, the van crept down a narrow path swarming with dead branches, wild brush and low-hanging limbs. The screeching of twigs scraping the sides of the vehicle was deafening.

The numbing pain in his leg pounded relentlessly, but he barely noticed. His mind reeled. This was obviously a gang, and he was their prisoner. They'd probably caught him for the reward.

He wanted to examine the door handles, but it was too dark. And his captors blocked his view. He spent the next few minutes measuring distances, trying to decide if he could force himself through a window. Not likely. He'd have to wrestle them. And since they were obviously in better physical condition than he was, any attempt on his part would be laughable. Even if he did manage to escape, his ankle wouldn't let him get very far.

The chick, smaller and slimmer than the others, could be their weak link. But experience told him how stupid that sort of thinking was.

Females were far more dangerous than dudes.

But this didn't change the status quo. Regardless of the risks, he had to escape. It wasn't important where this group was taking him. They moved silently, efficiently. Their indifference made Kyle feel even more helpless. Though they weren't dressed like cops, they could nevertheless be a police detachment. Their clothing would enable them to move about undetected, their rubber-soled boots silent as they snuck up on their prey.

They were probably taking him straight to the rendering plant.

***

After what seemed an eternity, the van slowed to a stop.

The driver lightly tapped his horn. The brush in front of them parted, revealing a narrow trail. Pinpoints of yellow light flickered straight ahead.

Kyle attempted another quick glance behind them and was immediately elbowed by the chick. He couldn't be certain but figured the brush had returned to its former position once the van had cleared it.

After about another mile, they stopped again. The doors opened. The driver and his companion got out, then the two flanking Kyle. The chick blocked the doorway. In the darkness he could make out the outline of a long-barreled pistol. She held it out at her side, the barrel pointed down. Although unusually large in her tiny hand, she had no problem holding it.

It might have been Allie standing there, for all he knew. *All right, Sonnet. You stole my car, left me in the middle of nowhere and embarrassed me in front of the Stone's friends. Now it's time for you to pay.*

Kyle's gaze lingered on the gun. He wondered if he could snatch it from her. He didn't think so; it looked like an extension of her hand. What would she do if he didn't get out of the van? Shoot him? She seemed as calm as her peers, but he could sense some impatience in her manner.

His ankle burning, he slid out. He landed on his good leg, then collapsed. Ignoring the jolts of fire shooting up his leg, he rolled down the slope, toward the wild brush that might lead him to freedom.

If he could make it down there, he could crawl away and—

Something caught him by the collar, pulling him back.

He turned over and lay there, looking up at her.

"Just needed a little tumble," he said lightly. "Exercise, you know."

She didn't reply. She merely jerked her gun toward the slope.

"Not in the mood for some fun and frolic?"

Still no reply.

He crawled back to the van and used the door handle to hoist himself back up. She stayed close.

339

He wasn't in the mood for all this. Getting shot might not hurt as badly as the scorching blister munching hungrily on his ankle. These folks might not want to damage the merchandise. They were, after all, being fairly careful with him so far.

Since he had nothing to lose, it would be interesting to see how far he could go. Trying to get away hadn't irritated them much; they were all still congregated around the van, watching.

"That thing loaded?" he asked.

She moved it a couple of inches closer. Even in the dark he could see her long-nailed thumb positioning over the hammer.

"Ease up, Alice," said the dude with the coach gun.

She lowered the gun and stepped back.

Kyle stumbled awkwardly toward the front of the van. His throbbing ankle heated up his entire leg, making it heavier. The roll down the slope hadn't improved his condition. He gave some serious thought to reaching for Alice's gun and shooting himself with it.

"Follow us." The dude with the coach gun joined the driver down the path.

Guided by the flashlight beam, Kyle hobbled over the uneven ground. He felt rather than heard the chick keeping close behind him, her light aimed at his feet, alerting him of exposed roots and underbrush. The scrubs and brush flanking them were at least ten feet away; he didn't think he could roll out of sight before Alice stopped him again.

Farther down, the driver and his companion stopped. The driver pushed some brush aside. Hazy orange light peeked through the bushes.

Alice bumped Kyle in the small of the back.

He hopped around to face her. In the dark she was just a slim shape with a lot of hair jutting out beneath her cap. The top of her head barely reached his chin. Her height, plus her narrow shoulders and skinny neck, made him feel superior. He tried to ignore the gun and the fact that he had only one good leg. "Listen…we had a really good time back there and you're a nice girl and all, but I just don't want to settle down yet."

The gun, twitching slightly this time, came up again.

"Alice!"

"What's her problem?" Kyle asked no one in particular. "Hasn't she had her shots? Or is she just happy to see me?"

Someone snickered softly.

A small travel trailer huddled in a grove of scrubs ahead.

Kyle couldn't imagine a gang taking their reward to such a place. Maybe this was how they did things. They could be more organized than he thought.

Or maybe this was a cop thing after all. If it was, Stoner would be inside, waiting for him.

"Go on in." The driver gestured.

"I really should tell you, I have another appointment—"

"Inside, Sonnet."

"If I don't make this appointment, some lady's gonna be very disappointed—"

"Now."

"Or what? You'll sick Alice on me?"

"You're wasting time."

"We must be on a tight schedule."

The dude stood there, waiting.

Kyle grabbed the wooden rail. To his left, a dozen gasoline cans covered part of the concrete slab. The wild brush behind it seemed miles away. His ankle screamed, reminding him how weak and vulnerable he was. Anyway, he was too tired and in too much pain to attempt any more foolishness.

If they were going to kill him, it would be nice if they did it now.

He just didn't care anymore.

# Chapter 48

A large, barrel-chested man with gray hair, a thick gray beard and tiny blue eyes sat behind a desk in the small cluttered area. A pair of black-rimmed reading glasses rested on his bulbous nose. Like the others, he wore a hunting shirt. He was writing something in a journal and didn't look up when Kyle hobbled through the doorway.

Computer equipment and other accessories sat on metal shelves behind the man's chair. A small portable TV rested on a metal table on his right. A large green gun safe covered a portion of the wall to his left, with a dozen or so green canisters marked *ammo* stacked beside it in the corner. A coach gun leaned against the safe.

"Close the door, please."

Please? Why would a kidnapper want to be polite?

With difficulty, Kyle did as he was asked.

"Kyle Sonnet?" The man still didn't look up.

"That's me." Kyle noticed the half-open window on the opposite wall. The woods would be only a couple of feet from the trailer wall. If the others were still out front, they wouldn't be able to see him. He could propel himself through it. He'd learned how to hide really well the last few days.

*But they still found you, didn't they?*

*With that damned chip, hiding's impossible.*

The chair creaked. The man dropped his pen and sat back. He took off his glasses and laid them on the blotter. His eyes went to Kyle's tattered, sweat-stained shirt, filthy jeans and mud-covered

343

tennis shoes. Then they focused on Kyle's face and stayed there. The large head tilted. *"You're* Kyle Sonnet?"

"Sure am."

"How old are you?"

"Nineteen in a few months."

Frowning, the man shook his head.

Kyle didn't know why this man should be so confused. Kyle's computer image had been altered, but the Government knew his correct age, what he really looked like. They obviously didn't communicate with one another out here in the boonies.

"They doctored the displays again." The man scowled.

"You didn't know that?"

"We don't exactly follow their, uh, exploits. But we know how they operate."

Something wasn't right...

Kyle's ankle trembled horribly. The empty chair facing the desk looked awfully inviting. "Mind if I sit? My ankle feels like it's about to climb up my leg and strangle me."

The big man got up and circled the desk. He was two or three inches taller than Kyle—which put him around six-four—and probably weighed close to three hundred pounds. The trailer shook with his weight. He opened the door, stuck his head in the gap, mumbled something inaudible, then closed the door. "Siddown, Sonnet."

Kyle dropped in the chair and stretched out his bad leg. Leaning back, he adjusted his butt on its thin vinyl seat. It was as comfortable as anything he'd ever sat on before. He must have been even more exhausted than he imagined.

The man went back to his desk, opened a brown folder and picked up his reading glasses.

"This is impressive." The man's gaze didn't stray from the folder. "Especially for someone as young as you are—now that we know you're *not* twenty-seven, with the mug of a cold-blooded serial killer." He scratched a fleshy jowl. "Any of these charges true?"

"Just about all of them."

"Which aren't?"

"I never tried to run over that cop."

"Why does this say you did?"

"They had a roadblock set up in Hadleyville. A cop snuck up behind me. He stood in my way when I spun the truck around. I was only trying to get away, dammit. He shouldn't have been back there. You can get hurt doing stupid things like that."

"What about George Manlon?"

"What about him?"

"Did you kill him?"

Kyle sat bolt upright. "Did I what?"

The big man consulted the folder. "This says you forced your way into the residence of a George T. Manlon, killed him with an assault rifle, set fire to his trailer and tried stealing his car when—"

"That's bullshit."

"It's on tape. We saw it on the news this morning."

"I don't care what you saw." Kyle suspected they might do something like this. He cursed himself for not seeing it coming.

345

"What really happened?"

"George picked me up in the woods and took me to his trailer. He fed me and let me stay there for the night. But I never got to. Cops surrounded the trailer, killed George when he tried to surrender, then set fire to the place. Why would I kill someone who helped me? I'm not *that* much of a shithead."

"How'd you escape?"

"The trailer once belonged to a man named Taylor. That dude had dug a serious tunnel beneath it. I found it, then stole a police car while those morons were running around in the woods, shooting at each other."

"Should I believe you?"

"I really don't care. It's the truth."

He returned to the folder. "So you didn't kill Manlon and you didn't try to run over a cop. What about the illegal firearm?"

"What illegal firearm?"

"You had one when we brought you in."

So they *had* taken it from him—probably while he was dead asleep.

"I found that in the cop car I stole."

"You didn't use it."

"I almost had to."

"When?"

"I met up with some drop-offs just below the Interstate."

"Kids?"

"Oldest was around sixteen."

"What happened?"

"I scared them with the gun and they scattered. Then the cops found them."

The man went silent. After a deep breath he said, "So you *were* a wagon driver?"

"Why the questions? It's on my sheet, isn't it?"

"Humor me. Why'd you run?"

"Cops were after me."

"I mean, why'd you leave the Department?"

"Listen, if you're gonna take me back to Stoner, why not just do it and spare me this crap. If it's the reward you're after, let's get on with it, okay? I'm tired and my ankle hurts so much, I'd have to blow my brains out just to feel better. And I'm starving to death. Can't even remember the last time I had anything to eat."

"Sonnet..."

"What?"

"Shut up and answer the question."

"Whaddya want me to do first?"

"What's that?"

"Shut up? Or answer the question?"

Traces of a smile touched the man's features. "Why'd you leave?"

Elden's image flickered before his eyes. Elden smiling from his rocker, tendrils of pipe smoke framing his lined face. "Those dirtbags killed a friend of mine."

"Who was that?"

"A harmless old man. Elden Jeffries was his name." He suddenly felt better, talking about his friend. "After work one day, I put on my street clothes and left the Station. Just needed to get away for a while. I found this friendly old man sitting on his front porch in one of those neighborhoods Stoner told me to stay away from. Elden was smoking

347

his pipe and watching life, taking it all in his stride. He was over ninety years old and had seen more than any of us ever will. He knew where we're going but seemed to accept it. He realized he didn't have much time left, so this was probably why it was so easy for him to understand everything. He told me how things were in his day."

"How were they?"

"Helluva lot better than they are now."

"Ninety years old, eh? Your friend must have grown up during the Seventies, when folks ran around making babies, didn't bother to get married, and made the Government foot the bill."

"But they didn't kill people back then."

"Sure they did. They were just more uptight about it and didn't do it out in the open. Back then they justified it with war. They had Vietnam, Nicaragua, then all that high-profile crap with terrorism. Then there were those nuclear reactor scares—which started the ball rolling with global disarmament and mass gun confiscation."

"Elden didn't dwell on any of it. I didn't have much time to spend with him, but he gave me the impression things were much better."

"How?"

"He said people cared about one another. Before computers, people actually talked to one another, spent time with one another."

"What else did this man tell you?"

"He told me about music and art, all the things I wanted to learn about." A wave of sadness washed through him. For Elden. For all the good things in life that were gone. And for the way things were.

"He sounded pretty sharp."

"He was, but he was old, and when he tripped on his front step—"

"They don't let you get that old anymore. Contributes to the overcrowding. Now the Government's working on something that'll let 'em euthanize anyone over sixty, regardless of health. They want it in effect in about five years."

"Will anyone be exempt?"

"Depends on how much bribe money's involved."

"I figure Stoner should be hitting the big one in a few years. I'd love to see that. It should really be cool. I'll get out the popcorn and watch it on TV."

"That's a cynical attitude for someone so young."

Kyle let out a breath. "Nobody's young anymore."

The big man sat back. "Where'd you get *that?*"

"This world has made everyone old and senile. Elden was the youngest person I knew. Go figure— *damn!*" A stab of heat raced up his leg; he sagged in his seat.

"Hurting?"

"Naw, turning purple's something I like doing in my spare time. I picked it up driving the wagon. Blends in with the yellow suit."

The man pressed a small button on the metal box on top of the desk. "I think we'd better get you in to see the Doctor."

Kyle swallowed loudly. "The doctor?"

"He'll fix you right up," the man said, and winked.

349

*Something about that wink...and the questions...and all that other buddy-buddy stuff that almost knocked me off my guard.*

*The same number Dennings tried on me in the squad car.*

Heavy footsteps outside.

"I'm okay. I really am." Kyle tried jumping up, but the sudden dizziness made the room start spinning. "I just need...to get away...for a little while." He lost his balance and felt himself falling. His shin smacked the desk on his way down.

A moment later, he vaguely heard the door open. The trailer shook as several pairs of heavy boots stormed in.

The lights dimmed. Kyle's limbs grew warm and heavy; his head weighed a ton. Everything faded into a quiet shade of soft gray.

Even his ankle quit hurting.

# Chapter 49

As if rising to the surface of a pond, Kyle drifted back to consciousness.

He lay on a padded table, covered in a white hospital gown. His arms were strapped at his sides. His bad ankle, elevated on a cushion of foam, was wrapped in a heavy bandage. His left hand and forearm were also bandaged.

What was going on? Why wasn't he dead?

The room, about twenty feet square, smelled of antiseptics. The metal walls were lined with cabinets and shelves, each shelf crammed with white boxes. Some sort of X-ray machine sat on Kyle's right. Beside it, one of those scary, tunnel-like contraptions they used for MRI's.

A chick crouched over an aluminum sink on the other side of the room. She looked really nice in her white blouse, jeans, and tennis shoes. Her long sandy hair, hanging in loose curls, gleamed in the ceiling fluorescent. She faced a mirror. He couldn't see her reflection but guessed it was probably just as nice as the rest of her.

"You're awake," she said, spotting him in the mirror.

"More or less."

She approached his table. Her eyes, a soft blue, were large and long-lashed. Only then did he notice the knife in her hand.

"How are you feeling?"

"I've been better." Although woozy, he perked right up when he saw the knife. "I never woke up strapped to a table before."

351

Tiny clefts showed at each corner of her mouth. "Are you in any pain?" She examined his bandages.

He moved his bad foot but felt nothing. No sensation below the knee. "What did you guys do?"

"Be right back."

"Was it something I said?"

"They told me to let them know when you came around." She replaced the knife on the sink counter on her way out.

The huge gray-haired dude from the travel trailer and a man dressed in a white jacket and black slacks came right in. The man in white was half a head shorter than his companion, slender and younger, with dark features, deep-set hazel eyes and high cheekbones. His black hair, peppered with flecks of gray, was brushed straight back from his high forehead.

"How're you feeling?" he asked.

"Like I told the chick, I've had better days." He wondered why everyone seemed so concerned. "Don't you guys talk to one another?"

"Told you he was frisky," the gray-haired man said.

"What *is* all this?" He couldn't help being curious. Why would they fix him up just so they could haul him to the plant? "What did you do to my hand?"

"You can leave now, Colonel," said the man in white. "Kyle and I need to chat."

The gray-haired dude left the room.

The man in white grabbed a metal folding chair and dragged it over.

None of this made any sense.

"Why didn't you just give me the needle? Why fix my ankle at all? And what did you do to my arm?"

"We removed your chip."

"You *what*?"

"Your chip. We took it out."

This was making even less sense than before. Why remove his chip if they were going to euthanize him?

He was beginning to suspect that these guys weren't actually cops.

But if they weren't cops, who were they?

"Guess it's safe to undo these now." The man carefully unfastened the leather straps pinning Kyle to the table.

"Why the straps?"

"You needed rest. I thought you'd be better off keeping that ankle and your hands immobile. Until the drugs wore off, anyway."

Kyle propped himself up. More dizziness. He closed his eyes and let it pass. The strong soap smell told him they'd washed him. He wondered if the chick with the big blue eyes had done it. Then he wondered what had become of his clothes.

"My name's Weston. Doctor Sam Weston."

"Doctor?" This was getting weirder and weirder.

"I've been one more than twenty years."

"I've never met a real doctor before. I thought they all—"

"All what? Died? Vanished? Got into something else?"

"I don't know. No one really talks about it. Just that the hospitals all closed their doors or went all loony."

"Everything just fell apart. Since the Collapse, there's very little need for private practice— especially since no one can afford treatment anymore."

"So why are you here?"

"Thanks to what they've done in the cities, it just isn't worth living there. Everything has become so damned political, you don't have a say in anything anymore. You treat this patient because his father's this, his mother's that. Points for this, points for that. Treat this guy, he works for the State. Treat this police officer. You have to treat TV newsmen because they can cause you serious trouble if you don't. Treat certain women because they're screwing political figures, or relatives of the Mayor. The whole thing became a farce, a joke."

"Why help me? You must know I'm a wanted man."

"Everyone knows that. We've been watching you on TV for the last week."

"Then why—"

"You've put the entire structure into absolute chaos. That in itself speaks volumes."

"They didn't give me much choice."

"They don't give anyone much choice these days."

"So what are you *really* doing out here?"

"What I was trained to do. I'm simply doing it on my own terms."

"Those guys who found me out there. Who are they?"

"They live out here on the compound. We've got a few parcels."

"So you operate a practice out here and rescue people who stumble onto your property?"

"Not at all."

"Why me, then?"

"Because of what you've done. But we first had to find out if you were legit. They've been using their own people from time to time to come out here. They report back to their superiors and tell them about our operation."

"Can't they leave you alone, even when you're a doctor?"

"They're not sure we're doing what we've been telling them."

"I don't understand."

"You know how difficult it is, buying raw land these days?"

"I've heard it's impossible."

"You can buy raw land only if they approve of why you're using it. If you're a doctor, they'll only allow you to do it if you're operating a rendering plant."

"So *that's* what you've got out here?"

He nodded. "But being a doctor, my operating such a disgusting thing is against everything I've ever stood for."

"Then you must be doing it because you're forced to."

"The law states that anyone running a plant must submit monthly reports, complete with notarized tallies and statistics. If the numbers aren't sufficient, we'll be forced to close the plant and the land will be confiscated."

"So you need bodies."

"Yes."

"How many?"

He sighed. "Too many."

"Where do you get them?"

"We fudge the stats. The only bodies we take to the plant are those we find. Sick people wandering over from other places, or dead animals lying around in the woods. We give the animals names and send the Government their copies, which keeps them off our backs for thirty days."

"How about people bringing in sick people for rewards?"

"We make it really difficult for them because we don't give them the money. We just fill out the necessary forms and send them to the Capital, and they handle it from there. You know how the bureaucrats handle bounty money, don't you?"

"Let me guess…badly?"

"It takes months to get any sort of reimbursement from the Government. Needless to say, these bounty hunters think twice about it after their first visit out here."

"And you were positive I'm who you thought I was?"

"It's pretty obvious. And Colonel Neil happens to be an excellent judge of character."

"What would have happened if I wasn't who you thought I was?"

"We would have sent your body to the plant. You would have suffered an injury, of course, warranting the euthanasia treatment. Everything legal and above board."

"You guys don't play games."

"Can't afford to. We don't want them out here."

Kyle gingerly touched his bandaged wrist. "My chip. I thought they got me in the ankle."

Weston smiled. "That's what they wanted you to think." The smile instantly vanished. "If you knew how many people have mutilated themselves digging into the wrong places looking for it, you'd have a renewed respect for the evils of society. Yours was in the forearm muscle near your left wrist—about half an inch below skin level. We used a scanner to find it. It's the only safe way we're able to find a chip."

"Good thing I didn't try going into my ankle."

"By the way, you must be starving."

"Sure am. Got any food lying around?"

"I think we might be able to scrounge something up."

"What did you do with my clothes?"

"Burned them. Don't worry, we've got fresh clothing you can wear. I'll take you to the storage shed. Then I'll have Kathy take you to our kitchen."

"Kathy?"

"She was here when you woke up. Pretty girl with sandy hair? Big blue eyes?"

"Ah. *That* chick. Nice stuff."

Weston beamed. "She ought to be. She's my daughter."

Kyle flushed. "She doesn't look like you."

357

"Thank you. But you're right."

***

A large Quonset hut sat half-hidden in the towering pines a hundred yards down the wooded path.

With the aid of an aluminum crutch, Kyle hobbled through the doorway behind Doc Weston. The overhead florescent flickered, revealing floor-to-ceiling shelves crammed with clothing, shoes, towels, tarps, plastic sheeting, tar paper, and other supplies. Weston found a new pair of jeans, a long-sleeve hunting shirt, and tennis shoes. Kyle shrugged out of his gown and carefully slid the jeans on over his bandaged ankle. Fortunately, the pant leg was larger than the bandage. The shoes weren't so easy. Weston slipped it over Kyle's bad ankle, but the bandage prevented him from lacing it. Kyle squirmed into the shirt and the two went back outside, where Kathy was waiting.

Using the crutch in the soft ground was difficult. Kathy was careful to maintain a slow pace, so keeping up was no problem. He was so excited by his new surroundings, he quickly forgot his discomfort. He'd finally reached the woods, found a bunch of really neat people, and would soon have his first meal in days.

Three long trailers sat on cement blocks at the bottom of the slope. Just beyond them, a creek shimmered in the afternoon sun.

Kathy led him down the slope, then helped him climb the wooden steps into the first trailer, which had been converted into a large kitchen. A metal table ran from one end of the big room to the other.

Two refrigerators, half a dozen microwaves, two stoves, a griddle, and three chest-type freezers covered one wall. Large pots sat simmering on gas burners, giving off delicious aromas.

Kathy opened a cabinet door and found a bowl. "I hope you like stews. We have them a lot. They're easy to fix." She uncovered a steaming pot and scooped out some of its contents with a ladle.

Kyle sat down and shoved a heaping tablespoonful into his mouth as soon as the bowl was placed in front of him. Dizziness came almost immediately, the waves making the room shift as if they were at sea. Nausea set in; he forced it away. His stomach protested. He sat back, closed his eyes and let it all flow through him.

"You okay?" She brought over two glasses of water and sat down.

He sighed, then smiled. The waves were already dying down.

"Daddy said you should take it easy and slow if you haven't eaten in so long."

Kyle opened his eyes. The dizziness was almost gone. He had a sip of water, closed his eyes and waited for the last of the warm waves to pass.

"You sure you're okay? I hope I didn't—"

"I'm cool. Really." He returned to his meal. The warm fullness in his gut made him feel much better. "You always have this great-tasting stuff going on in here?"

"The workers like to eat whenever they have the chance. And they're *always* hungry."

Kyle continued eating, savoring each mouthful.

"How bad was it?" she asked after a short silence.

"Whaddya mean?"

"Working for them. Picking up bodies. I can't understand how anyone can do something like that. I get depressed when Daddy has to drive out to the plant in the morning to see if anyone's been brought in during the night."

"I couldn't do it." He saw the shadow in her blue eyes and knew exactly what she was feeling. Everything suddenly seemed so long ago, but he knew he'd never forget any of it—not even if he lived another hundred years. "I thought I could at first, but I couldn't. Not when I saw what they were capable of. I just can't stand watching people die."

"Well, we all know you didn't kill that man and set fire to his trailer."

The heat came back. "George helped me. Cops shot him down, then blamed me."

"We figured that's what happened."

"What's everyone do out here?" he asked, more curious than ever about this exciting new place.

"Well, as you can see, we're pretty self-sufficient. We've got carpenters and electronics people living with us, as well as electricians and architects. Ted's our electronics expert. He used to work with the cable companies until the Government took over and started their censorship program. We have satellite dishes and antennas everywhere. We've built Quonset huts and sheds for our supplies, and mostly everyone lives in A-frames, trailers or earth homes. Colonel Neil and his contractor buddies have been busy ever since Daddy bought this land. And about half a dozen of us work with Daddy at the clinic, helping people who come here for treatment."

"And no one bothers you?"

"We're well-protected. Artie has his own arsenal. He's the one who found you, incidentally. He's an architect and a former security installer. He helped design the compound's security system, but his hobby's guns. He's got tons of firepower and likes going out into the woods, where he has his own range set up. The guys like going out there with him on a Saturday or Sunday afternoon."

"I take it you've got no close neighbors."

"There's Government land on the other side of the Interstate, and a few Asian parcels on the opposite side. It used to be farmland, but all the dumping contaminated it. The Government doesn't want to buy it back and develop it. At least not yet."

"How much land?"

"Several sections. Five or six square miles. I guess you can say no one's here but us. And since Daddy's operating a rendering plant, no one likes getting too close. Why do you think the cops didn't look for you in the woods? They probably figured someone would take you in for the reward."

A thought struck him. "This Artie. What's his last name?"

"Taylor."

Kyle laughed. So they didn't get him after all.

"You know Artie?"

"George Manlon told me about him. It was Artie who actually saved my life."

"How?"

"I found his tunnel. I'd be dead if I hadn't stumbled across it. But what happened? I was told they caught him."

"They did."

"But how? I mean, how'd he make it out here if he was dead?"

"I'll let Colonel Neil tell you what happened," she said, a smile touching her fine features. "It's really a great story."

# Chapter 50

That evening, Kyle and Colonel Neil strolled down the path leading to the lake.

Kyle felt pretty good despite the dull pain in his ankle and wrist. Doc Weston's painkillers, a nap on the couch in Colonel Neil's trailer, and more good food were just what he needed for a recharge. It was the first time he'd been able to rest in days.

Now, as he hobbled down the wooded path, the orange glow of the setting sun dancing on the lake, he wanted to throw away his crutch and do a cartwheel, even though he'd never done them before and always thought them silly. But now he wanted to do as many silly things as he could think of. For the first time in his life, he suspected that he might actually be able to do all of them.

But he also wanted to ask questions. This was going to be his new home and he wanted to know all about it. The man walking beside him, huge and imposing in his hunting shirt, boots, camouflage pants and baseball cap, might not know as much as Elden, but he just might know the important stuff.

"So Doc Weston owns all this land?"

"Some of us helped by cashing in our stocks and bonds, but it's in his name—mostly because he's the only one in our group who can legally own raw land."

"How much is there?"

"About two thousand acres."

"Must have cost a fortune."

"Dirt cheap, actually."

"Toxic land?"

"It's bordering toxic land, but two thousand acres is a lot of dirt no matter how you slice it. And this location sure does cut down on meddlesome neighbors."

Three dudes huddled close to a canoe, repairing a hole in the side. A guy with a long dark ponytail sat on a stump near a Quonset hut, splicing wire from an electrical box.

"Like it here?" the big man asked.

"I've wanted to live in the woods since I was little."

"Not many conveniences, though—not like in the city."

Conveniences. Things you don't need.

"What conveniences?" Kyle asked, trying not to sound too bitter. "Having to share a room with a bunch of other dudes? The same shower? Standing in line for food? Trying to brush your teeth with three guys slap- ping you on the butt?"

Down the path, the wind whispered through the branches of the pines.

"Aren't you guys worried about the reward they have out for me?" Kyle asked. "I've heard it's pretty big."

Neil chuckled. "You actually think the Government wants to fork out all that jack when it doesn't have to?"

"What do you mean?"

"A few weeks from now, a news story will break. They'll say you joined one of these savage gangs living out here. The story will say you were trying to rob someone when one of the gang members got greedy and slit your throat, then hauled you out to the rendering plant. News coverage will be extensive, close-ups high quality."

"So *that's* what they'll do…" For some reason, he hadn't thought of that.

"See, the Government no longer has the funds available to support the manpower it would take to hunt anyone down. The National Force nearly bankrupted it during that three-year gun-confiscation farce. Good for us, though."

"Speaking of guns…Kathy told me to ask you about Taylor."

"Good ol' Artie." Neil shook his head. "They did quite a job on the old boy. Really fine work, actually. Caught him at a garbage dump retrieving some of his old guns. Got several nifty close-ups. Artie loves watching that tape."

"Computer-enhanced?"

"What else?"

"I guess it's much easier than actually catching and killing him."

"Serves their purpose. It spreads the fear. People are afraid, they'll do most anything you tell 'em."

"Did they get you, too?"

"We're *all* dead, kid. Everyone except the doc, Kathy, and the nurses working at the clinic. Cops did a great job on every one of us they couldn't catch."

"And no one questions what they see on the news?"

"I've been around a long time—more than fifty years. Those news rascals have been doctoring things ever since I can remember. Long before that,

365

I've been told. Hell, the biggest news broadcasters of the last century were also the biggest liars. Worse than politicians, even. Ever hear of the *paparazzi*?"

"Tabloid reporters?"

"What the hell do you think *they* are? Reporters—just like those well-dressed, smiling idiots you see doing the news. The news is only what they want you to believe. People have been content with that for a long time—why upset everyone with the truth?"

The setting sun rested lower on the surface of the lake, turning the water into a bright sheet of flickering gold.

"What did you do before coming here?"

"Contractor. Worked for a firm of developers."

"What happened?"

"Got tired of the bullshit. A developer is the lowest breed of animal. Take somebody like you...You look at a beautiful place—the woods, or a lake. Whaddya see?"

"A place where I can sit by myself and hear myself think."

"A developer sees money. Buildings. Wasted space. The bigger the space, the more money he can make. Asshole's foaming at the mouth to ruin everything. Doesn't care, so long as he can buy up a parcel of land, strip it bare, then sell it to some other asshole to stick another worthless strip mall on it. Or condo. Or golf course."

"So how'd you piss them off?"

"Got together with my buddies. We boycotted 'em. I'd been around a while, knew all the reputable heavy-equipment boys. Hell, we'd been drinking buds for years. Pretty soon no one would work for these hotshots, and being the sick bastards they were, they made some calls to *their* buds and put out a contract on me. Can you believe that? I make it a little tougher for them to operate and they come after me with a hit squad. Little extreme, wouldn't you say?"

"Slightly."

"I had to go into hiding. After a while, they got tired of looking. Or maybe they did one of their famous budget studies and decided they were spending too much on manpower. So they fabricated my execution a few weeks later on the nightly news. Apparently I went crazy, holed up in a deserted warehouse in Cleveland, my hometown, and took potshots at passing cars before some concerned citizen called it in. The police showed up and surrounded the place. Couple of snipers got me. Both received citations. It was really a good piece of work, I admit. They did a fantastic job piecing everything together."

"There was a corpse?"

"Got it from one of their homicide cases."

"And it looked like you?"

"*Was* me. My mother would have gone nuts, had she been alive. Kid, the cops have their own specialized committee of visual/graphics experts. They use 'em a lot nowadays. You can't tell what's real or what's not anymore. They just piece together what they want with actual news stories and superimpose the appropriate image. It's strange, watching yourself getting shot, zipped up, and tossed in the wagon."

"What about obits?"

"As accurate as the videos. Makes for entertaining reading. Got mine taped to my fridge. The news boys know how to turn everything around, make things real, get everyone scared and shook up. Amazing what a little computer work'll do. Ain't exactly the same world your old friend lived in, is it?"

Once they turn you, you're as good as dead.

Kyle could visualize Elden sitting in a lounge chair by the lake, smoking his pipe, watching the stars, having a grand old time.

"That's why he told me to get out," he said softly.

"Smart man."

"I thought so."

"The cops have slit their own throats." A wry grin took over Neil's broad features. "The National Police Force made it bad in general, but it was their own fault. Their strategy worked against 'em. When you wanna turn someone into a criminal, your first step is to tell him he *is* a criminal. Then tell him his guns are illegal, and he can't have 'em anymore. So now you've not only called him a criminal, you've violated his freedoms by taking away his rights. You've not only made an enemy, you've destroyed all trust and respect."

"I'm glad the nuns didn't let us know what was going on. If they had, none of us would have wanted to leave the Home."

Colonel Neil shook his head sadly. "Look at us. Even when some of us practiced birth control years back, the baby makers fucked it all up. Thank God for Family Planning—although that came about much too late. And it's impossible to implement in the underdeveloped countries."

Farther down, two women in shorts and halter tops sat on a dock, chatting away.

"Things have been screwed up so long," Colonel Neil said, "we'd have to go back to the beginning to fix 'em. What they're doing now? The wagon? The needle? Ridiculous. Like shooting the horses once they hightail it out of the barn."

"Why'd you guys decide to come out here?"

"The decision was made for us."

"By the Government?"

"The Collapse did it. It happened right after the Government started taking away our freedoms. But they were smart about it. They didn't do it when anyone was watching. They did it when we were all vegetating."

"Vegetating?"

"For the last century or so, Society's been sitting on its ass, getting fatter and dumber. Everyone's too busy to pay attention to what's really going on. All folks really care about is the stupid boob tube, their computers and earpieces, and if there's enough beer in the fridge and potato chips in the cupboard."

In a clearing beyond the trees, more than twenty vchicles were parked in a neat row underneath a huge aluminum roof. Three travel trailers were hooked up to pickups.

"We've been alienating ourselves a long time. With TV, with privacy fences, with security doors and burglar bars and home alarm systems. When the Internet arrived, it sealed our doom. People could stay home, performing useless services without having to heave their butts out of their chairs."

The Internet. Elden was right after all.

"When we lost our right to obtain competent medical care," Colonel Neil said, "that was the ball game. The bigwigs could finally pick and choose who they wanted to survive. Society had finally devised a fool- proof system of selecting its own team."

"Yeah, by killing everyone."

"Not everyone. Just those they've chosen as liabilities. If you've got enough money to stay alive, now that's another story."

"Or outsmarting them."

"Not everyone can. But at least they know there's a small bunch of us that just won't lie down and die. They don't have the manpower to find and kill us so they kill us on tape and forget about it. They know we hate them enough to stay out of sight, so they don't have to worry about dealing with us anymore. And those sheep living in the cities believe what they see. And that in itself makes the cops—and the Government—more powerful."

"I just hope we never see them out here."

"We've got a doctor operating a clinic and a small plant out here. He's got some medical assistants living with him and others taking care of the place. He does his job, performs a much-needed service, and pays his taxes. No reason at all for them to come out here and disturb the status quo."

# EPILOGUE

Kyle sat on a grassy knoll by the creek, thinking.

It seemed so long ago when he'd first seen Allie in her drab tee shirt and jeans, that cold, unsettling stare on her pretty face, those big dark eyes taking him in. Her lavender scent.

The coldness hadn't been part of her—not at first. That was developed out of necessity—purely as a defense mechanism. When you're a quiet, sensitive young girl, you're afraid of being hurt. You're fragile, can break very easily.

To cope, you're forced to develop a rough outer core. But while doing this, you also change those other qualities that once made you special. You turn into something tough and rigid, destroying every wonderful thing that had once been part of your past.

The woman who'd betrayed him at the lake was the woman she was destined to be the rest of her life. Far removed from the sensitive person she'd once been, she would forever remain the strong, invulnerable force forged and shaped by society. A cold-hearted woman unable to understand the simple truths about life or the evils society had wrought upon itself. A bitter, unapproachable creature with soft skin and dark, brooding eyes.

He wondered how things would have turned out if Allie hadn't let society break her. If her childhood memories had never dimmed. If her personal traumas could have been overcome with the help of a man who truly loved her.

If she'd been able to keep her treasured past with her, she could have joined him in his escape. They could be here together, sharing what might be a bright future.

But he knew better. Allie could never be happy here because she could never be happy anywhere.

"Mind if I join you?" Kathy Weston, slim and sexy in her jeans and loose-fitting tee shirt, stood at the top of the grassy slope. Her hair, shiny and full, smelled strongly of lilacs.

"Not at all." His thoughts of Allie instantly evaporated.

Kathy came down the hill and sat in the grass a few feet away, curling her legs up under her. "Daddy just told me you like art and music."

"And sculpture."

"I like those things, too. I also like to paint. You can come see some of my work, if you like. Daddy and I have a small place on the other side of the hill, where the road branches off and takes you to the clinic."

*God... Was this real*? Or was he dreaming?

Maybe he got everything backwards. He could be in the wagon, being taken to the rendering plant. Those dudes waking him in the woods...the big guy in the travel trailer...Doc Weston in the Infirmary...and this sexy chick...might be the actual dream.

His palms had become wet. The back of his head tingled.

A hand on his shoulder startled him. "You okay?"

It was Kathy. Her big blue eyes searched his.

372

He sighed; his pulse settled down.

*Calm down. This is as real as it gets. This chick's right here, concerned and worried, and she smells awfully good. What else do you need to convince you?*

"I'm...fine now," he said, enjoying the warmth of her hand.

*You're home now. You escaped Hell—remember?*

"I realize it must be a shock, finding out about this place," she said.

"*That* sure is an understatement."

"Well, you're here now. That's all that matters."

"I didn't think anyone felt the same as I do. No one liked me at the Home because I spent so much time by myself."

"I've always been a loner too. When we lived in the city I wanted to paint murals and things on the walls of our apartment but our landlord said we had to repaint everything when we moved out. I couldn't bear the thought of covering up my work. It would be like burying someone you love."

"I've always wanted to do things like that but never had the chance."

"I'll let you see our art supplies whenever you like."

"I never thought anything like this would ever happen to me."

"I'm sorry you had such a terrible time getting here."

"I just hope I can forget what happened...before I got here."

373

"Actually you'll probably be too busy working here with us to think too much about it."

"As long as it's different work, I won't mind."

"Well, it won't be hauling bodies around—I can promise you that."

"Cool." He tried a gamble. "By the way, do you like old movies?"

"How old?"

"The ones they made more than a hundred years ago, with real actors and actresses. Nothing with computer-enhanced characters, images, or wires making everyone fly around like birds."

"We've got stacks of them in one of the supply sheds. We've also got all kinds of books."

"You mean audio books?"

"The paper kind you have to read for yourself."

"Novels?"

"Fiction, non-fiction. Classics, along with newer stuff. We have shelves filled with them. I've got a couple of hundred in my bedroom."

This was getting more amazing by the second. "Where'd you find them?"

"People toss them in the trash all the time. I noticed that when we lived in the city. I started rescuing them when I was a little girl. Most of us read, so it's no problem picking up a couple of dozen whenever we go into town for supplies. As far as movies go, we must have two or three thousand of them. Tapes, DVDs, micro disks. They sell them for pennies in flea markets and yard sales because they're kind of useless if you can't play them. We pick up a few on each trip, bring them here, drop them off in the supply shed, and play them when we have time. Daddy's got a big screen, Colonel Neil's got one, and Artie's got two or three screens in his trailer. We'll get together, bunched up on the couch, munching popcorn while watching a movie. It's just like the old days Daddy and the others are always talking about, before the theaters all closed."

Kyle couldn't believe his luck. "So you've actually seen some of them?"

"Oh yes. Daddy's got a couple of players. There's a stack of them in the supply shed. You're welcome to anything we have. We pick those up at yard sales, too. We even find them in dumpsters while scrounging around for building supplies. Most were old and broken, but Ted fixed them and now they all work like new."

His heart wanted to jump out of his throat. There were so many questions to ask. "Are they as good as I've heard?"

"You've never seen any?"

"The nuns told us they'd interfere with our studies."

"That's sad."

"I read about the old films and found things on the Net when I had time to surf. Everyone says they make you feel good and give you the illusion the world is better than it actually is."

"They're very romantic. When you're watching them you get this warmth inside you. It's almost like you're actually there. You know they're only make-believe, but when you're watching them you forget about that. Or maybe you don't care. And the really special ones make you sad when they end because you don't ever want them to."

Kyle sat, mesmerized. His dream had actually come true.

"You'll be able to see how people used to live," Kathy said. "How they felt about things, did things."

*How people used to live. How Elden used to live. Right there on the TV screen. And he could watch them whenever he wished.*

Elden's spirit had come here after all.

"What about music? Got any old CDs lying around?"

"They're in a big stack with the movies. We also have LP's as well."

"Vinyl? You're kidding…"

"Not at all. Daddy told me those LP's last a lifetime. Most of them are over a hundred years old. They're warped and scratched, but they still play. We also have a stack of players to play them on."

"Amazing." He'd actually come back in time…

"Have something in mind?"

Kyle couldn't help smiling. "An old song a very special friend told me about."

"We've got most of them categorized. Any idea when it was recorded?"

"I figure around the early seventies."

"Do you happen to remember the title?"

"It was called "Dust in the Wind.""

"We can see what we've got. I can't promise we'll have it, but we just might. We've got dozens from that time period. I think Artie told me his great-grandfather was heavily into music back then."

Kyle didn't reply.

"Is something wrong? You've got a funny look on your face."

He shrugged. "This all sounds too good to be true."

She laughed. "Don't start thinking everything will be fun here. When your ankle heals, Colonel Neil plans to put you right to work. We're constantly building new homes, and there's always repair work to be done on the vehicles, trailers, or fences. Occasionally you'll be asked to drive to town for supplies."

"Is it safe? I mean, I *am* a wanted man, you know…"

"Didn't they tell you what will probably happen?"

"That's right. I forgot. They're gonna kill me on the news stations. How silly of me." For a moment he'd forgotten. "What else do you guys do?"

"We always need someone to help us with medical stuff—supplies, cleaning up, that sort of thing."

Yes, this was all so wonderful. He was free, among people just like himself. If he closed his eyes, he could almost hear Elden's voice.

*You got out, son. I'm proud of ya…*

"When can I see your movie and music collection?" he asked eagerly.

"We can check them out right now, if you'd like."

Kyle jumped up, stumbling when his leg gave out. Kathy grabbed him and held him by the waist until he positioned his crutch. Her touch gave him a warm rush.

"Is there...a boyfriend hanging around anywhere?" he asked softly.

She blushed. "I've been...sort of waiting."

"For what?"

"For someone like you to come along."

He wanted to kiss her. If he was lucky, that would come later. He also wanted to jump up and down...and do that cartwheel...and scream at the top of his lungs.

That could come later, too. When his foot healed.

He strongly believed that his foot—as well as the rest of him—would heal at a very rapid rate, now that he had finally come home.

# ALSO BY DAVID BERARDELLI

THE APPRENTICE
DEMON CHASER
DEMON CHASER II
STEPPING OUT OF MY GRAVE
ESCAPE CLAUSE
FATAL INNOCENCE
THE FUNNY DETECTIVE
JUST A SIMPLE ERRAND
COLORS
WORKING FOR A MOB BOSS
AND DARKNESS FELL
AFTER DARKNESS FELL
DEMON CHASER III
IN ANOTHER REALM
BEYOND RECOGNITION
THE NIGHTMARE COLLECTOR
HIDDEN
DEMON CHASER IV
BEYOND GUILT
A RIPPLE IN TIME